Donegal

BRIAN PENTLAND

To my dearest friend

Christopher

Order this book online at www.trafford.com
or email orders@trafford.com

Most Trafford titles are also available at major online book retailers.

Print information available on the last page.

ISBN: 978-1-4907-9253-8 (sc)
ISBN: 978-1-4907-9252-1 (hc)
ISBN: 978-1-4907-9256-9 (e)

Library of Congress Control Number: 2018966608

Trafford rev. 12/12/2018

 www.trafford.com

North America & international
toll-free: 1 888 232 4444 (USA & Canada)
fax: 812 355 4082

CHAPTER 1

A Funeral

CHAPTER 1

A Funeral

'Dominus vobiscum,' intoned the priest.

'Et cum spirit tuo,' was the response.

'Benedicat vos omnipotens Deus Pater, et Filius et Spiritus Sanctus.'

'Amen,' the congregation replied.

'Ite, missa est,' replied the priest, dressed in black vestments and the final reply from the congregation was, 'Deo gratias.'

The priest followed the two altar boys out, and the congregation stood to watch the funeral directors wheel the coffin to the door and then it being carried to the hearse, which slowly pulled away from the front of the church.

'Hello, Catherine,' said a tall good-looking man of about thirty four. She turned to see Mark standing behind her. She kissed him and said, 'Mark, I haven't seen you for ages. How are you?'

'I'm fine,' he replied.

'You'll obviously miss Jean. I am so sorry.'

'So am I,' was the clipped reply.

'Listen, why don't you join us for lunch?' she added.

'Another time.' He moved off toward his car, parked some way from the church.

'Shall we be going?' Catherine said to her husband and arm in arm they made their way out onto the street on a very cold and overcast day with a wind that blew the autumn leaves in all directions.

'It's hideous,' she said. I can't believe ecclesiastical taste has dropped to such a low ebb and the damn church probably cost a fortune. So much for Australian architects.'

'I agree,' said Dermit. 'Just such bad taste.' They drove to the hotel where they had stayed last evening, coming direct from Melbourne late afternoon.

'We'll have lunch and then leave for home,' Catherine suggested, 'unless you want to inspect Jean's house.'

'I might have a quick look.'

'Mark hasn't changed much, has he?' Catherine commented over lunch. 'Still as non-committal as ever, but he will miss Jean.'

It had been the oddest of relationships, that between Mark and Jean. Mark's parents had divorced when he was young, so somehow, from an early age, he was shunted off to Aunt Jean's for every vacation. She had never married and had lived in the same house all her life, a forties weather-board dwelling of no style at all and this description suited Jean as well. The house was in the middle of a street and the pale, faded green with white trim had never altered all her life, except that the colour became lighter, as Jean always said to the painters that she wanted it the same but with time and as the original paint had faded each new paint job had matched the faded shade.

One entered from a tiny front porch into a narrow hall with a bedroom one side and the living room the other. Nothing had altered from the time of Jean's parents. The same stern relatives looked down from dark oak frames that were virtually frame to frame all around the walls, suspended at different levels from the picture rail. The furniture was nondescript and the only addition to this room, which always had an odd smell, was a large television set. The predominant colour, with the cream gloss walls, was brown – in the autumnal leafy carpet to the 1940s large divan and two large arm chairs that matched, in a brown toning in Genoan velvet, a fifties buffet with a solid front door and two side glass doors, which were sand-blasted with a peacock on each door. There were numerous little tables, all covered with doylies and each one had an ornament of no character whatsoever perched on it, not to mention a ghastly standard lamp. The whole house followed this pattern, not so much sad as something that functioned but in a terribly old-fashioned way, and nowhere was that more evident than in the kitchen, where no updating had been done since it had been installed.

It was to this house that Mark had come for his vacations, year after year, even through his university years, and up until now he continued the same pattern with his life. He was, as Catherine described, uncommunicative: one word or perhaps two but a whole conversation was out of the question. Catherine was never sure if he was extremely shy or just bored with the world. But be that as it may, he was still an exceptionally handsome man.

'What is this odd smell?' Catherine asked Dermit, as they walked through Jean's house.

'No idea. But it's always been here. I have always thought my sister used the wrong cleaning fluids.'

'You can say that again,' she remarked. 'Who gets the house?'

'Mark. He is the only young relative. We don't want it and now both his parents are dead he was the obvious choice. I have seen the will. I would assume Jean and he were just an odd couple.'

'Yes. She was thirty or so years older than him. I can't imagine them together, as neither of them had much to say or perhaps that's why they did get along. I don't think Mark has many friends. I have never seen him with anyone, have you?'

3

'No, never. Perhaps he has friends from work. Who knows?'

'Oh God, look at this kitchen! It's unbelievable! Nothing modern ever entered here. Look at the old-fashioned gas hot water system – a trifle primitive! Poor Jean.'

'She never changed anything, so I guess she never saw these things as a problem,' Dermit said.

'I suppose you're right.' She looked about in this time warp. 'Come on, let's go, otherwise we shall be late. Remember we have a dinner party this evening.'

Dermit looked up as they walked to the car. He said, 'I'm my sister's executor, so unless she hasn't changed her will, Mark gets the lot and it's all very straightforward. I suppose I shall have to go to the reading next week. Oh, what a bore! It's sure to be at an inconvenient time.'

They got into their car and headed towards Melbourne.

Catherine and Dermit had been married for thirty years. They were an example of a success story, both dynamic, both very good-looking and they both had the drive to succeed. Dermit had his own real estate company and it was very successful – money was good and plentiful and as a result of his work they had upgraded their homes until now they were most content in a large Victorian mansion in George Street, East Melbourne. Little by little it had been restored and renovated to their taste and a more elegant home would be difficult to locate. Catherine was very much a socialite and held important positions on several charities. These took up a lot of her time. She was still a very handsome woman at fifty five: she seemed ten years younger, with hardly a line on her face. She was tall, with a mane of auburn hair, green eyes and lips that always betrayed a hint of a smile. She dressed extremely well and as a result of Dermit's now six real estate offices she received for her birthday every year a substantial piece of jewellery which she wore very well and often, and she was well aware of the catty comments passed by the other women. Dermit was seven years her senior and he doted on her. He was still, at 62, a very handsome man, tall, with bushy hair turning grey at the sides. He had twinkling eyes that seemed to follow you wherever you went, a fine strong face, with a cleft chin, strong arms that ended in large, strong hands. He was charm itself, but when it came to business he could be quite ruthless. He made every cent do a dollar's worth of work. He was very popular with his staff and they worked very well for him.

'Well, there is only Mark and me left,' he said in an offhand way, having a drink before going out to dinner. 'The rest are gone.'

'Darling, what an unnecessary comment,' his wife replied, looking at him. 'I shall invite Mark over for dinner this week. I think he must be feeling a bit lonely now Jean is gone.'

'Yes, he must,' agreed Dermit. 'Come on, let's get going or we shall be late. Who did you say was going to be at this dinner party?'

* * * * *

After several telephone calls in the following week, Mark finally replied.

'Darling, do come for dinner on Thursday night. Dermit said that there is to be a reading of the will in the late afternoon so I shall expect you for drinks afterwards.' Then she quickly hung up so as not to give Mark the opportunity to refuse.

The early part of the week had been frenetic for her. She had had two meetings to do with her charity organisations, both, as she described later, a complete waste of time, as members of the charities tended to think they had a captive audience and so spoke on about useless things interminably, wasting everyone's time for nothing achieved; a rush to the antique shop for a look at a pair of chairs and then onto the town hall to glance at the paintings on show in preparation for the auction on Friday. She wandered around with a catalogue, checking numbers and writing in her neat hand comments about the paintings she was interested in. There were several in the European Paintings as listed in the catalogue and she looked very carefully at a pair of 18th century noblemen in their finery and wondered what price they would finish up at.

'Catherine, I am so sorry. I am late!' cried Faith Roberts. 'But it has been one of those days!'

'It's not a problem,' replied Catherine. 'What do you think of these?' She pointed to the two noblemen.

'A bit damaged, but they should go for a good price, I would say. Oh, Catherine, I am so sorry to hear about your sister-in-law. What happened?'

'Well, it appears she just had a heart attack while she slept and that was that.'

'Oh, well, I suppose it's the best way to go,' said Faith, looking about. 'I can't tell you what a day I have had. One of my nieces has just left her husband. They have been married only two years. I can't believe it. Such a mess and they are both, it appears, to blame. Oh, why do they bother to marry? I haven't a clue. They seemed so happy just living together and the minute they married the trouble began.'

'It's an old story,' answered Catherine.

'Do you have nieces and nephews?' Faith asked, suddenly realising that she had never asked Catherine before.

'Only one nephew, Mark, and a more distant person you would never find – almost anti-social.'

'You're lucky,' laughed Faith. 'My tribe are exactly the opposite and are just impossible. Are you finished here?

'Yes, I don't think Dermit's bank account is going to reach to the large 'Streeton' in the main hall but I will make a bid for this pair.' They left and walked up Collins Street to their club and sat comfortably having a drink and re-discussing relatives.

'What do you mean – you don't know him?' Faith asked.

'It's the truth. I may see Mark twice a year and he calls me for my birthday and that's it. Never a social engagement, ever.'

'How odd!' Faith said and they moved on to more interesting gossip about friends they knew.

Faith and Catherine had known one another from art school and had remained firm friends - in fact on Catherine's part her only close female friend - through thick and thin. They had always remained close and that was not easy as Dermit loathed Faith's husband and the sentiments were reciprocated. So Faith always accept a dinner invitation to Catherine and Dermit's home, but was unable to offer the same hospitality to Dermit, who was quite fond of her. Faith had two children, two boys, now in their late twenties and both still at home. She complained bitterly, but everyone knew she would not have had it any other way. Her husband, Richard, barely communicated with her, so the boys made the house much more lived in.

'So your nephew Mark gets the house of Jean's, does he?' she asked.

'Yes. Dermit said he had read a copy of the will, so there are no problems, and Faith, dear, who would want the house? Nineteen forties suburban! It's ghastly! I don't know how Jean managed to live in it like that.'

'Perhaps she never saw it.'

'What do you mean?' asked Catherine.

'Well. There are lots of people who just use houses as a place to eat and sleep and that's it. They probably couldn't give you a description of the hall table if you asked them.'

'Perhaps, but Jean lived her whole life in that house in that seaside resort. I don't think she ever saw the sea, just the supermarket, the newsagent and Mass on Sundays. That's about it, according to Dermit. I didn't really know her at all. I may have seen her a dozen times in my whole life.'

'What did she look like?' a curious Faith enquired, and then interrupted as she signalled the waitress for another round of drinks.

'Well, she is hard to describe, a bit like the hall table!' She laughed. 'She was solid, but with no real shape, a round face and small eyes. If I remember, she wore glasses but never any make-up and had thick arms and legs. I remember I saw her one summer, years ago, and she always looked tired. She dressed in a dowdy fashion and I never saw her in pants, always frocks that seemed to be stretched to the limit.'

'And sensible shoes,' Faith added, with a wicked smile.

'If you're talking about her sexual preference, I don't think so. She appeared asexual, a little like Mark, strangely, now you mention it. Mark's beautiful but he has the same look, also a bit tired all the time, as if he has been working all night.'

'Or playing all night.'

'Oh, I hope so,' laughed Catherine. 'I would hate to think this beautiful creature was asexual – what a waste!'

Catherine moved to the large gracious living room overlooking the street, filled with good quality antiques and fine paintings and accessories. A large vase of chrysanthemums in a shade of burgundy stood on an inlayed cabinet at the side of the room as you entered.

'Well, how did it go?' Catherine asked, standing up and moving to Dermit and Mark, kissing them both.

'It didn't,' said Dermit.

'Whatever do you mean?' she said, facing Mark.

'Aunt Jean wrote another will before she died but just didn't tell anybody. But as the will is a public document it was read just the same.'

'Well, what was in it?' asked Catherine, curious, pouring three glasses of champagne.

'It appears,' Dermit began, taking a seat and motioning Mark to do the same, 'that Jean was very much a woman of mystery. I never realised my sister had another side to her. You see, she had written a new will which automatically cancelled the will where I was the executor. The solicitor for Jean is here in Melbourne. She must have caught the train, come to town, made a new will making the solicitor the executor and gone back home telling no one about the change.'

'Well, what is in the new will?'

'It states that Mark, myself and a certain James O'Donald are to share, one third each, but here is the odd bit. No one knows who this James O'Donald is. The solicitor has written a letter to his address but received no reply, but – you tell Catherine, Mark.'

'There is not just the house where she lived at Time Street. There is another property and we don't know what it's like. It faces onto the lake system somewhere and how big it is is unknown. The will just says 'my other property facing the lake' with an address, but in all the years I have known Aunt Jean she never ever mentioned another property.'

It was Catherine who noticed that, for the first time, Mark was talking and joining in the conversation. About time, she thought. 'Did your parents have another property?' she asked Dermit.

'No, not that I'm aware of. You see Jean was just so – how can I put it – ordinary. She didn't do anything out of the ordinary. She was totally predictable, so where did this extra property come from? Because it wasn't there when I helped her write her other will five years ago and who the hell is James O'Donald?' Mark seemed to Catherine to be very agitated and she could not work out why. He was quite wealthy in his own right; he didn't need Jean's house. He worked for an investment firm and at thirty four had risen to be assistant manager on a fantastic salary. He had a face that gave nothing away and some of his investments for the firm were, to say the least, very unsure, but every time they came through, and his face or body never betrayed a moment where he seemed insecure about an investment. He had inherited money from both his mother's and father's estates, both having divorced, so he was financially very secure. Catherine wondered why he was so concerned about a 1950s house in a suburban street, and now it appeared another property as well. And, of course, he now only had one third of it all, whereas in the earlier will it was all left to him.

'I don't understand why it was kept a secret,' he said. 'It's just so unlike Aunt Jean.'

'Yes, it is,' Dermit agreed. 'Jean always spelt everything out so carefully, so there was never any confusion and yet somehow in these last five years she had gained another property unbeknown to us and another beneficiary, a certain James O'Donald.'

'Well, what happens now?' asked Catherine.

'Nothing until James O'Donald is located and we have a look at this other house that is overlooking the lake. I don't understand why she didn't tell us about it all. You know I invested some money for her some years ago.'

'No, I didn't know at all,' Dermit said, surprised. 'Where did the money come from?'

Mark look at them in surprise, 'But I thought you and Catherine gave it to her.'

'No,' said Catherine. 'If she had been short of money, we should have sent her some at once, but she never asked us for a cent, so where did the money come from then – and how much was it?'

Mark looked at both of them as he drained the glass which Catherine then refilled. 'Seven hundred and sixty thousand dollars,' he said.

'What?' came Dermit's astonished reply.

'How much is in her bank account now?' asked Catherine.

'We don't know. The solicitor says that he will have to locate the bank account number and he won't tell us until the three of us are together. Yes, our mysterious James.'

'I don't understand at all,' said Mark. 'Perhaps with the money, and good investments, I must have doubled her money so she just decided to buy another house.'

'Well, that's feasible, but where did the initial $760,000 come from and who the hell is this James person?'

'Let's have dinner,' interrupted Catherine, and they all moved to the dining room.

'It's a fabulous room,' Mark commented.

'Thank you, darling,' Catherine said, and it was indeed a fine room. There was a beautiful early Victorian table in walnut with ten matching balloon-back chairs covered in black leather and heavily buttoned and a beautiful sideboard again in walnut, with a separate wine-cooler that looked like a miniature coffin that slid in between the two pedestals that supported the top section which was plentifully covered with large pieces of silver. The walls were papered in the palest celedan green with matching silk curtains. The whole effect was one of subtle and the large chandelier in crystal just finished it off.

'I don't mind the sharing at all,' said Mark. 'In fact, I don't need the house, but I am so confused about Aunt Jean's secrecy.'

'I'm exactly the same,' agreed Dermit. 'In fact if you want the house you can have my share, as I most definitely don't want it.'

'Thanks, but neither do I. I went to stay with Aunt Jean because I always felt she was so lonely but looking back now perhaps I misunderstood her completely.'

'I think that all the time you spent with her was fantastic and I am sure she looked forward to seeing you every time.' Mark's reply was non-committal and unsure.

'Well, how do we find this mysterious James' Catherine asked.

'I suppose the solicitor will have to contact the police. And why didn't she use her usual solicitor? It's all very, very strange and totally out of keeping with her character. I have a funny feeling all is not right.'

'Well, we shall have to wait and see, unless you want to go up and have a look at this other house,' Mark suggested.

'I'll come with you, if you want some company,' Catherine offered. 'I'm most curious to see what type of house Jean purchased and I just wonder why.'

'Very well. Let's do it. What about next Friday early? We could be there in a bit under three hours. I'll telephone the solicitor again for the exact address and see if we can also speak with James O'Donald.'

'That's fine with me,' Catherine smiled, and the three of them chatted on about all manner of things. 'Mark,' she went on, 'I don't exactly know where you live.'

'Richmond,' was the reply, but no further information was forthcoming. 'You have so many beautiful things here,' he said, glancing around.

'Thank you. It's the result of a few years of collecting,' Catherine told him.

'A few years!' Dermit exclaimed. 'It's a lifetime's collection. Catherine spends more time at the auction houses than she does at home,' and laughed heartily.

'Well, I think the whole house looks marvellous and perhaps one day I shall have something like this.'

'I'm sure you will, Mark, and if you ever need a hand, just give me a call.'

'Be careful,' he smiled at her. 'I may just take you upon on that.'

She thanked him for coming and said she would see him early on Friday morning. They said goodnight and she closed the front door. She was very surprised. 'You know, Dermit, he is quite charming. Do you know this is the first time I have had a discussion with him without the responses being yes and no.'

'He is a great guy. I think he is just shy.'

Catherine murmured, thoughtfully, and then said. 'Oh, Dermit, don't forget tomorrow night we have dinner with Paul and Gerald.

'Oh gosh! I had quite forgotten. Great! I'm looking forward to it.

Paul and Gerald were Catherine's closest friends. They had been lovers for years and the three of them were always at auctions or galleries together, laughing and joking. Dermit adored them and when possible they were guests at the big house in East Melbourne, laughing away until the small hours. Paul was an interior designer and Gerald a chef at an international hotel in the heart of Melbourne, so most activities socially were worked around Gerald's nights off. If there was no possibility of his joining them because of work, he inevitably called in for a drink after work at East Melbourne, collected Paul and headed home.

'Welcome to the hovel,' cried Paul as Catherine and Dermit entered their beautiful terraced house in Richmond. It was a very broad terraced house, so extremely spacious and decorated very tastefully. 'I've had to use the whip in the kitchen, but all is well.' Paul laughed. Dermit had always got along with Catherine's coterie of gay friends very well. He loved the attention and genuinely liked them. It was the married men that Dermit found heavy going, as with Faith's husband and others, so his close male friends were nearly all gay.

'Oh, this James is probably fourteen years old and has been Jean's lover,' laughed Paul, who was the sparkier of the two. He was as tall as Dermit, with the most mischievous pale hazel eyes, a handsome face and very well-toned body, as a result of going to the gym twice a week. Gerald was shorter and quite thin, with slightly receding blonde hair and the most gentle, soft face imaginable. His pale blue eyes and pale olive skin set him above the general look of men., His capacity in the kitchen was supreme and quite often at East Melbourne he just took over Catherine's kitchen with Dermit as his assistant, while Catherine and Paul chattered on venomously about people they knew.

'Oh, darling, I am sure he isn't fourteen years old.'

'Oh, well, you never know. A new house and a young lover. It's been done before, you know.'

'I'm sure,' she smiled, 'but Mark last night was great. I can't believe it – so chatty.'

'What does he look like?' asked Paul, refilling the glasses.

'Oh, he is divine. Tall, dark and handsome, but aloof - or perhaps, as Dermit says, just shy.'

'How old is he?' Paul asked, narrowing his eyes.

'Thirty four, darling, and not married.'

'Hmm. Have you met the boyfriend?'

'Paul, what are you talking about? I think Mark is probably asexual. He is beautiful, but like a fine painting: you can only look at it and then you move along.'

'Catherine, what beautiful man unattached at thirty four and wealthy do you know?'

'None,' she replied, with a laugh. 'The wolves take them at once. Oh, what about Jenny Walls? Can you believe it? That mangled old crocodile has a lover half her age and not too bad at all. I can't imagine what she is paying him.' They both broke into hysterical laughter.

Jenny Walls was indeed a predator in every sense of the word and without pity. After two husbands, a nice house and a secure bank account, she had taken quite publically this young Greek lover. She was aptly described by Gerald as an arch-bitch and all heartily concurred. Jenny dwelt under the illusion she was chic itself, as Paul remarked. He wasn't even sure if she could spell the word! She dressed atrociously. Gerald always described her as clash, clash, clash: one outfit in large horizontal stripes of red and green did not do a great deal for Jenny from behind, but in her mind she was the suavest women in town. She disliked Catherine and was very envious of her jewellery collection. Paul's comment, one evening at a party, when he was with Catherine decked out in sapphires, to Jenny that he adored junk jewellery, did not endear him to her at all.

'Oh,' interrupted Catherine, 'I have seen a pair of portraits at the showing at the Town Hall. I think I will get them; they need a bit of restoration but I really like them.'

'Are they the ones in the very decorative gilt frames? One man in reds and the other in blue?' he asked.

'Yes, that's them. What do you think?'

'I think they are divine. I was going to make a bid for a client, but I shall be a very generous friend and bid for something else.' Catherine thanked him.

'Come through! It's on the table,' cried Dermit, and arm in arm, Catherine and Paul swept into the dining room.

'I'm sure Jean had a secret lover. Perhaps this James is the pensioner. Who knows?'

'I bet you'll get a surprise when you meet him,' Paul added.

'I'm sure we shall,' Catherine agreed. 'You see,' she continued, addressing the boys, 'Mark and I are going up on Friday for a look at this new house, so perhaps we shall meet this mystery man.'

'Oh, how exciting,' exclaimed Gerald.

'This food is delicious,' Dermit said. 'Every time it's just better.'

'Marry me, big boy,' laughed Gerald.

'You'd better look out,' smiled Dermit.

Friday morning arrived, and as previously organised, Mark was at East Melbourne for breakfast. Dermit chattered to him while preparing the food.

'Hello, darling,' cried Catherine, as she entered the streamlined stainless steel and marble kitchen and sat at a table overlooking the manicured back garden. 'Just coffee for me, thanks.'

'So you're the chef, Dermit?'

'Yes, Mark, he most certainly is,' she stated. 'My culinary skills are strictly survival or a dash to the nearest restaurant.' She laughed. 'Do you like cooking?'

'Yes, I do, but I am a bit lazy. It really doesn't seem worth the work to prepare it just for yourself.'

'Oh, if that's the problem,' Dermit told him, 'you only live ten minutes away and this kitchen with the ingredients awaits you.'

'You'd better be careful or I may just take you both up on that offer.'

'Just tell me when,' Dermit insisted. 'I could do with a break from the constant housework,' and laughed loudly.

'Catherine is hopeless.'

'Thank you, darling,' came a sharp reply. 'I wasn't going to bring it up but now you have started, it is my birthday next month, just a reminder.'

'No need, darling. It's already purchased.'

'Oh, Dermit, you are divine,' she cooed.

'I don't know why there is so much traffic,' complained Mark, as they drove in a stop-start fashion until they entered the freeway system and headed for Lakes Entrance. Catherine realised that she actually knew very little about this handsome nephew beside her, in fact her only relative, and so she began to try to draw him out, but Mark was very reticent at handing on information about his private life, so she just changed the subject and they spoke about his holidays with Aunt Jean. But even here he gave only brief outlines and nothing detailed. She was aware that he was more than just curious about James O'Donald and constantly returned to the subject. But when it came to paintings and antiques they found they had common ground and this was the topic that kept them occupied until they reached Lakes Entrance, almost three hours later. With all the information to hand, they first drove to the Police Station to see if they knew of a certain James O'Donald. The best they could help them with were two O'Donalds in the telephone book but that was it.

They thanked the policeman on duty and drove to the first address. It was a smarter type of holiday home and a well-dressed woman opened the door to them. She said she was sorry but no male in her home carried the Christian name of James. They had great difficulty in locating the second house, as it was in a forgotten sand track that went between two houses and at the end were three small cottages. The one on the left, the most run-down, with high uncut grass and a broken picket fence, carried the number they were seeking. Catherine and Mark looked at one another, took a deep breath, opened the gate and walked to the front door. They knocked, but there was no response. Mark took from his pocket a pre-prepared letter, stating it was necessary to contact the solicitor at once, and left the telephone number, as well as his own. This they poked under the door and returned to the car.

'Well, it doesn't seem Jean's Mr James O'Donald is exactly the wealthiest man in town, does it?' she said.

'Perhaps that's why she left him the third share,' Mark suggested. 'Let's see if we can have a bit more success with the real estate office.'

They drove to the Main Street and with difficulty found a parking place.

'Good morning. May we help you?' asked a young girl. It was then that Mark and Catherine realised that they didn't really know much about what they were seeking – just a house facing the lake. They gave the girl the address of it as Mark had copied it from the will.

'Oh, that's nowhere near here. That's right over near Metung. Ask when you get there or you could check here at the local post office. They should be able to help you.' Mark thanked her and they headed off to the post office.

'Oh, the post girl has left. You might catch her on her mail run but I can't help you,' said a stout matron. 'Perhaps if you can come back very early tomorrow morning, before the mail run, the girl will be able to help you.'

'Not exactly a successful day,' Catherine commented with a sigh. 'As we are here, let's go to Metung and see what we can find. What do you think?'

'Fine! If nothing else, we can have lunch at the Metung Hotel.'

She thought it a great idea, and they walked back to the car then headed off in the direction of Metung.

Mark glanced at the scenery. He did not know it well, as, when here on vacation, he generally remained with Aunt Jean or spent time at the beach, never touring around, so he was quite interested in the landscape – as was Catherine. They idly chattered away, until, both together, they saw a little red van with 'Australian Post' written in white on the side, heading in their direction. Lots of flashing of headlights and use of the horn, and the little red van slowed down until it was parallel with Mark's car.

'Give us a look at the address,' demanded the post girl, in a very efficient manner, and Mark handed her a copy.

'That's nowhere near Metung, mate. If you continue along this road for about three kilometres, look carefully on the left and you'll see a broken-down cottage with no windows. Turn down that road beside it and go on for about another killometre, but be careful. You could make a mess of your smart car. See ya!' and she began to speed off. 'Oh,' she yelled from a distance when she had braked, 'the property's called Donegal. There's a sign on the gate,' and she once more took off at a rapid rate, sending dust and gravel up from the sides of the road. The second time around they located the cottage, due to it's being immersed in a jungle of overgrowth, a very forlorn sight where vandals had really left their destructive mark. They turned down the sand road just as it began to rain, so the driving was very difficult, as the potholes were quite deep. The speed was virtually nil. They crept slowly down the uncared-for road as the rain became heavier.

'Oh, Mark, do you think we should call it a day? This road is dangerous in these conditions.'

'It's not very promising, is it?' but he slowly drove on through the rain. And now the wind started to blow the gum tree branches in all directions. Mark stopped his BMW and just looked ahead.

'How far do you think we have come?' he asked.

'I've no idea. It's difficult to tell in these conditions. I'm not sure I should like to live here, would you?'

'I don't know,' he replied in an odd way. 'It might be fun living in such isolation.' He started the car again and they crept on, dodging one pothole after another.

'You don't think we've passed it, do you?' Catherine asked, seriously.

'Goodness knows! We missed the damaged cottage. Oh, if only the rain would stop!'

'Well, we haven't come two kilometres yet I should think.' All of a sudden, the road became a little better.

'If we can't find this place in ten minutes, we'll turn back,' Mark announced, as he drove now through driving rain; the black sky ahead did not promise any better conditions. 'I think we must have passed it. Let's turn around a go back.'

'There's a gateway. We can turn there,' Catherine suggested, and Mark turned in. Just as he was starting to reverse, Catherine cried out, 'Look, Mark, this must be it.' He braked and looked ahead but could see nothing.

'Where?' he asked.

'Look at the gate,' and sure enough, in faded, washed-out letters on the top rail of an unhinged gate that was wired up, was painted the name Donegal.

'Well, at least we know where it is,' said Mark, but in those conditions it was impossible to look around, as the rain was teeming down.

'Mark, it's obviously not just a house,' Catherine remarked. 'It must come with a certain amount of land, as from here at the front gate we can't even see the house.'

Mark agreed. 'Perhaps the house is up behind that bank of trees. Let's call it a day and go back.' He reversed and began to navigate the potholes, heading for the main road.

'Well, it hasn't been a great day,' Catherine sighed. 'No James and the rain is such we can't even see the second house. By the way, Mark, are you hungry?'

'Starving,' came the reply and they found themselves a little restaurant-cum-take-away in Dairnsdale, and reviewing their day of lost achievements.

As Mark headed out to the highway and back to Melbourne, they began to converse softly about the things they liked and places they enjoyed being at, but it was quite impersonal. Mark kept everything separate in his life and he never mixed things, so it was basically Catherine who kept the conversation going.

'I never thought we should arrive,' she smiled. 'You must stay for dinner or Dermit will be furious.' He smiled at her, and they entered the big house in East Melbourne arm in arm.

'Well, tell me about the mansion!' laughed Dermit, who had been well-warned via the telephone about the evening meal.

'We have no ideas,' Mark began, sitting down in the kitchen and staring ahead. 'It was raining so heavily we saw only the gate and that was all. And as for James O'Donald, I think we found a very run-down cottage but that was all. I left a note, or should I say an envelope, under the door with all the information and the solicitor's telephone number but I'm afraid our day of discovery was anything but that.'

Dermit asked Catherine why she thought Jean would want to purchase a property in the middle of nowhere, but she said she had no idea at all, and she was sure Mark was also confused, despite having known Jean better than she had.

'It makes no sense to me,' agreed Mark. 'Aunt Jean was never one to want to live in isolation, in fact she liked to have someone around to help her as she got older. To purchase this Donegal makes no sense at all,' and the three of them, over dinner, ran over the same information again and again. No one arrived at any idea that would resolve this odd mystery.

'Let's do a title search and find out exactly how big this Donegal is,' Dermit suggested. 'I am sure it's probably an old house on one or two hectares but on Monday morning I'll find out.' They all moved to the informal dining area of the sleek kitchen to a splendid meal of fish, as this was Dermit's speciality.

On Monday morning, Dermit, through his office, ordered a title search on Donegal and late afternoon all the information was ready for him after he returned from viewing two large properties for sale. He said he felt tired, 'but what was Donegal all about?'

'One hundred hectares of coastal landscape and one house,' came the reply.

'What! I don't believe it – one hundred hectares! What the hell was my sister thinking of?' He telephoned Catherine with the information; she was equally surprised.

Thursday evening saw Catherine and Mark seated together at the art auction and both were surprised at the way the prices ran up. 'Hi!' called Faith, as she bustled through the crowd and took a seat beside Mark. 'So you are the handsome nephew! My name is Faith,' she said, smiling at him.

Mark said, 'How do you do,' very formally. Catherine leaned over and said, 'The prices are astronomical. Unless they drop a bit I am not touching anything.'

The auctioneer silenced everyone and continued the auction. The early Australian paintings fetched very high prices and Mark looked at Catherine who just shook her head, but the moment the important pieces had been sold and the equally important dealers left, the prices began to drop considerably and minor pieces became affordable toward the end of the auction. The European section was auctioned and bidding was very slow. Several did not reach the reserve and finally lot number 232 arrived. 'Two eighteenth century portraits, damaged' and the bidding began. Catherine bid quickly and in a short time the other two bidders dropped out. 'Bang' went the hammer and Catherine was the owner of the two portraits.

'A good price,' smiled Mark. They were just about to stand up to go when the auctioneer stated, 'Lot number 233, no reserve,' and they all looked at this extremely large canvas in a huge gilt frame of a dark landscape. The bidding started slowly due to the size of the canvas and suddenly, to Catherine's surprise, Mark began to bid. The bidding was in only ten dollar lots but with his ever-straight face he raised his card again and again. 'Bang' went the hammer. 'Sold to number 87' which was Mark's number for the sale.

'Darling, what will you do with it?' asked a confused Catherine.

'Probably use it at Donegal,' he said in a non-committal way.

'Of course,' she replied, pretending to understand.

'Let's have a drink,' suggested Faith. 'It looks as if you two are the winners tonight. I personally would have killed for the Streeton, but the price! Forget it! I may just go back to art school - painting in the manner of,' and they both laughed.

Seated in an international hotel close to the Town Hall, they ordered and Faith quizzed them on Donegal. 'We can't tell you anything, can we, Mark?'

'No. I'm afraid Catherine's right. We went down to Lakes Entrance but all to no avail. The problem is we now know that Donegal is not a house but a property, but we don't know who this James O'Donald is, as one third of this is his as well, so I suppose we just have to wait until he pops his head up.'

'And calls for the cash?' Faith asked.

'If it's only money he wants, we have the properties valued and, depending what Dermit thinks, sell the house in Lakes Entrance, work out his third share and then Catherine, Dermit and I may just decide to keep Donegal.'

'Oh, really?' said a surprised Catherine.

'Why not?' He smiled.

'Why not indeed,'Catherine heard herself saying.

'Well, it looks as if you three are going to become country folk,' Faith laughed.

'We may just have to see what Dermit thinks, but it is close to the sea, though this lake view bit is most confusing.'

Ever since Jean's death Mark had become closer and closer to Dermit and Catherine. He lived barely twelve minutes away and ate with them at least twice a week now. Mark, like Dermit, was a good cook, so hearty laughter was heard from the kitchen zone in the big mansion in East Melbourne. Catherine found herself depending on Mark socially for a dash to an auction or an antique shop. It was now possible to coax him to a day at the races, which with Dermit and Catherine in the members' stand he had to admit to himself he quite enjoyed, so, from the non-committal nephew, he was developing into a good friend. Catherine often wondered about Faith's comment about the boyfriend and she hoped if this was the case that very shortly Mark would introduce him. But he was very secretive about his private life and as Dermit said, if it was possible for him to join them whenever they called, logically there was no other person he had to consider. The more Catherine got to know him, the more she was convinced about Dermit's reasoning.

Another appointment was made to go to see Donegal but this fell through, due to the winter weather now setting in, so they decided to wait until better weather, but most weekends were generally poor. Still the solicitor had not heard from this James O'Donald, so nothing could be finalised and the solicitor was now preparing to engage the local police at Lakes Entrance to help, in order to wind up the case. Dermit warned against it.

Catherine was determined, as it was her birthday, to invite Mark and also Paul and Gerald, because they were her closest friends. But she was also more than curious to see how Mark handled the situation. Drinks were first at East Melbourne and then on to a fine restaurant in the city.

'Come in, Mark,' she said. As he entered he heard voices laughing and the sound was coming from the large front drawing room. Catherine entered on Mark's arm. 'Mark, this is Paul and Gerald.'

23

They put their glasses down, stood and shook his hands. Catherine noted that he was very quiet. That might well have been the result of Paul's taking over the conversation and relating a funny story about Jenny Wall, she thought. The doorbell rang again and Catherine went to answer it. Dermit sensed that Mark was ill at ease and moved over and stood beside him.

'Well, I believe you think we should take a country residence together. I think it's a great idea, and if it needs a bit of work inside, we may just be able to coax Paul here to do some for us.' Mark smiled.

'Hi, Faith!' Gerald called out and went over to give her a kiss, as did Paul and Dermit. Mark very formally shook hands.

Once seated, the banter began and Jenny Wall yet again came into the firing line. Dermit went out and returned with his present for Catherine. She had forbidden the others to bring gifts, but was more than happy to accept Dermit's. The diamond and ruby bracelet was exquisite, an art deco design, with the perfect setting for the stones.

'Darling,' said Paul to Dermit, 'I hate to tell you, but my birthday isn't far away and something like that would be divine.' Everyone laughed.

As they moved to their cars, Gerald and Paul take Faith and Mark went with Catherine and Dermit. 'How do you like them?' asked Catherine. 'I have known all three of them for most of my life.'

'It took me a while to get used to Paul,' laughed Dermit, 'so don't worry, Mark, he is actually good fun and an extremely loyal friend.

'Did you think I wouldn't be able to cope this evening?' Mark asked and Catherine replied at once, 'Darling, I have no doubt at all that in any company you would cope splendidly and as we three are the closest of friends I know you will enjoy the others as well. This has been the first chance for Dermit and me to show you off to our closest friends.

'We both think you're great,' smiled Dermit, slowing down in a crowded street.

'Thanks,' Mark said. 'I think you two are great as well and I am sure once I know the others they will also be part of my life.' Here he stopped and then slowly began again, like a little boy who wants something and isn't quite sure how to go about it. 'Are you really interested in the property, or are you just going along with it to please me?'

'I think it's a great idea,' Dermit replied, 'especially the three of us. You see we had a beach house at Portsea but we never used it and as there were just the two of us we decided that we would get rid of it. So I sold it, with no regrets at all. I didn't miss the people or the place, but a place that is both country and seaside sounds another adventure altogether, especially as we are together.'

Mark thanked him and placed a hand on his shoulder.

* * * * *

After Catherine's birthday party Faith called the following morning to thank her and Dermit for their hospitality and for a fun evening. Then she said, 'He is beautiful – so elegant and he was quiet, not that anyone could get a word in edgeways with Paul on stage! But I have decided not to tell Terry about him yet. I don't want complaints filtering back to me.'

Terry was the younger of Faith's two sons and he fell in and out of love with the most amazing regularity. As Faith said, she could never keep up with this constant changing cavalcade of beautiful men, but if Terry was having a good time his father most definitely was not. The fact that his son was openly gay annoyed him greatly and Terry, realising this, made every move a winner, in that he aggravated this relationship and gained great pleasure out of it. Terry knew very well his mother would never throw him out of doors and the other power factor he had was the knowledge that the great majority of the money in this household came directly from his mother's bank account, not his father's, who had worked in a local bank for years. So the shouting matches were loud and often, and, as usual, Terry won, having developed a very sharp set of social teeth. His repartee could be poisonous. So as time went on, the small television room became exclusively Faith's husband's domain and the rest of this large house in South Yarva Terry's, where had had no compunction in bringing home his friends who inevitably ended up being Faith's friends as well. Terry's older brother, Colin, just smiled, took it all in and went his own way, seemingly oblivious to the fractured relationship between his brother and his father. Paul and Gerald had also called to ask why Mark had been kept a secret for so long and wasn't he just divine!'

* * * * *

The following week saw a great change in their relationship. Mark invited Catherine and Dermit to dinner at his home, which was the first time an invitation of his kind had been offered and to say Catherine was curious was an understatement.

'Oh, you didn't have to,' said Mark, as he welcomed Catherine with a large bunch of hothouse roses in her arms and Dermit with two bottles of wine. They were shown into the front sitting room of a beautifully restored double-storey terrace house on Richmond Hill. The décor was in the best of taste, but lush, nothing minimalist in this house and the warm interior was exceptionally welcoming. The large overmantel mirror reflected a wall covered in paintings in gilt frames with beautiful furniture covered in fine objects. There was just so much to see one had to concentrate on speaking to Mark and not letting the eyes drift off to yet another fine object or painting tastefully arranged. After the first drink, Mark took them on a tour of the house. It was all the same, well furnished with marvellous and strange objects that gave the whole house a sense of someone who lived there who cared very much about the contents, with every piece in perfect condition.

'Darling, it's marvellous,' Catherine enthused, reseating herself and having another drink. Mark left the room, asking them to excuse him for a minute, only to return with the roses in a large silver vase which he set on a cabinet.

'The house is great,' said Dermit. 'I hope you plan to do the same with Donegal,' and then, laughing, 'but we have to see it first. I wonder what it's like. I'm more than curious to know why Jean purchased it – it was so unlike her.'

They moved to the dining room, papered in a Victorian paper in lilac, gold and violet, an extremely dramatic room, again heavily furnished with fine pieces and lots of silver everywhere. Dermit look around as they began to eat.

Mark laughed. 'This whole house is the result of an unhappy childhood.'

'Was it unhappy?' asked Catherine.

'Not so much unhappy as lonely,' he told her. 'You see, I was only ten years old when my parents divorced. I was bundled off to boarding school and every break or holiday I found myself with Aunt Jean, as my parents re-married and I guess they saw me as unnecessary. I was always grateful to Aunt Jean. She never once forgot my birthday or my name day – ever. And every Christmas, from when my parents divorced, I spent with her and we always, even last Christmas,' he laughed', had two bonbons each. One we exploded before the meal and the other at dessert, which was always a big Christmas pudding with money in it. But you had to give the old currency back and Aunt Jean would give you the present currency.' When Catherine asked why, he told her, 'Aunt Jean was convinced the present silver currency tainted the pudding whereas the old currency didn't.'

'I suppose you must have assumed that as an uncle I was hopeless,' Dermit said, slowly.

'No. I guess everything and everyone has their time and place. Now that Aunt Jean has gone you and Catherine have slotted into my life and I couldn't be happier. I think,' and at this point he frowned, 'that everything is pre-destined. What do you think?'

'I couldn't agree more,' Catherine replied, 'but on the subject of responsible relatives, I agree with Dermit. We were both failures in your case.'

'Not at all. I'll now make sure you make it up to me!' and he began to laugh, before changing again. 'You know, you shouldn't say things like this but when my parents died I didn't feel anything at all. I suppose it was their guilt, that they left me, independently, their money, but that was it. I was happy to take it but there were no sad thoughts at all.' He poured more wine.' I am glad Donegal has a lot of land. I would like to have a garden, a large one. I have never had one before.'

'Sounds great!' said Dermit, 'on condition I don't have to do the weeding.' He laughed.

Catherine was aware that at every opportunity Mark returned to the subject of Donegal as if it were like a new chance in an odd way, an avenue he had waited for all his lonely life and then there it was, Donegal, and he hadn't even seen it – just a faded piece of lettering on an old wired-up wooden gate.

'You know,' Dermit said, 'your father and I didn't get along. In fact we hated one another.'

'You and the world,' was Mark's reply.

'When we were kids together we were always fighting, or he was. I always saw my elder brother as a bully and I guess your mother arrived at the same conclusion, hence the divorce.

'I never really knew him' Mark said. 'As a child I have no memory of him at all and after he divorced my mother I think I only saw him half a dozen times. I have no real recollection of him at all.'

'And your mother?' Catherine asked.

'Well, it's not much different. She married at once. He had two children, so she moved into a ready-prepared family, and there wasn't room for me. Besides I don't think the new husband was all that fond of me. His kids came first, so I just stopped seeing them and at every opportunity went and stayed at Aunt Jean's. She always said that people should have to sit an examination before they should be allowed to have children.'

'She was absolutely correct,' Catherine agreed and then changed the subject. 'Where on earth are you going to hang that huge painting you bought at the auction?' She looked around as there was no space on any of the walls.

'Well, yes, it will take some organisation but we shall see. Perhaps it will fit in better at Donegal.' And he laughed again.

Towards the end of the meal, Catherine told him he had been a great success and that Faith and the boys thought him adorable. He just smiled, but didn't pass a comment. But this smile was sufficient for Catherine to organise dinner parties with the same six of them, with four of them (and she included Dermit in this group) offered the opportunity to eat and also feast off the good-looking Mark. It had once or twice crossed her mind that Dermit was not blind to a good-looking man and in the past this had not worried her at all, as from her time at school with Faith their male friends had all been gay and many of them, like Paul, had remained their friends ever since. Dermit had fitted in with Catherine and Faith's friends without any problems at all, in fact Dermit now had very few straight male friends. And now Catherine saw him begin to take a real interest in Mark socially and she was sure it was not all guilt stemming from the fact he had virtually ignored Mark growing up. This re-discovery of the handsome Mark, she thought, was probably triggered off by a certain sexuality. e never knew it well as when here on vacation he generally remHH

CHAPTER 2

James O'Donald

CHAPTER 2

James O'Donald

'I don't believe it! It's raining again! What a bore!' Catherine complained loudly as she carried plates through to the dining room and began to set the table. The best china was brought out and she passed a pleasant hour preparing everything. Then she left the house and dashed for the car to drive to the supermarket in order to acquire exactly what Dermit had written on his list. Then she made for home, having meantime collected the flowers which today she took a great deal of time arranging. But the little thought that flickered back and forth in her mind was Donegal : it had now started to move into a fantasy, a big house in the country and Mark, oh yes, Mark, he was also part of this fantasy, the three of them enjoying life, laughing, telling jokes, confiding in one another and the guests they could have in the summer. Oh, how marvellous, Catherine thought and then something crossed her mind. What if Donegal wasn't a big house? What if it were just a tiny cottage? Goodness knows there was a strong chance of that. What would they do then? Sell all? No, she thought, we shall build something fantastic. And yet again her mind worked tiny miracles, imagining guests arriving, good food and wine and, of course, the nucleus of all this – Mark.

'But Mark,' asked Paul, 'what would you ideally like to do with this property?'

'I think I should like a secure hideaway from this world.'

'Wouldn't we all!' Paul exclaimed. 'Gerald and I were going to buy a holiday home at Merricks, but they are so expensive and the maintenance – and let's face it, most of these holiday houses are the pits.'

'I couldn't agree more,' Faith joined in. 'Hubby and I spent an exhausting four days at Portsea in the most expensive architect-designed house and it was terrible. Every time you moved in one room you could be heard through the entire building. So smart, it was hideous. I am so sick of it all. If you lay travertine flooring you are smart: who says so?'

'I'm with you, Faith,' Gerald agreed. 'Paul and I stayed with a business colleague of mine. Oh, the house was unbelievable but I will let Paul tell you.'

'The pits, darlings,' he said, looking at Mark. 'So designer that you thought you were in a hotel in Dubai, and everyone totally unrelaxed. A really fun weekend. I think that the ideal holiday house has to be a home as well, not designer chic or the other extreme, furnished exclusively with left-overs from others houses. Something soft and very comfortable. What do you think, Mark?'

'I agree totally with you. These travertine floors are great and so are the bathrooms but everywhere in winter they are freezing.'

'Absolutely,' said Faith. 'Polished floors, nice rugs, good antique furniture and paintings, not to mention good wine – that's my idea of a holiday home, and no, absolutely no neighbours.'

'That's essential,' said Mark, and everyone looked at him, waiting for another comment that never came.

'But when the hell are you going to get this super Donegal?' Gerald asked.

'Who knows?' was all Dermit could say. 'Perhaps this James O'Donald is in a nursing home and that's why they can't find him. It's taking ages. We know the address but no one returns the mail. The police aren't that helpful. I guess it's going to be necessary for us to go down in Spring and sort this mess out ourselves. You can bet this solicitor will give us a bill like you won't believe.'

'Isn't the legal world divine!' Paul commented sarcastically.

'But if we do need some help with this Donegal I trust we can rely on you, darling,' said Catherine, smiling at Paul.

'Well, it depends,' he replied in a theatrical way, 'whether my clients will let me go.'

'Oh., don't carry on!' exclaimed Gerald. 'They will throw you out!'

'Careful, sweetie,' came the sharp reply, which had the rest of the table laughing.

'Oh boys,' said Faith, 'I don't suppose I can interest you in a twenty-six year old whose hormones seem to be in the high randy position, can I? I need to get rid of Terry for a week.'

'Forget it,' shot the reply from Paul. 'We did the baby-sitting once.' He looked at Mark as he went on, 'A disaster! This wretched, beautiful child decided to use our home as a disco for stray cats, it seemed. A disaster! The police were called, the neighbours put in complaints to the council. Oh God, he is cute, Terry, but so irresponsible. No, darling, unless he is interested in being chained down for a few days. Forget it.'

Dermit laughed. 'I can just see you as Madam Lash, in leather, and whipping all into submission.'

'You'd better believe it, big boy!' Paul replied.

'Oh God, I'll have another drink,' Gerald sighed, gazing at Mark, who smiled.

'Why on earth do you have to get rid of Terry for a week?' Catherine wanted to know. She was exceptionally fond of him.

'It's hubby's cousin and wife we have coming to stay with us and Richard says that if Terry remains in the house he is leaving and staying at the Hilton.'

'I guess he's anticipating trouble,' suggested Dermit.

'Oh yes,' Faith explained. 'Terry hates them. He calls them suburban upstarts. I think he has shot that line once or twice to his father, so you can imagine what a state I am in. I don't suppose I can interest you, can I, Mark? He is good looking, but a handful.'

'Thanks, but children are not really my scene.'

'And what is your scene exactly?' smiled Paul, like a cat waiting for the mouse.

'You will have to wait for that,' Mark replied.

'I will.'

'No takers,' moaned a forlorn Faith.

'Oh, darling, if it's only for a few days Terry can stay here. No partners, though, that's the deal.'

'Oh, Catherine, you are a darling. He adores you and Dermit. He always says Dermit has the same fine taste as he has.'

'Oh, really?' asked Dermit.

'Yes, you both loathe Richard!'

'It's not hard to,' Gerald chipped in. 'He is the pits. I don't know why you haven't divorced him,' Paul went on in an uncharitable way. 'He is so anti-social, not to mention anti-gay. Oh, he is like someone from the dark ages. I suppose he must have been good-looking once?'

'Once,' was the sad reply.

'Oh, Mark, I forgot to tell you,' Catherine interrupted. 'The restorers have called me and your painting has been cleaned. They say you won't recognise it. It looks great with all the old brown varnish cleaned off.'

'Thanks. I'm looking forward to seeing it. And the paintings you bought?'

'They say another month or so, as the tears in the bottom of them are going to take longer to repair.'

'I suppose this large painting is Donegal-bound,' Paul smiled.

'Of course,' Mark said, simply.

* * * * *

Terry moved in with Dermit and Catherine for the five days and despite a certain anxiety he was fine, but he had the most spontaneous laughter. He did virtually nothing : Faith supplied the money so he didn't see why he should waste time on a nine-to-five job, so he was basically company for Faith and anyone else who wanted either fun or sex, or preferably the two together. This was the point that angered his father into screaming matches but they were rarer these days as his father had just decided that Terry was a no-hoper and would finish badly. He, for one, couldn't care less.

On the third day, Catherine returned late and instead of the usual gales of laughter and loud chatter with Dermit, there was a soft murmur from the kitchen zone. Catherine walked through toward this sound and to her utter surprise she saw Terry on a tall stool with eyes focused in only one direction, that being Mark. It happens, this effect of one's adrenaline pumping, and it doesn't follow that it is a two way effect, but for Terry this was the first time he had had this sensation where he just felt overwhelmed in the presence of another man. Mark never having met him before assumed that this was the real Terry. To say Catherine and Dermit were surprised was an understatement. The effervescent Terry had changed into, as Catherine said later to Faith, a loving Labrador waiting for his beloved master to take him for a walk. The evening was, to say the least, artificial. The only one who didn't see it as such was Mark, who continued as normal with two enormous brown eyes that never strayed from him for a moment.

The next day saw Terry going to the top and then plunging to the bottom. The questions about Mark never stopped and then Terry began to plan how to conquer this beautiful man and sweep him to paradise. This view pattern was not shared by Mark, obviously, and when Catherine explained to him that Terry was infatuated by him he casually shrugged it off with no enthusiasm at all. Catherine knew that now Terry was in for a rough time emotionally. When he returned to his parents' home, Faith was most confused by his behaviour. He became quiet and at times moody, but still found time to spar with his father.

'Oh, goodness,' said Faith to Catherine, 'I am not sure I didn't prefer his over-enthusiastic approach before. Now what am I going to do?'

Catherine and Dermit were overwhelmed at Mark's complete indifference to Terry's state and in fact he never spoke about him again, unless someone else brought his name into the conversation. Paul thought it all fitting justice and it was high time Terry learned this lesson, as in the past he had been ruthless with his lovers and for the first time the tables were reversed.

* * * * *

The telephone call had been sharp and to the point. Catherine sank down on a chair in the hallway and just stared ahead, not seeing anything or feeling anything. She hung up the phone feeling completely numb, like a robot. She dialled a number and a voice responded. 'Catherine, how nice to hear from you.'

'Mark,' replied an empty voice, 'Dermit is dead.'

'Where are you?' he replied in a business-like voice.

'At home.'

'Don't leave. I am on my way.'

Twenty minutes later the front door bell rang and Mark saw a white-faced Catherine staring at him as if he were invisible. He stepped in and held her in his arms. It was this spontaneous gesture that released the floodgates of tears and he held her for some minutes before they moved into the living room, where she sat down weakly.

'I don't know what to do,' she kept saying and again began crying. 'It just isn't possible. It just isn't possible.' Her whole life with Dermit began to flash like short videos in front of her eyes. 'My whole life was with Dermit. What shall I do now? I'm all alone. There's no one.'

'I am always here, Catherine, never forget that,' he said and from the sideboard poured her a stiff drink. 'What happened?'

'It was a multiple heart attack. Oh, what shall I do?'

'Nothing. I shall take care of everything. Don't worry. I think you had better lie down for a while. Later, I'll prepare a light meal for you. There is nothing you can do except pray.'

Catherine frowned and looked directly at him. He had seen the death of both his parents and recently of Aunt Jean and so instantly she saw him as a strength at this moment in her hour of need. But she felt numb. As she lay down, a certain unreality seized her. All the most ridiculous small things swarmed together and like a vicious group of mosquitoes attacked her. It was in this state of helplessness that she cried herself into a light sleep but not before she had gone through her past with Dermit into about ten agonizing minutes.

Catherine and Faith had met him at a party when they were in their final year of art school. They had attended an evening with a group of their gay male friends and it never crossed either of their minds that the very handsome Dermit did not fall into this category. But it appeared that this was not the case – or was it? She now wondered and if so, why had they married and been so genuinely happy? They had not had children, this being due to a low sperm count on Dermit's part, and to be implanted with donor sperm was simply not on as far as Catherine was concerned and so they had just lived extremely full lives but ones where harsh comments and bitter recriminations just never existed. Instead it had been a life of security, happiness and love, but a love based on equality and sharing, not to mention laughing. All these long years together and now her husband, lover, companion – all gone. 'I am so sorry,' the voice at the end of the telephone has said, 'but your husband has suffered a heart attack and has collapsed and died.' All she could hear now in her ears was the word 'died, died, died'!

A knock on her door aroused her and Faith entered and sat on the bed beside her and held her hand. 'Darling, I am so sorry,' she whispered, 'and if there should be more appropriate words I haven't got them.' She leaned over and hugged her. 'Come on. Let's go downstairs. Mark has done everything. When I came he dashed home, collected his things and he will stay here for a while until you sort everything out. He is very worried about you.'

Catherine thanked her but said that she might just stay where she was.

'No, darling. If you stay here now, you won't sleep this evening and that's not going to help you at all. Come on.' She spoke in a commanding way and the two women walked down the staircase arm in arm. They went into the kitchen area and took a seat overlooking the meticulously manicured garden. Mark produced three champagne glasses and filled them. He then said, very boldly, as they charged their glasses: 'To Dermit' and the response was 'Dermit.' The conversation was fairly static, with Catherine at times losing track of the subject, though she grasped the fact that everything – undertaker, solicitor, everything - had been taken in hand by Mark. Faith said she had to be going but not before she withdrew from her bag a little bottle of pills. These she handed to Mark. 'One each evening for a week,' she directed. 'They are strong and will do the trick.' She looked at Catherine. 'Darling, this next week is going to be hell so you do exactly what Mark says. Take one each evening and the next day you will find things just a little easier.'

After Faith had left, Catherine said she was exhausted and began to cry. Mark held her in his arms and then escorted her upstairs. When she had changed and got into bed, he came back into the room with a glass of water and the pills.

'No, Mark, I don't need them.'

'You had better take one, anyway,' he smiled at her, and perhaps it was the smile, just for her, that didn't make her feel quite so alone. The pill took its effect and Catherine slipped into a soft world without any problems.

Mark had taken time off from work as he was owed quite a lot of time and spent the first three days fine-tuning organisation and answering the telephone. Faith, Paul and Gerald rallied in strongly and Catherine, although she cried in private, held up well in public. But it was the funeral that she dreaded, that final parting, the last moment of someone she had loved dearly all her life.

The priest entered, wearing black vestments as had been asked for. 'In nomine Patris et Filii et Spiritus Sancti.'

'Amen' was the response.

Mark looked sideways at Catherine, dressed totally in black, as were they all, but she seemed quite fragile in her black suit with a mantilla in black Brussels lace.

'Gratia vobis et pax a Deo Patre nostro et Domino Iesu Cristo,' the priest intoned.

'Benedictus Deus et Pater Domini nostri Iesu Cristi,' came the response and the funeral Mass continued.

As they left the church, following the coffin, which had had the black velvet pall removed, the bunch of white roses that Mark had organised for Catherine were lifted off and then with the removal of the pall replaced on the coffin as it was moved to the hearse. There had been a packed church and toward the end Catherine was aware she was becoming quite tired thanking everyone. Faith also saw this and told Mark to take her home; she, Gerald and Paul would join them.

As she entered the house, the smart façade gave way and she wept bitterly in Mark's arms. He just held her and let her cry. It was an outpouring of everything that she now was to go without, namely Dermit's love and companionship and so these five or so minutes were for Mark very difficult. He moved her to the sitting room and sat her down.

'Did you see?' she asked, a little like a child, and slid the sleeve of her jacket up to expose the diamond and ruby bracelet.

'Dermit would have approved,' he smiled.

'Yes, I am sure he would have.' And for the first time Mark recognised a tired little smile.

Faith, Paul and Gerald arrived and in their own way began to short circuit the enormous loss. It was Faith, when Mark was in the kitchen organising lunch, who said to Catherine, 'I had to be firm with Terry and told him not to trouble you today – or should I say, not to trouble Mark.' Everyone smiled. Terry was still besotted with Mark. The more Mark ignored him the more infatuated he became and to see him dressed all in black and so sophisticated, thought Terry, as he watched Catherine on Mark's arm leave the church.

The next two days were slow and Dermit's solicitor, a friend of Catherine's arrived at the house in the late afternoon to read Dermit's will. Catherine inherited everything and then the solicitor said that a month before Dermit had added a codicil to the will which left a large terrace house in South Yarra that was tenanted by Mark to him. To say Mark was surprised was noticed by both the solicitor and Catherine and he handed Mark a letter. Dermit had been a very wealthy man, but a very intelligent investor. He owned a great deal of property and this now all reverted to Catherine. Mark opened the letter, read it and then handed it to Catherine. It began:

Dear Mark, To begin to know you at 34 years of age only points out to me my irresponsible behaviour of the last 34 years, where I left my sister Jean to pick up all of the responsibilities. Since you came into my life after Jean's death you have been someone I can honestly say I love and I hope you feel the same. To share with you has given me the greatest of pleasure as I am sure it has Catherine. This terrace in South Yarra is just a little something I should have done 16 years ago for you, so please forgive me. I hope this letter won't be read until we have shared many happy years at Donegal. Love, Dermit.

Catherine let the solicitor out and returned to a very circumspect Mark. 'I can't take the terrace in South Yarra. It's your property,' he said.

'And you cannot refuse it, as this codicil was obviously added to the will not so long ago, so this is definitely what Dermit wanted, and so do I.'

'I think we could do with a drink,' and they moved to the kitchen area, overlooking the garden, and sat down together.

'It's strange,' said Catherine,' but I feel so much more at ease now that Dermit wrote that letter to you, for you see he really did love you. We spoke about it one evening. He didn't see you as the son he never had but more like an adult discovery of someone he had lost but then relocated, you, and he was immensely proud of you.'

'He was extremely kind to me,' Mark replied slowly. 'I have never had such a close relationship with a man,' and then he looked at Catherine and smiled, 'or with a woman. You have both been great to me, eating with you both at least twice a week, the races, the theatre, restaurants – it has been a new way of looking at life for me.'

'I hope these expressions are not all about the past. I should like to think we two can continue in the same way.'

'Absolutely,' he said, 'and you realise that you are now a one third owner in Donegal.'

'Yes, Donegal' and she smiled and glanced into the garden as a blackbird jumped about, pecking at an invisible meal.

It must have been a fortnight after Dermit's funeral and Mark was still living at Catherine's home. She had not been out, except for one evening meal at Gerald and Paul's with Mark, but she was beginning to face the world and she knew only too well that this was due to Mark.

'I'll get it,' she said, going to answer the telephone. 'When? Oh yes. I think we can be there. What time?' She listened to the solicitor's instructions. 'Very well. Goodbye.' She hung up and made her way into the kitchen to find Mark preparing an early dinner. 'Well, we have been summoned to Jean's solicitor's office next Wednesday at 10.30 to finally resolve this Lake Entrance mess. At last some progress!

At the weekend, they all decided to go out to a restaurant Faith knew, and just before Mark and Catherine left the house she asked if she could have a word with him. 'Darling, I have two things to ask you but I don't want you to make any decision until tomorrow. Is that clear?'

'Certainly. What's the mystery?

'I should like you to move in here permanently. The house is vast, so there is no shortage of space and your independence is totally guaranteed. The second is this: Dermit has left six real estate offices and a good rental agency, plus all the properties he has acquired over the years. I don't know what your attachment is to your present occupation but I would be only too happy to hand over the entire running of these investments to you. Do think about it.'

'Catherine - -' he began.

'Now, Mark, nothing said until tomorrow. Oh, I forgot to tell you. I do hope you won't mind being adored all night. Faith says Terry is threatening suicide if he can't join us this evening. I hope you don't mind.'

'Not at all. He is actually a nice kid.'

'Well, my advice is don't tell him that or you will be pushing him out of bed this evening.' She laughed as she said this and was aware that she was laughing again.

'Let's go,' he suggested, and they walked arm in arm to his car, parked in front of the house.

Faith had never seen Terry and Mark together. Goodness knows, she had certainly heard enough about him at home as that was now the only thing Terry seemed to talk about, so this evening Faith was in for a shock. Terry barely said anything and if he did he directed it to Mark with his eyes wide open, hoping desperately for a reply that was longer than yes or no.

'So, Wednesday is the day you finally get to meet Mr Mystery man,' said Gerald.

'Yes, I'm more than curious. We are told that he is coming down by train.'

'I hope there is not a wheelchair problem,' laughed Paul.

'Oh, goodness, do you think this James will be that old?' asked Faith.

'How old was Jean?'

'She was only sixty five,' replied Catherine and then realised that Dermit had passed away at sixty two and that both of them should have had at least another twenty or so years ahead of them, but Paul's infectious laughter brought her back into the conversation. 'Sorry! What did you say?'

'Just a joke about a wheelchair. I am sure your Mr. O'Donald will be a perfect old gentleman as he is probably only a few years older than Jean.

'Do you and Catherine plan to live in this Donegal house?' asked Terry, directing this question, as all others, to Mark.

'We don't know yet. We haven't seen it and as Catherine says it may be quite tiny. We have no idea what we are doing until we sort out Mr James O'Donald at 10.30 on Wednesday.'

Wednesdy morning at nine the telephone rang as Mark moved his clothes into the large guest bedroom permanently and wondered what the role of Managing Director of O'Brian Real Estate was to offer.

'Hello,' he answered. 'Yes, yes'. Then he sighed. 'I suppose so. Goodbye, Catherine,' he called out and she made her appearance at the bottom of the staircase. 'It appears that we have to collect this geriatric from Flinder Street Station. Something about him not being very orientated in the city, so we shall have to leave earlier.

'What time?' asked a buoyant Catherine.

'I'm told the train gets in at 10.30, in a bit less than an hour. In case there is traffic. You know what it's like.'

'Darling we won't find a parking place. Let's say we do all this by taxi. It just has to be easier.'

'You're right. Where on earth does one find to park in Flinders Street?'

Very shortly after she called out, 'It's here!' She gathered up her handbag, still wearing only black, and they entered the cab and sped off in the direction of Flinders Street Station.

'It's platform one. I remember catching this train regularly to Aunt Jean's,' said Mark, and Catherine reached over to hold his hand. He replied with a smile. She now depended on Mark much more than she had on Dermit. If Mark was late, she began to worry, whereas with Dermit and his job it never worried her at all.

'We go through here,' he said, and they entered the noisy country platform with a loudspeaker that defied understanding. They stood, waiting for the train, as people pushed and hurried around, seemingly in great haste but where were they all going? Eventually the train slowly pulled in to the platform and it was then that Catherine said, 'Mark, how on earth shall we recognise him?'

'I don't know, but if he is looking for someone, as we are, we must find him.'

'Why didn't we write his name down on a piece of cardboard like they do at the airports?'

'Yes – I never thought of it.'

The train came to a halt, the doors slid open and the passengers began to file out and flood the platform, making for the exit as quickly as possible.

'If we can't find him,' Mark said, 'I'll have an announcement put over the loudspeaker system,' but Catherine said she thought she had spotted him. They made their way over to an elderly man with white hair, looking confused. Just as they came near him, he waved and headed off toward someone who had signalled him. Catherine looked at Mark. 'Perhaps he missed the train,' she said, as their eyes scoured the now-emptying platform, but after another few minutes they were becoming concerned. They were relatively obvious, Mark and Catherine extremely well-dressed and Catherine as elegant as usual, so they stood out in this environment.

'Hello,' said a voice, and Mark spun around. He just froze. He didn't or couldn't say a word. It was Catherine who took over. 'Are you James O'Donald?' she asked in an odd way, aware her voice was higher than usual.

'Yes,' was the quiet reply and there he stood. He couldn't have been more than sixteen or seventeen, thought Catherine, and had obviously been in an accident. He had a black eye and a bad cut down the side of his face. He was tall with black or very dark hair cropped very short, with a good face except for the obvious damage and a happy smile. But the eyes were amazing – long, black lashes surrounded a pair of cobalt blue eyes. The look was electric. He had broad shoulders but seemed very thin, though this was hard to tell as he had on a short jacket that was torn on one sleeve and his jeans were marked, but, as Catherine thought, this was probably as the young wear clothes nowadays, having seen some of Terry's outfits when he was ready to tackle the town and the bars. The boy looked out of place and moved from one foot to another. 'Shall we go?' she suggested, and they headed out to the taxi rank and took a cab directly to the solicitor's office.

'Come through,' was the secretary's request and the three of them filed through into a very plush office.

'Well, Mr O'Donald, you have kept us waiting. Why didn't you reply to my letters?' James started to say something but then thought about it and stayed quiet.

'Let's get this done,' said Mark and James turned and looked at him. It was the first time he had heard this deep voice say anything.

'Well,' began the solicitor, and read through the will. There was silence. 'I take it all is clear. In the case of Mr Dermit O'Brien having passed on, his share goes into the estate that is now the property of Mrs Catherine O'Brien. May I have your bank account number, Mr O'Donald. I can, at the end of the week, have the cash divided and it will be placed in your accounts.'

James looked completely confused. He had brought and handed to the solicitor a statuary declaration of who he was but no one had said anything about a bank account number. 'I, I - -'he began. Mark stepped in and said, 'I'll phone it through this afternoon.' The solicitor thanked him and said that all was done. They stood up, shook hands and left the office. While waiting for the lift, it was obvious to both Mark and Catherine that something was very wrong with James.

'Are you returning home this evening?' Catherine asked. His quick response was 'How?' Mark looked at Catherine and then at James. 'I don't understand. I haven't any money. I thought the solicitor would give me some and everything would be OK but now I need a bank account.' Tears began to well up in those big blue eyes.

'Mark, I am sure we could manage lunch at home, couldn't we?' He agreed and was aware that he was not only smiling but felt very happy about the arrangement. 'First, we stop at a bank and open an account and then lunch. How does that sound?'

'It's OK,' was the quiet reply.

They took a cab to Catherine's bank and, knowing the manager as an old friend of Dermit's, the account was opened with two hundred dollars from Catherine's account and in less than twenty minutes they were in another taxi headed for East Melbourne.

'George Street, please,' and the taxi driver looked at Mark sitting beside him and without a word headed off to the required destination. Conversation was virtually nil, with Catherine wracking her brains to think of a subject to begin with, but before she knew it the taxi had pulled up. Mark paid and out they got. They both noted James's look as he glanced from side to side of the façade of this large house in awe.

'Come on, James. I am absolutely certain we are all going to be the best of friends.'

Catherine did not realise exactly how prophetic this statement was to be. Mark noticed that James walked strangely and moved his back oddly, but said nothing. Once inside, James was truly out of his depth and looked very embarrassed. Catherine, sensing this, moved him into the kitchen's informal dining area, thinking he might feel more comfortable. Mark left them for a moment and telephoned the solicitor with James's bank account details, then returned and put a hand on James's shoulder, only to notice a grimace and movement that suggested pain.

'James, how did you get these injuries?' he asked directly. James cast his eyes down in embarrassment and did not reply. 'James,' Mark repeated, much more softly, explaining they were there to help him in any way they could.

'My father belts me,' he whispered. Something rose in Mark that was somewhere between fury and the re-arming of a firing squad. 'Come with me, James,' he said gently and he took him upstairs to his bedroom and through to his bathroom. He removed James's coat and jumper and then underneath he removed the tee shirt, all with no resistance. To say Mark was shocked was an understatement. James was marked all over his back with what must have been the result of a belt used so the buckle was the main part of the weapon, and it had cut into the skin badly. Mark immediately went to the cabinet and withdrew a tube of Huridiord, a cream for reducing bruising. It had been a new tube, as his old one had been misplaced in moving to George Street but most of the tube was used on James's face, arms and back. He re-dressed and looked at Mark.

'Mrs O'Brien said you were a good guy and she was right.'

Mark started to say something and just gagged. 'Let's have lunch and then we'll work out what we are going to do with you. Come on.' He lightly placed one hand on James's shoulder. James turned a little and smiled. 'Thanks.' He grasped Mark's lower arm and they went downstairs. He sat at the table with Catherine, who offered him a drink and suddenly realised she didn't know how old he was.

'I'm just over nineteen,' he said.

'So would you like a glass of wine or champagne?'.

'Whatever you two are having.'

Catherine noticed that his eyes moved about the room but always returned to Mark. She let Mark take over in the kitchen and little by little began to draw out of him his sad story.

'He always beats someone up, especially when he's drunk. He used to beat my mum up all the time.'

'Where is your mother now?' asked Catherine, and there was an odd silence, then on a sudden movement he swung his head up and stared directly at her. 'She's dead. She couldn't take it anymore.' Catherine was aware of reaching for her glass and drinking quickly.

'How did you know my aunt?' asked Mark, as he realised they hadn't even reached first base in this conversation.

'Miss O'Brien was the only nice person I knew. I used to get her her paper and a carton of milk each day, but when you were there,' he looked at Mark, 'you did it but she paid me the same. You see, I wasn't good at school and I didn't have any friends. Everyone was afraid of my father. He is mad, you know.' He spoke in a flat tone.

Mark brought the food to the table that Catherine had laid while the conversation went on.

'The only person he was afraid of was Miss O'Brien,' he went on, eating hungrily. 'Oh, this is good. I didn't have breakfast this morning. You see, now Miss O'Brien has died there is not much food around.'

'You can have as much as you want,' smiled Mark. 'Do you work?'

'How can I? Every time I get a job my father comes and yells and screams and so they fire me. They say I am bad for business.'

'Do you have to go back to Lakes Entrance this evening?' asked Catherine.

'I don't suppose so,' he replied.

'Good. You are going to stay with us for a while. If that's alright?' There was a slight smile. 'It's alright with me,' and little by little, as the afternoon drew on, he began to tell his life story to two people that were going to be a dominant part of his future.

'I didn't do well at school. The kids gave me a hard time. They used to make jokes about my clothes being bad and holes in my runners. They called me names all the time, but they were all really scared of Dad, who would make a fuss whenever he could. So I left school as soon as I could.

'When did you meet Jean?' Catherine asked.

'When I was still at school. My father beat me up one day and I ran out of the house and I just walked and walked, crying, and I guess I ended up in front of Miss O'Brien's house. She must have seen me and came out. She offered me dinner, as I hadn't had anything to eat all day and I told her about home and then she helped me. Dad was real scared of her. It's strange but he used to sweat when she was near him. It's strange, isn't it, she was the kindest lady I ever knew. Whenever I had trouble at home I used to stay at her house. She used to give me some money for watering her garden and helping her do some weeding. We used to go fishing. I really liked it. She was a good fisherman.'

'Mark was surprised. 'I never knew. When I stayed with her life was very quiet. It's odd. She never said anything to me about you.'

'Oh, she talked about you all the time,' James replied. 'She said that you and me were alike,' and then blushed with embarrassment.

'I'm sure we are, if Aunt Jean said so. You realise that she has left you one third of the house.'

'Yes, I heard what the solicitor said.'

'But what can you tell us about Donegal?"

'Oh, you mean the farm? Well, one Sunday after –' there was a pause '– my mother went, I was having lunch as usual with Miss O'Brien after Mass. She insisted that I go to Mass with her every Sunday. You see, that's how I knew you at the station. I remembered seeing you at her funeral. It was nice in Latin. She loved it. Anyway, we were talking about things we had always wanted and it turned out we both had always wanted to live on a farm, and not long after she took me one Sunday afternoon, after lunch, to see our –' he proudly said 'our' '- farm. Well, it's not in good shape but every Sunday after Mass we used to take a picnic lunch and eat it there. I really like the place.' Here he stopped and began to eat again.

'Is it a big house?' asked Mark.

'I think so. It has windows in the roof. It's really nice but it's falling down a bit and there is no electricity but it's really nice.'

'Do you drive?' Mark asked.

'Yes. Miss O'Brien paid for my lessons and helped me study for the questions.'

'You can have her car when we go to Lakes Entrance. I will have all the papers changed for you.' James beamed his thanks.

'Do you want the house in Lakes Entrance to live in?' asked Catherine.

'I haven't any money, so I couldn't afford to maintain it,' was his quiet reply.

'Well, that's not a problem for the moment, but you must be settled somewhere where this father of yours has no access to you. Do you understand me?' James said he did. 'So now we three have to decide what to do with Donegal.'

'We could sell the house in Lakes Entrance and live at the farm. Don't you think that would be nice? That's what Miss O'Brien and I were going to do.' He looked forlornly down at what was left on his plate and ate in silence.

'Catherine and I will have to talk about this but I don't see any reason why we can't honour Aunt Jean's wishes, do you, Catherine?'

She agreed, and then leaned over and lightly touched his arm. 'Wow!' was all he said, but the broad smile showed that once again, in a strange way, Jean O'Brien was coming to his rescue.

They stopped the questions and turned to lighter conversation but it inevitably returned to 'our' farm and all the things he and Jean had thought of doing, on those summer and autumn picnics. This property had become an escape from the ordinary world, two extreme people who had been bound together in a fantasy world that they both believed firmly would become a reality.

The afternoon passed pleasantly with Mark and Catherine coming little by little to know or understand James. In the late afternoon Mark took James to a pharmacy and he purchased two tubes of Heriodiod and that evening after dinner, as they had all decided to have an early night, Mark once again applied the ointment to the damaged skin.

'This will never happen to you again,' he said in a determined voice, but James did not reply. Mark was very aware of the sensuality of rubbing the cream into James's back and upper arms. He was very thin but had a particularly broad set of shoulders. This skin was not white but a soft, olive colour, as if he had lain stretched out in the sun all summer and the tan was beginning to fade.

'It's been hard for me,' James admitted, 'since she died. She was my only friend and now when Dad gets drunk I sleep in the park or on the beach.' He turned around and held Mark's hand. 'Thank you very much. You are both very kind,' and continued to hold Mark's hand a little like a child receiving security from the knowledge that the strong hand meant safety. But Mark felt a different sensation that swelled his whole being into a wonderful warm state that was tinged with sexuality. Pyjamas were located and James said goodnight and settled down in this mansion, not really believing his good fortune. Mark went downstairs to find that Catherine was still there, having filled her glass as well as Mark's

'Well, it appears we have the third party for Donegal after all,' and looked at Mark. He slid his hand over and held hers.

'I am certain Dermit would have been very proud of your kind offer to include James in Donegal.'

'Yes,' she sighed, 'but isn't it odd that Jean had this other life with James.'

'Perhaps she didn't,' he replied. 'Perhaps this was her real life and we were just the others.'

'Yes, I hadn't thought of it like that. I suppose it depends from what viewpoint you look at it.'

'Let's hang on to the two properties. James can live in Aunt Jean's house for now and when we fix Donegal up he can move there and then we will sell Aunt Jean's house. What do you think?'

'Yes, that is the most practical way of looking at it. But the father – how on earth can a father beat a nineteen year old?

'You should see his back,' said Mark. 'I think when we go down to Lakes Entrance this weekend, I shall go to the police and make an official complaint about this form of behaviour. It's absolutely unacceptable.' He was aware his voice was rising.

'He's a very handsome boy,' Catherine remarked.

'Yes, very.' Catherine noticed for the first time in Mark a different side to him, not just being helpful but James was bringing to the surface another Mark, a vulnerable one, without the social shields in place.

'I'll photograph the lesions on his back and arms tomorrow morning, not to mention the black eye and this may well do to convince the police to keep an eye on him.'

'Mark, did you understand when James was talking this evening what happened with his mother?'

'No, not at all. She's dead. He obviously didn't wish to talk about it.'

'So Jean virtually looked after him from when he was at school. I wonder how old he was when this feral father began beating him?'

'No idea. But with time perhaps he will tell us all the story.'

'But no money. What the hell are they doing at school that allowed it to escalate to this level. I just can't believe it. That no one in all his years of schooling didn't notice that something was wrong.'

'I couldn't agree more,' Mark said, and they finished their drinks and headed upstairs.

'Well, we shall be able to dream of dormer windows tonight,' Catherine laughed as she kissed Mark goodnight and went to her room, but when Mark pulled the blankets up around his neck it wasn't dormer windows that were on his mind, it was a battered nineteen year old with the most beautiful, sensual face in the world.

The next morning, James was not convinced that photographing him in this state was a good idea.

'Look,' Mark argued, softly, 'let's take the photos and keep them as an insurance policy for the future. No one will see them unless your father becomes very difficult.' So a reluctant James allowed Mark to take the photos. Then Catherine gave him a tour of the whole house and James said he had never seen anything so grand and beautiful.

'Oh, just wait until you see Mark's terrace house.'

'I thought he lived here?' said James and Catherine explained about Dermit's death and the fact that now Mark was permanently in residence here and now James was as well, who was welcome to stay whenever he wanted and for as long as he wanted. 'Remember, we are all owners of Donegal,' she said.

'I never thought I would ever own anything. It's fantastic. I just can't believe it. When I woke up this morning in that fabulous bedroom I just sat up and looked around for ten minutes before I got out of bed. I felt really good.' He laughed. It was the first time Catherine had seen him laughing. With those big blue eyes and his sensual lips open he seemed another boy altogether.

'Would you like to meet some of our friends for dinner?' she went on.

'Yes, that's OK with me, but my face is a bit of a mess.'

'Darling, they won't notice it at all.' And how right she was.

When Gerald and Paul swept in to George Street on Friday night, the black eye, especially to Paul, was invisible. 'Paul is going to oversee the renovation of Donegal,' said Catherine.

'What would you like it to look like?' smiled an ever-cautious Paul, sensing immediately that Mark had very territorial claims on James.

'I saw Mark's house this morning, so I guess if you could make Donegal something between here and Mark's house it would be great.'

'Well, that's quite an order, but we'll have to see what we can do,' and a very pleasant evening ensued, though James would not be drawn into any part of his past life, only the future, and that was Donegal – or was that all? Paul noticed the movement of eyes between Mark and James and was certain that James had found the invisible key to unlock the hidden Mark that the rest of them had been unsuccessful with.

'Oh, won't our Terry be ready with a meat cleaver!' thought Paul.

The next morning, they left very early for Lakes Entrance. James was looking a little better and certainly better dressed, due to his being thinner but approximately Mark's height, so his torn jacket had he had arrived in on Wednesday was gone and a beautiful black leather jacket that fitted perfectly from Mark's wardrobe had taken its place, not to mention shirts and jumpers from Dermit's wardrobe. It had James looking a happier young man. The bruises were still noticeable but the black had turned to a murky brown, still obvious, but much less so. And so were the marks on his back and shoulders. He still refused to discuss how or why this beating came about and so they just left the subject alone. The closer they came to the turn-off with the vandalised cottage, the more excited James became. After three hours of travel it was, in Catherine's mind, quite a feat. They turned down the road with the pot-holes and although the wind blew a cold whisper across from the lake system there was no rain. 'It's always raining here,' said Catherine and turned back in her seat, almost to touch face to face with a very agitated James.

'Keep going, keep going!' he exclaimed and they did exactly that, at the slowest pace, due to the shocking road surface.

'It wasn't here, you know,' James said and when Mark asked him what he meant, he said that the road was new. Mark was surprised, thinking that a new road should not be quite as bad as this long stretch of pot-holes was.

'You see, the only access to Donegal was by the lake. This road here now was put in only ten years ago. Before that, to go to Donegal and the house beyond, you had to take a boat from Metung or Lakes Entrance and there are big stairways going down to the water.'

'You mean, originally, all the timber for this house was brought in on boats?' Catherine asked.

'Yes, everything you wanted had, until ten years ago, to come in here or go out by boat, so you were very isolated.'

'Sounds great,' commented Mark, dodging another pot-hole.

After what seemed an eternity, they arrived at a gateway that almost proudly proclaimed that they had made it to Donegal. 'If you go further up this road,' James explained,' there is another house, but I have never seen it. When we got this far it was enough!' He laughed.

This time, Mark looked at his tachometer and from the main road in it was much closer to five kilometres than the original estimate by the post girl of two, so Donegal was isolated but only because the road system was so bad. They parked the car at the gate as James said you couldn't go beyond there and on foot they headed in. 'Isn't it great?' he cried enthusiastically - and all Mark thought was, 'Isn't he great?'

The house couldn't be seen from the road. There were groups of scrub and trees that obviously masked the house from the road and after quite a walk they turned and entered behind yet another group of trees and there it was. Both Catherine and Mark stood transfixed. They just stared at this amazing structure trapped in the middle of nowhere. How on earth, thought Catherine, could you possibly have moved all this timber, door frames, windows, roofing, all the way from Lakes Entrance by boat and then hauled it up the cliff side and assembled it all? The thought that went through her mind again was, 'Why?' But James was ecstatic. It was his world and even if he didn't have any money he was the richest man in the world. 'Isn't it fabulous?' he said, and in his enthusiasm grasped Mark and embraced him. Catherine noticed clearly that the indifferent man suddenly lit up like a Christmas tree and they still had five and a half months to go.

The house had, on closer inspection, once been symmetrical. The classic front door had panes of glass from halfway up and a window either side with twelve panes each, but at some stage the left hand side had been extended, throwing the symmetry out of line. Another matching window had been slotted into the extension and so the two dormer windows were much closer to the right hand side of the roof section. On the same side as the extension there was also a skillion addition which made the whole façade one of progress, not to mention necessity. The veranda ran across the front and halfway down the right side, and a rail and narrow pieces of criss-cross wood made up the balustrading, but only in one part. Between the veranda posts the rest had obviously collapsed with time. The weather boards were painted a chalky cream colour which once might have been white and all the detail was picked out in brown. There was no cast iron trim, just fretted wooden brackets at the top of each side of the veranda posts. From first impressions, the two dormer windows seemed to have the glass intact. On the left side of the front door along the handrail grew a thick hedge of blackberries, which, it appeared, had been eaten back at the bottom by sheep or cattle, of which both had left their distinctive marks. Oddly, there were no chimneys to be seen. Either side of the main block grew large, bushy trees to the height of the roof in a dull green and it was possible to see another building or at least the roofline of it behind. One solitary post standing in this well-grazed field denoted that once it had been the corner post of some form of domestic fencing that surrounded and protected the house and garden but of these all that remained was the one lone one.

James's enthusiasm was contagious and they moved forward for a closer inspection. 'It's a pity the door is locked,' said Catherine, trying the panelled door, which was picked out in brown and cream, but with very little paint remaining on the bottom section.

'Just a minute,' and James ran around the veranda - or on what boards were still left in place - and returned with the key. With a certain flourish he unlocked the door and they all went in. It was a cold, late morning in early spring so the interior seemed completely forgotten and sad. There were six main rooms of a fair size, plus the skillion, which had two rooms, and up a steep stairway were two bedrooms. The front windows overlooked where they had come from but the back had a view from this height between the trees to the lake system. The house itself was built back from a cliff and from the upper windows you could just see a type of wooden railing that had steps that went down to the water. Mark was quite excited. 'I think it's fantastic,' he said. 'I love it!' He smiled at James as he went downstairs and wandered around. What must have been the living room held an old wooden table and two chairs but nothing else. The old holland blinds were in shreds and a ragged, printed cotton curtain hung listlessly at the window. The whole of the interior of this house was lined in lath and plaster, some of the rooms having pine lining ceilings. The hall was also half-lined with vertical pine lining, topped off with a finishing in wood to give the impression of wainscotting. Old twisted electrical wiring supported naked bulbs but it was evident from outside that the electrical supply had been cut off many years before. Yet despite all the run-down, negative points about the house there was a feeling of hope Catherine had the odd feeling that with just a bit of work here and there it could once again return to being a large, cosy, family home, and then in a reflective mood she thought of a man she had loved dearly all her life who would not be sharing it with her. She roused herself from this thought and stepped outside onto the damaged veranda to see Mark and James returning from looking at the old stairs that in two turns arrived at a tiny pier at an acute angle at the bottom: this once had been the only method of contacting the outside world before the road had been put in only ten years before, now in such poor condition.

'Boys, will you bring me the large box from the boot of the car.' They returned, laughing, with the box. Catherine dusted off the table top and the two chairs and from the box set out a deluxe lunch for the three of them. James went to an outer shed and returned with a wooden box which, upturned, served for the third seat. There was a white damask cloth, co-ordinated crockery, glasses and serviettes and champagne ready to open, Catherine glanced at the open fireplace and then realised that outside there were no chimneys.

'They must have closed them off at some stage. How very strange!' Mark commented.

'Perhaps they were built badly and just fell down,' James suggested, as he lifted his glass. 'Here's to Miss O'Brien.' He smiled and they all charged their glasses. 'It's great, isn't it?' He looked at both Catherine and Mark.

'Yes, it is,' Mark agreed, 'but you are going to have to make some decisions, James.'

'Oh? What do you mean?'

'Well, now that we are at Donegal, and I think we are all in agreement to keep it, what do we do about the house in Lakes Entrance?' Do you need it?'

'No, I should like to stay here.'

'Well, for the moment that's rather difficult,' Catherine said, looking around. 'For one thing there isn't any electricity, which means no hot water and no light, so until this is all put in order it appears you have three choices.'

James held his breath and two large blue eyes crossed between Catherine and Mark expecting to hear problems.'

'First, you could return to your father,' and James narrowed his eyes, 'secondly, you could live in Jean's house in Lakes Entrance independently, as by the end of next week you will have money in your account, or thirdly, you could come and live with Mark and me in Melbourne until everything is sorted out here. Which would you like to do?'

James put his glass down slowly on the table and turned it around. Catherine was aware that there was not only one anxious man at the table.

'If it's not a problem, I'd like to –' and here he stopped to look directly at Mark '– go back to Melbourne with you both. Is that OK?'

'Yes, James, that's perfect.' Catherine smiled and also noticed a much more relaxed and happy Mark sitting opposite her. 'Let's have another look about the house before we clean up.' They retraced their steps and gave the house a full inspection. It was then they realised that the large detached section at the back of the house held the kitchen and servants' quarters and as Catherine said, 'If these two buildings were joined together it would make this a sizeable dwelling.' They spent another half an hour walking about, living out fantasies and then coming back to reality about furnishings and gardens. Behind the kitchen block were a number of service buildings, a stable, sheds for agricultural equipment but all in poor condition.

'I wonder why they didn't open up the road originally?'

'I guess because it went across someone else's property and they were just not co-operative about letting them have access, or perhaps the original owner or owners just enjoyed the isolation of the property.'

'Yes, but isn't there another house further down the road?' asked Catherine.

James told them that there was and that it originally had access to the main road from behind it. He thought that when the road was opened up they just put a gate at the end of it so they had two entrances.

'We must get the telephone number of the real estate agent; perhaps Paul and Gerald might be interested in it. What's it called?'

'No idea,' James said. 'There is just that 'For Sale' sign on the post near the gate we saw when we arrived. It will have the telephone number on it. Why don't we clean up here and have a look at it?' Mark agreed.

Having returned everything to the box, James carried it back to the car and they walked down the road to the other property for sale. It was a fair walk in and it was obvious that the roadway had not been used for years. Then they came upon the oddest sight. Here was a largish weatherboard house with a veranda on three sides with a faded red tin roof but the oddest thing was that the weatherboards were painted in alternate colours, one blue, one cream, one blue, one cream,. This effect continued under all the veranda, with the rest of the house painted a cream shade. It was in much better order than Donegal, with a garden fence surrounding it, but a very overgrown garden. It looked as if it had not been inhabited for at least six months or so. All the blinds were drawn, so it was impossible to see inside. They noted that the farm buildings were in working order, so perhaps although no one lived there the farm as such was still working. They turned and headed back to the gateway, closed it, and Catherine said, 'I wonder who is grazing Donegal?' as they could see the grass was quite short around the house.

'No idea,' replied Mark, 'but for the moment whoever it is is doing us a great favour.'

'I wonder if it's the farmer who owns the property that's now for sale?'

'Time will tell,' and she took yet another photograph on her digital camera.

'I think that must be the two hundredth photo you have taken,' laughed James.

'Well, it's a good idea to record everything. I'm sure, otherwise, we should forget something.' They got into the car, traversed the terrible road for the five kilometres and headed back to Melbourne with a very contented James on board.

CHAPTER 3

A New Breeze

CHAPTER 3

A New Breeze

Estelle was five foot nine, thin but with slightly broad hips, which annoyed her no end. She was vain and saw herself as the desired woman. She had a sharp face and all her features followed suit. When she laughed, which was rare, or smiled, the look she gave was uncomfortable but when unhappy or discontented, which was her regular state, those pale green eyes narrowed and she had the habit of straightening her short, reddish hair with her left hand. She had worked for Dermit all her life and she was a good, if not over-determined, worker. It couldn't be said the staff liked her, but every one of them was well aware of her business capabilities. She had no pity at all: they were all there to make O'Brien and Company money and that was that. Many a new employee in the first fortnight was told they were not the sort of person she was looking for. She dressed as for someone much younger and sometimes that made her look even harder. She had been having an affair for some time with the manager of one of the branches of O' Brien and Co., Rodney Taylor, who, needless to say, was married with two children. Estelle brushed all that aside saying the wife was a bitch and poor Rodney had been conned into the marriage. This was obviously not correct but it suited Estelle's point of view. She had this manner of closing cupboards or drawers that made her mood known immediately to the staff and this morning, after having waited, like the entire staff, for Catherine to determine policy, as the business was now hers, the slamming of a cupboard door made it very obvious to all that the telephone call she had received did not suit her at all. She had assumed that when Dermit died she would have automatically been elevated to Managing Director of this prosperous company but to be told that Dermit's nephew was to take over galled her no end. Who the hell was this nephew, she wondered.

If there was one person in this world Estelle loathed it was Catherine. She saw her as the success story a rich woman in her own right and with Dermit, the good-looking Dermit she had tried every trick in the book to make him her lover, but it was Catherine, always Catherine who won, not Estelle. Among many things that annoyed her about Catherine was that when she entered a room everybody stopped and looked at the elegant woman who was expensively dressed and jewelled. Estelle had thought a teaspoon of poison in her champagne glass was an excellent idea, and here she was, Catherine, dictating that Dermit's nephew would take control of the company, not her. She immediately called Rodney Taylor to pass on the news and vent her spleen, stating that she was surprised Catherine hadn't sold the company and pitched them all out on the street on their arses.

Catherine was not unaware of Estelle's attitude to her and warned Mark to be very careful. 'She works well and knows exactly what she is doing, but be careful. She will undermine you at every turn. If,' Catherine smiled, 'she becomes just too difficult, fire her.' With that she finished her drink.

So the first day at the new job as Managing Director Mark saw Estelle at her most obvious. She had been pleasantly surprised that Mark was so good-looking and assumed with her charm he would be easy to control in bed and out of it. It was here she was in for a shock: he virtually ignored her, calling for his secretary or rather Dermit's, a certain Maggie Thompson, a very stocky woman in her mid-fifties and she dressed as such, always with a smile and equally always with a scowl for Estelle. It had been Estelle's idea to get rid of Maggie as soon as possible and in fact in the first interview with Mark she suggested strongly she had to go – 'too old to keep up with the business these days' was her comment. 'I will hire and fire as I see fit,' was Mark's clipped reply and the later slamming of Estelle's office door alerted the staff to the fact that the new Managing Director was not going to be controlled by Estelle. This gave Maggie, especially, a great deal of satisfaction, and as a result she lent over backwards to assist Mark in his new position.

The end of the first week saw Estelle at her worst. She managed to find out that Maggie on Thursday evening had been invited to Catherine's home in George Street for dinner and not her. Maggie had arrived and although solid she had the most charming, happy face, well made-up and topped off with a magnificent head of thick black hair, perfectly coiffured. She got along very well with Catherine and had regularly dined with Dermit and her, and now this was repeated with Mark and in Dermit's place was a young man she noted called James, who was a very attractive person. She wondered where he actually fitted in.

It had been an evening of laughter and funny stories, of which Maggie had lots, but the stories she loved telling the most were at Estelle's expense. One that was dear to her heart, which had Mark and James in hysterical laughter, was when Estelle had arrived at work with scratches on her face and was limping. 'This was due,' Maggie smiled, 'to an adventure with Rodney Taylor.' Rodney's wife and children were staying at the seaside and due to a confusion of dates he assumed that the coast was clear and so for some odd reason Estelle went to Rodney's home for an afternoon of love-making, when, to Estelle and Rodney's horror, his wife and children arrived home. Estelle dressed rapidly and thought to save the situation but make-up everywhere was definitely going to be the give-away. Rodney opened the bedroom window and Estelle tried to escape but the tight skirt was a problem, so it was necessary for Rodney to lift her onto the window sill and, hearing the children, he pushed her out of the window and closed it afterwards rapidly. The mistake he made was in not telling Estelle the distance between the window sill and the ground or garden level, which was considerable, as the house was built on an incline. Down she went, flat on her face into a row of hydrangeas, scratched and very crumpled, having twisted her ankle. She limped off to her car and sped off.

Maggie was now laughing with Catherine. 'Can you imagine, one minute in the arms of one's true love and the next moment catapulted into the hydrangeas! I have no idea how Rodney explained the flattened bushes,' she laughed.

Maggie genuinely liked Mark and so evenings like this were relaxed and enjoyable but she was still curious to know if James was Mark's lover or if he were simply a relative.

James had become for Catherine exactly what she needed at this time. The loss of Dermit had been extreme and she was only too grateful to Mark and James for constantly keeping her company. While Mark was at work at O'Brien & Co. it was James who was always with her and she enjoyed having him with her and so his social education began. His bad bruising was now gone and at Catherine's insistence he was letting his hair grow so all round he was a very desirable companion. He learned fast. Catherine only had to explain something once to him and he remembered it. Catherine was now teaching him about the art market that was her passion and he enjoyed the opportunity to see and learn. Although the cash from Jean's account had been transferred, or at least his share of it, into his bank account, he rarely used it as either Mark or Catherine paid for everything. His relationship with Mark was still slightly formal. It was as if they were good friends but the sexual undercurrent was strong, but with neither of them prepared to make a move. Mark was totally dependent on James socially. From the loner this was a big change and nothing pleased Mark more than to arrive home to find James and Catherine chatting or laughing over a drink and this was for him the first time he had experienced a sensation that he likened to family, not having any concept of one from the past.

This evening Paul and Gerald were invited to dinner and the main topic of conversation was Donegal, as Paul had driven up and had a look at the property as well as the property for sale at the end of the road.

'You must use an architect that lives close. It's no good using one from Melbourne and then you find you have a problem in the country three hours away. It will hold all the work up and you will have to pay for lost time.'

Mark asked whom he suggested. 'Well, there are two architects in Bairnsdale. I suggest you use Peter Symonds. He is a nice guy and very thorough but not very innovative, so I suggest that Peter does the drawings as the house stands now, then we decide what we want and give him the brief. He can do the finished designs, we check them again, he submits them to the council and when cleared he takes over the work. And that should be it.'

'Well, it seems feasible,' said Catherine. 'Can you call him and tell him to start.'

'Certainly. Oh, I will have another slice of that pork. It's delicious. Gerald had some burnt offerings on the table last night. I can't begin to tell you.'

'Careful!' Gerald warned. 'The truth is, the oven is automatic or should be, but as it didn't turn itself off Sunday lunch was eaten with smoke masks on.' CAtherine laughed and said she could just see it.

'See it!' cried Paul. 'The damn smell permeated the whole house. We had all the windows open. What a mess!'

'So what did you think of the other house?' Mark asked.

'I like it, but there is a problem with the owner about the land. He hasn't decided if he wants to keep some of the land or not, so we shall have to wait until next month. But I must say Donegal is just charming, though it's in terrible repair.'

'It's fantastic,' James joined in. 'I know it's going to be just great when it's finished.' They all turned to look at him, and he smiled back at them, then looked directly at Mark.

'Yes, it's going to be just great,' he replied.

It hadn't taken Paul and Gerald long to catch the sexual undercurrent between Mark and James, but as they said later whilst driving home, 'There is something odd about the set-up with the two boys. I don't think they are sleeping with one another.'

'Yet,' came Paul's quick reply, 'James seems totally concerned about Donegal, don't you think?' Gerald agreed. Catherine had said that it was his escape from the world, or the terrible family he had, so he guessed he could understand it. Paul agreed. 'He has had a rough beginning but he seems to have landed on both feet with Catherine and Mark.'

'Well, especially with Mark. Not bad at all and for that matter without the bruises our James is not bad.'

Paul saw fit to ignore the comment. 'I believe that the house of the aunt has to be sold in Lake Entrance as James said he doesn't want to live in it. Some of the money will go to restoring Donegal, but they are going to need a great deal more than that to finish the renovations.'

'Money is not a problem with Mark and especially with Catherine's wealth,' Gerald concluded, 'so Donegal is going to become a reality for James. Let's see if Mark and James together form a real situation.'

'No doubt of that, sweetie!'

Catherine lay in bed. She became aware of an odd sensation. Here she was, without Dermit, but her house held two men that, if she thought about it carefully, she did not know well at all, her nephew Mark and this mysterious youth called James. She rolled over and thought about it again, then came to the conclusion that although she missed Dermit terribly these two young men were just marvellous.

It cannot be said, though, that everyone followed the same thought pattern. Faith had diplomatically explained to Terry that James was now in residence with Mark and Catherine and a quick glance at his narrowing eyes made it very clear to her that son Terry did not think this a satisfactory arrangement at all. Terry was still infatuated by Mark and the more distant Mark became the more intense Terry's feelings were, but now, with a third party on the scene, Terry's jealousy became fine-tuned. Faith had warned him that one wrong step with James would cancel any chance he might ever have with Mark.

'So they are lovers, are they?' he spat.

'No, I don't believe so. They have separate rooms.'

'Really? That doesn't mean anything. They are probably just being discreet for Catherine's sake.'

'Terry, don't be so terrible. I don't know their relationship and nor do you, so give it a rest.'

He made no reply but his exit from the dining room and the slamming of the door made it quite clear that he was out for blood, preferably James's. The first time he had seen James was with Catherine and Mark at a concert and he was genuinely surprised at how good looking James was. He had moved over to see them and was charm itself, complimenting James at every opportunity, to which James's sixth sense told him to be very careful. He saw him for what he was, a rival for Mark, but he felt no danger at all in that situation, strangely, and just graciously accepted Terry's compliments. But it was Terry, later, who realised he had real competition for the man he lusted after and every skill in the book was going to be necessary to separate the two of them, one way or another, and it came to him in a delicious, calculating way that divide and conquer was the only way. That meant taking James to bed first and in all honesty that wasn't going to be such a hardship, then declaring it and collecting the grieving Mark. Oh, so simple, he thought. 'I can't imagine why I didn't think of it earlier,' and a much cheerier Terry passed by Faith and suggested they eat out together as Dracula was sure to be glued to the television all night for the Grand Prix. To say Faith was surprised by this sudden turn about only alerted her to her son's capabilities to organise everything to suit himself and with that situation she felt very uncomfortable.

The relationship with Mark and James was still forming; this had a great deal to do with Mark's personality. He found it difficult to touch anybody except in a moment of need, as he had in holding Catherine after she had discovered Demit had died, and in a much more physical way when he administered the cream to James's back and shoulders, but to suddenly embrace someone was still a step ahead that he had to arrive at. For him, at this moment work was all absorbing; fitting into a new role wasn't easy and it was Maggie who rounded off all the sharp corners, much to Estelle's annoyance. The agencies worked directly with head office, that being in South Yarra, but the managers of each branch of O'Brian & Co. in district suburbs were virtually autonomous in promoting sales and each branch had a letting agency. It worked very well, as the managers were completely responsible for promotions, sales and rents, and as such each year, depending on their capacity to force successful sales, took a bonus and a healthy one on the year's take. It was Estelle at Head Office who always claimed the largest bonus. She worked her staff hard and always produced results and it was for that reason alone that Mark, for the moment, let sleeping dogs lie, even though Maggie had quite firmly suggested getting rid of her. This change of administration was not so different from what had been before. Estelle couldn't have Dermit and after a week or so realised, ever more clearly, that Mark was out of the question. But it didn't stop her pushing and casual flirting, that Mark disliked and found very threatening. For that reason, everything now had to go through Maggie and nothing annoyed Estelle more than that. The repartee between the two head women in this company was poisonous and the staff enjoyed immensely the banter between the two of them, with Maggie always winning and always finishing a sentence with a very patronising comment. The slamming of Estelle's office door always meant she had lost, at least for now.

Her relationship with Rodney Taylor continued on this thin ice existence, with both being very careful not to say too much, as this might just, by the new manager, be construed as bad public relations for the firm. So these fleeting moments of passion were now becoming few and far between. This was absolutely not to Estelle's liking at all, and so, like Terry, she decided to hasten things along. She was, in fact, quite similar to Terry in the pursuit of affection; work-wise they were opposites. Terry had no attachment to a career or, for that matter, work at all, hence his father's constant criticism, but when it came to love, he and Estelle, although they had never met, were very similar. They were capable of organising the most irresponsible intrigues only to suit themselves. If someone else became hurt in this exercise it was the luck of the game as they saw it. Neither Terry nor Estelle gave a damn for the loser, providing it was not them.

Estelle realised that there was no win in the Head Office. She could go no further than she had achieved and she realised quite well that Maggie would knife her whenever she could with Mark. She decided to move sideways for a while, which meant taking over one of the other branches as Manager, so she immediately began research to locate which branch was producing least. This, she reckoned, would be seen as a noble act on her part and she could get exactly what she wanted. But to her horror, when all the information of the last financial year was in front of her, it was Rodney Taylor's branch that was not producing well. All the other managers held on to their lucrative jobs firmly and even

Estelle recognised the difficulty in dislodging them. 'Hmm!' she thought, 'Rodney!'

Terry was also beginning to move forward as well and at an informal drinks at Gerald and Paul's, seeing James by himself for a minute without the ever-present Mark, slowly moved in. The compliments were subtle and Terry saw James as easy prey but he was more than surprised when James spelt out very clearly that he was not interested in going to bed with him now or ever. He smiled and, leaving Terry, crossed the room to join Catherine and Faith. Terry now saw James as the enemy and his attack changed. He would now have to get rid of him once and for all. He had heard his mother recount James's story and as his background was exceptionally vague Terry realised that it would be reasonably easy to discredit him. A theft at the house in George Street would instantly throw a shadow of doubt over him. 'Of course,' he thought, 'straight for the jugular vein.' The vicious determination to destroy James was not ending his passionate desire for Mark, but the fact that a very attractive nineteen year old boy had openly refused him struck him hard. He still felt weak when he saw Mark but now every time he saw James he disliked him more and more, as he saw him as the victor, not him.

It took less than a week for Terry to put his plan into operation, at a dinner party at Catherine's. He knew the house very well, having stayed there for a week not so long before. On an excuse to use the bathroom, he sped upstairs and straight to Catherine's bedroom and there it was, fate was playing right into his hands. She had taken it off and left it on her side table, the bracelet in rubies and diamonds, the last gift from Dermit. Terry quickly removed the top drawer of her chest of drawers and placed the bracelet right over the back on a flat piece of structural timber so it was completely invisible. He then slid the drawer back in and hurriedly dashed down the staircase to collide with Mark as he rounded the corner. 'Oh, we must keep meeting like this, and linked arms as they returned to the front sitting room. The linked arms did not go un-noticed by anybody.

While Terry had the satisfaction he had won, Estelle meanwhile was deciding how to axe Rodney Taylor nicely. Their relationship had indeed tapered off. Rodney had never forgotten the close shave he had had with the wife and children returning to the family home as he pushed Estelle out of the window. It was a fact she hadn't forgotten either, so Rodney was now being very careful. He knew several of the management staff were aware of the affair and was terrified that someone at a drinks party just might, for one reason or another, see fit to inform his wife, so with a relationship wind-down Estelle reckoned that Rodney had to go and armed with the figures for four financial years she placed them in front of Mark and bluntly asked him what he was going to do about the branch manager who was not performing. He cautiously asked her what her ideas were to lift the branch and was surprised how tough she really was.

'Fire him! The figures for four years speak for themselves. He is in a good area and obviously has no drive so we, or should I say, you and Mrs O'Brien are the losers. But,' and here she stopped and glanced at him in a hard way with narrowed eyes, 'give me the position as manager of the branch and I will bring the figures into line within six months. Think about it.' She smiled and turned, then closed the door behind her.

Mark glanced at the sheets and then called Maggie in. The two of them studied very carefully the sheets and both had to admit Estelle was correct. The branch should be showing much better results. 'Estelle thinks we should fire Rodney Taylor. What do you think?'

'Well, you do realise they have been lovers for years, although I hear on the grapevine that their relationship has faded, but he is a good man, Rodney. He works hard. Just a moment – I've got it! Why don't you just get Estelle to do the dirty work? If you bring Rodney into Head Office here, he is going to see you as the demon, so why not get Estelle to do it for us, as Rodney will see the administration as supporting him, not censuring him, so he is bound to work better, especially as he will take over Estelle's office. What a scream! Oh, let's do it, Mark.' She laughed at the idea. 'The company can only benefit.'

Estelle was genuinely surprised when her telephone rang and she was summoned to Mark's plush office.

'I have thought it over,' he said, 'and I agree.' Here he hesitated, and Estelle immediately began to finger her short hair. 'If you want this position, you will speak with Rodney and inform him of the change. I will not fire him, but you will inform him he is to take your position here at Head Office on Monday morning.'

Estelle was bright, and she now waited for the second round. 'And I accept your offer to turn his branch round and I will expect a different financial statement in six months' time,' he added.

'I accept, on one condition,' she said, sharply, which made Mark feel it was he who was being disciplined.

'Really What?'

'That I have a free hand in re-organising this branch and no interference from Head Office,' which obviously meant him and Maggie.

'Fine,' was his clipped retort. 'You start on Monday but remember you must inform Rodney as soon as possible.'

The glare before she departed acknowledged that she still had one hurdle to cover, Rodney.

His cellular telephone shrieked as he was going to his car. 'You will meet me for lunch,' and Estelle gave him the address.

'Sorry, Estelle, I have another appointment.'

'Oh no, you don't, darling,' she retorted sharply. 'You will be at the restaurant or you may well be looking for a new job,' at which she hung up.

Rodney knew Estelle very well and that tone of hers simply meant trouble. He walked into the chosen restaurant and to his surprise Estelle was seated at a table waiting. It had always been the reverse. She did not rise as usual and kiss him, but just waited until he had seated himself.

'Help yourself,' she said, in an offhand manner as he poured himself a drink.

'What's this all about?' As he spoke, a shiver ran up his spine. He had never seen Estelle like this before. He had seen her deal ruthlessly with staff but never with him and now he had a terrible feeling he was in for trouble.

'You will, on Monday morning, move to the Head Office, where you will be placed in a position that you will negotiate with management.'

'And if I don't go along with this,' he started, defiantly.

'Oh, that's easy. You're fired.'

He began to breathe regularly but deeply. 'So I am to work with you, am I?' he asked.

'Not at all, Rodney. I shall be taking over your manager's position on Monday morning, so it's one in one out.' She stared at him.

'You've organised this to suit yourself. You are completely irresponsible.'

'Not at all, darling,' she replied in a calculating way. 'I am anything but irresponsible.' With that she stood up, collected her handbag and smiled. 'Give my regards to your wife. Oh, Rodney, before you make it to Head Office, get yourself some decent suits and ties, darling. You have never had any taste.' She disappeared out into a busy lunchtime crowd, leaving Rodney completely numb. It was only when he phoned Head Office and Maggie replied to assure him that these were in fact the arrangements that he understood full well Estelle had sacrificed him for her own gain.

Estelle swept into her new position with a force that shocked the employees. She demanded better work productivity, which obviously would show dividends in six months. She was without mercy, an architect she knew was called in and the somewhat tired real estate office was completely overhauled giving it what Estelle thought was a much more corporate look. Within the first week she had fired two staff members and advertised for more, so the staff were very much on their toes and writing was on the wall: 'Make better sales more quickly or you are fired'. Estelle's interviewing technique was terrifying. She showed not the slightest interest in what they had to say and somehow gained a great deal of satisfaction criticising their dress sense.

The result of Terry's theft of Catherine's bracelet was not immediate. In fact it took twenty four hours before she realised it was gone and she called Mark in to speak about it, without James.

'Mark, I can't understand what has happened to it. It can't just have gone astray.'

'Are you sure you haven't place it somewhere safe?' he asked.

'No, I have looked everywhere.'

'But who was here that evening?' he asked and they went through their friends who had dinner with them.

'Mark, it just isn't possible. We know everyone so well. What has happened to the bracelet?'

They both looked at one another and an automatic split occurred between them. Mark had known the friends of Catherine and Dermit only for a short time, so they were all suspects to him, except, of course, James. But for Catherine it was exactly the opposite. She had known all these friends of hers and Dermit well, all except Mark and especially the mysterious James. They glanced at one another over the breakfast table, trying to make a logical decision about the theft.

'But why?' asked Catherine. 'I have known everyone for ages. It doesn't make sense.'

And so this hovering sense of not knowing became a very uncomfortable living situation where everyone who had been at the evening when the bracelet went missing could have indeed made the trek up the staircase, stolen the piece and no-one would have been any the wiser. But it was James who felt that a certain finger of blame or suspicion was aimed at him, as the last in, and he defended himself over dinner sharply.

'I didn't take it. Why would I? This is the first time in my whole life I have found two people I like really well. Why would I steal from one of them?'

'Darling,' Catherine insisted, 'no one is accusing you of anything.'

'Well, it looks like it to me,' he said, looking down at the splendid meal Mark had prepared for them. 'I didn't touch the bracelet.' He repeated this, and although Catherine supported him verbally he was not convinced that she believed him. 'If you don't trust me, then there is no point at all in my remaining here.' He looked at both Catherine and Mark. The thought of James not being with him gave Mark a very sudden jolt. The idea that he might not be with him to share his every moment was just impossible. Mark was now utterly distressed and both Catherine and James saw this. It was the first time in his whole life that Mark had loved another person and as much as he kept it very formal, love it was.

'No one, James, would dream of asking you to leave. The three of us just fit together very well. I am sure the bracelet will turn up.' But none of them that evening believed for a moment it was going to be that easy.

The missing bracelet also had a negative effect on the rest of the group who had been present for dinner that fateful evening and it was Faith who discussed it with Terry.

'Well,' he said, in a calculating way,' who do you think stole it?'

'Terry, please, I haven't an idea. The finger of suspicion points to all of us, I'm afraid.'

'Oh, I don't think so,' he said, in a nonchalant manner. 'My bet is James helped himself to it. Remember he comes from a background that is anything but clear.' He reached over and refilled his glass. Faith said nothing at all, but stood and moved to the kitchen bench to begin to prepare dinner.

Gerald and Paul were much more talkative about the social dilemma that they were involved in. 'I am certain it's not James,' said Gerald.

'Well, sweetie, I am unfortunately not certain of anything. It could have been any of them, even Mark. But I haven't a clue and certainly it's not Catherine, unless she was looking for attention and hid it so she became the star of the show – you know, the post-Dermit routine.'

Gerald just stared at Paul without saying a word. Paul looked around, feeling most uncomfortable. 'And don't look at me like that,' he said. 'I don't have a single outfit I could wear the ruby bracelet with, anyway.'

It was then that Gerald began to frown. 'For heaven's sake, what's wrong?' Paul asked him, nervously.

'We are so stupid. It wasn't stolen for financial gain. Think about it for a moment.' He raised his glass and then returned it to the table.

'You mean it was taken to discredit someone? But who?'

'Well, who is it that at the back of our minds we probably wouldn't be surprised if he was found with it on his person?'

'James.'

'And who do we know in the group that is the one to benefit if this happened to be true?' Paul turned his head a little and then narrowed his eyes.

'Of course. Terry. I heard James knock him back on an offer of a night together.'

'And not only that,' exclaimed an excited Gerald. 'Who is Terry madly infatuated with?'

'Of course, of course,' cried Paul. 'Mark!'

'Good thinking. This is a set-up to discredit James so then Terry can step in and take what he wants most, Mark. Why didn't I think of it before? It was when you said about Catherine perhaps seeking attention that I realised that there was another person seeking attention – Terry from Mark.'

'Well, I must say you seem to have worked it all out but how the hell do we get Terry to return the bracelet and confess?'

'Yes, that's the tricky bit. He may be attractive but Terry is a real bitch.'

The two of them muddled through plan after plan but to no avail. They just couldn't think of a way of forcing Terry's hand on this theft.

Catherine said to Mark and James that she was having a dinner party on Friday evening and she was intending to invite the same group again. 'If we don't fight fire with fire then everyone is going to think that we are just afraid to confront them for one reason or another.'

'I suppose you're right,' Mark agreed.

'If you don't want me to come, it's OK with me,' said James, quietly.

'James,' Catherine spoke sharply, 'if you are not present it is going to look as if you have something to hide and I for one don't believe it, so the three of us will welcome our friends on Friday night with the knowledge that one of them knows more about this missing bracelet than the rest of us.'

'I must say Catherine's game,' Paul remarked, drying himself as he stepped out of the shower. 'I hope she has all her other jewellery under lock and key.'

'Don't be silly,' Gerald protested. 'Terry has done what he wanted to. To do it twice would be just stupid.'

'To steal the bracelet in the first place was bloody stupid,' Paul went on, dressing.

'Be that as it may, he is very, very determined to get Mark into bed.'

'For this whole period after the theft, Mark was even more supportive of James than ever, something Catherine took note of, but he was also very disturbed about the theft. Catherine took the matter of trust evenr further and left two pieces of jewellery of high value lying on her chest of drawers and not in the safe. It wasn't that she thought she was tempting James or for that matter, she reasoned, Mark. What she was doing was proving mainly to James that she trusted him. James was aware of Catherine's stand and felt very supported, even if the finger of blame seemed to be pointed in his direction a little more obviously than at any of the others.

'Come in!' shouted Catherine, as everyone arrived together. Faith was obviously a little nervous and Terry, as infatuated with Mark as ever and as gushy as ever. But this evening it was the quietest of them all, Gerald, who began ever so subtly to lay a trap for Terry and, of all people, he did it with the aid of Mark. Drinks were supplied and at one stage Mark left the room for another bottle, not an unusual occurrence in this house, but when he turned around from closing the refrigerator door he was very surprised to find Gerald close behind him.

'Gerald!' he exclaimed, looking at him and noticing he had put a finger across his mouth to silence him. Gerald drew him close and whispered his theory of the theft and told him that no matter what happened this evening he was to trust him implicitly. Mark nodded in agreement and the two headed back to the drawing room, talking in a slightly artificial manner. Mark was now agitated and furious that it had been Terry that had cast a shadow of doubt over James. He had the urge to take James in his arms and tell him that he had always believed in him - but had he, he wondered?

They all sat down to dinner, chatting, but a certain tension was there. Gerald began to bait Terry and Terry, being so sure of himself, didn't even see the trap that Gerald was clearly laying for him. The conversation in this elegant dining room touched on their usual subjects but not this evening on jewellery, until Gerald began his planned attack. He addressed most of the conversation at Mark, not the others. Paul, usually the centre of attention in the dining room, fell into silence as the dangerous game began.

'I believe you said, Mark, that the police have some evidence about the theft.'

'That's right,' Mark replied, not having any idea where this conversation was going but following every move Gerald offered. The table was now silent and the cutlery on the china seemed to make a deafening noise. They all now stared at Mark.

'Mark, you didn't tell us that you had brought the Police into the situation.'

'I think it was very wise to have handled it like this, Mark,' said Gerald. 'When did they say that they would have the results of the finger prints ready?'

'I'm not sure,' he replied weakly.'

'Well, that obviously means that we shall all be finger-printed and then the situation will be quite clear. It was very clever of you to have that policeman you know so well, Mark, do this job discreetly. Didn't you tell me that once proven this crime carries a jail sentence.'

'Yes, if we press for it,' Mark smiled, finally catching on to the game. Everyone looked at one another and here Paul stepped in on the act.

'Oh,' he said, raising his glass and smiling, 'you mean that if the bracelet was returned,' and here he turned and looked at a very nervous Terry, 'or located the Police would just forget about the issue?'

'That's right,' Mark told him, surprised that Paul was now part of the act.

'Oh, I do hope they use the digital finger print machine and not that tacky black ink. It goes everywhere.'

Faith had the odd sensation that something was very wrong and if she felt strange, Terry was genuinely worried. It had never crossed his mind that Mark knew a policeman and that they had taken the finger prints the following day and his were sure to be amongst them. He knew no matter how he twisted the truth there was no convincing way of explaining his prints in Catherine's bedroom. He had emptied his glass and refilled it rapidly but did not say a word.

The meal continued and at one point Terry stood up to use the bathroom. Gerald glanced at Mark and then frowned as the others were talking amongst themselves. Suddenly Mark caught on. 'Oh, Terry,' he said, very quietly as he passed behind him, 'use the bathroom upstairs. There's a problem with the one down here.'

Terry left. Gerald winked at Mark, who was starting to feel very hot and the conversation about art prices was something he wasn't interested in at all. Gerald and Mark waited patiently for Terry to return and Gerald could see Mark was very nervous. He leaned over and put his hand on his and smiled. This did not go unnoticed by James but it was Faith who was becoming agitated and sensed something was afoot and said sharply to Gerald. 'What's going on between you two?' glancing at Mark and Gerald.

'Nothing, Faith. We were just discussing some receipts for hot curry.'

'Really!' she said in surprise. Terry returned and the stilted conversation continued.

'I don't feel so well,' he said and looked at Faith.

'Oh, Mark,' said Gerald, ignoring Terry's so-called complaint. 'Paul and I' – and by this time the table had fallen to salience – 'are very proud of you and your love for James and your support of him in this period. We think you both make a splendid pair, don't we Paul?'

'Absolutely a perfect pair!' Paul chimed in.

Mark took a deep breath and looked directly at James and taking all his courage in both hands replied in a strange, business-like way, 'I am very proud of James.' There was a slight pause. 'And I am very much in love with him.' Strangely he felt neither embarrassed nor awkward and smiled at James. This was reciprocated.

'Oh, boys, how wonderful!' Catherine exclaimed and a radiant smile was seen, the first, it must be said, for many days.

'Can we leave now?' asked Terry, looking at Faith, and he was genuinely feeling ill. But it was a type of nausea brought on by fear, not to mention the possibility of exposure. Faith rose and they all said their goodnights and as Catherine returned from closing the front door she noted a lot of smiling. She resumed her seat as dessert had not been served.

'I'm sorry Terry isn't feeling well,' she said, in a charitable way.

'Wait a minute,' cried Paul, not listening to Catherine's remarks. He raced upstairs to Catherine's bedroom, and when he returned he had a countenance that looked like the cat that had got the cream.

'Well, well,' he said, 'how nice you knew Constable Plod, Mark. Such a helpful man!'

'Mark, I had no idea you had called the Police. Why didn't you tell me?' Catherine asked.

'Simple,' answered Gerald. 'Because Constable Plod remains trapped in Enid Blyton's books.'

'What are you talking about?'

It was obvious at this stage that James had also lost the plot, but despite this he was looking very happy.

'Close your eyes, Catherine,' Paul insisted, which she duly did and then opened them to see Paul with the bracelet around his wrist.

'Paul!' she cried, surprised. 'How - where - I mean, where did you get it from?'

'I shall not tell you until Mark serves the champagne and Gerald serves the dessert. I say, I probably could wear it with a white shirt after all!' He burst into laughter.

Over the dessert and champagne, Gerald explained the whole story. 'But, Gerald, how on earth did you work it all out and how did you know Terry would return it?'

'Simple! Because he did not take it. He hid it, to discredit James, so he had no trouble finding it and leaving it on top of your chest of drawers, so Paul tells me. And here he is, wearing it like the Queen of May.'

'Careful, sweetie,' Paul warned. 'No one said that with gloves and a felt hat you were a ringer for Jane Marples.'

Everyone laughed, but Catherine suddenly put her hand to her throat. 'Oh,' she exclaimed, 'what about Faith?'

'I think the idea is simply to keep this drama to ourselves,' Gerald told her, very seriously. 'Terry will know we know he hid the bracelet, so he is hardly likely to say anything. If we don't, as well, and we tell Faith it was discovered in your bedroom as a result of falling somewhere, she won't lose face and hopefully this cretin Terry will be much more circumspect before he thinks of doing anything so stupid as this in the future.'

'Let's hope so,' Catherine agreed, receiving the bracelet from Paul.

'Funny,' he added, with a smirk. 'I hadn't realised how rubies suited me so well.' Everyone started to laugh again.

The evening drew to a successful close and a happy one, with a certain tension dissolved. It was later, alone with James, that Mark, as a result of his declared love for him, began for the first time in his whole life to hold in his arms the young man he wanted for the rest of his life.

They sat and talked and kissed but for this, the first real night of their lives, it stopped there. The promise of something else to come was something they were both waiting for but strangely it was Mark who was much more nervous about making the first move to bed with James and he was to discover that although he himself had no sexual experience before, James was not able to claim that at all.

Estelle had fired two of the eight staff at Rodney Taylor's old branch in the first week and another later, but the fourth firing was much more explosive. In the second week, it was a receptionist, a certain Kylie Smith, who was young, attractive, carrying a little too much weight, but an efficient worker and always cheerful. When Estelle took over, the original staff were anything but pleased. Here was a dynamo who was making all their lives difficult. Not a word did Estelle pass that was not a criticism. It made no difference if a good sale had been made, she criticised that it could have been better, and so it continued. Kylie sized Estelle up at once and knew exactly what she was up against, but she had one great advantage and that was her lover companion, Christian Hall. Christian was thirty one years old, tall, with thick, wavy black hair, a brilliant body and fine olive skin, but the cobalt blue eyes said it all. He was employed by O'Brien & Co. to photograph all the properties that were for sale and his photography was good. It always showed the house or apartment in the most subtle way in order to convince a client that this visual image was just what they were seeking. He didn't work just for Estelle's branch; he also worked for other branches of the company, so although he did work for Estelle she had no control over him. She became besotted with him. The concept of tall, dark and handsome was really what she wanted but, and oh, but, there was Kylie in the middle. To fire Kylie was easy, but she realised that that would automatically alienate Christian from her, so she suffered a few smart comments from Kylie that she most certainly would not have accepted from any other staff employee, just to keep in line for Christian. Kylie was not stupid. She knew exactly what Estelle was about and Christian only had to step into the branch office to find Estelle immediately take over and spend some time in her closed office talking over the value of this photo or that. She was objective on this level, but at the same time she was making every move a winner.

'It's difficult to make this apartment on Howard Street look interesting,' he said to Estelle, who looked at his photos on the computer.

'Forget the façade – it's hideous,' she answered. 'Look, we'll use the photo of the kitchen and the living room – that should be sufficient. It's always difficult to sell these 70s apartments, unless a decorator has been in before.' She smiled at him. Christian, although warned by Kylie of 'Crocodile Features', as she called Estelle behind her back, was conceited enough to think that although the other staff had real problems with Estelle and he didn't, that his work and his charm had her at his feet, a foolish mistake, especially as Kylie was to say if you know Crocodile Features you should be very careful. Christian was not.

This constant work with Estelle checking every photograph to be placed in the front sales window was not always to Chrstian's advantage. He took some hurried shots of a house as he and Kyle were late for a dinner party and when they were handed over to Estelle two days later a raised voice in her office made it quite clear to the beautiful Christian that he most certainly did not have Estelle under his control, and as a result of this was much more formal with her, which, on a professional level, was fine, but on the level of a projected sexual exercise was exactly what she didn't want, so she was trapped, and seeing a smiling Kylie day in day out did nothing to make her any happier.

All these antics seeped back to Head Office and it was Maggie who kept Mark well-informed over gales of laughter about Estelle's attempting to move in on Kylie's boyfriend, the beautiful Christian, who, as Maggie said, was better than a poke in the eye with a sharp stick, and then left Mark's office in stitches of laughter.

CHAPTER 4

Consolidation

CHAPTER 4

Consolidation

Ever since the dinner party, where Terry had ever-so-cleverly been discovered as the villain in the theft of Catherine's bracelet, James and Mark had been closer than ever. James had felt that all eyes were originally on him as the thief but to have Gerald and Paul, not to mention Mark, declaring his love for him, he settled down and was now more than happy to be in Gerald and Paul's company, which made for a much happier and relieved atmosphere. But like the others now, he was very aware of what Terry was capable of and although this time Gerald had saved the day both James and now Mark were extremely cautious of Terry, knowing his capabilities.

A major problem remained and that was Terry's desire for Mark and although this time he had his tail between his legs it would not be long before he worked out another scheme to convince Mark of how much he wanted him and to demand the same in return.

But what James worked out was another scenario. The person who had gone in to bat for him was Gerald, not Paul, and so he became much closer to Gerald than Paul. It was not obvious to begin with but with time everyone realised James was quite attached to Gerald. He and Paul were an institution. When Paul met Gerald so many moons ago, Gerald was a professional tennis player and with time his talents had moved to the field of chef and as such he was now employed by a major hotel in the city as Head Chef. They were always together, Paul and Gerald, although night engagements with friends were always difficult due to Gerald's working arrangements.

'Perhaps for a late drink' was the usual response from Gerald.

He was now thirty six. His large mop of light brown hair had been cropped back to a very short stubble and it was seen to be receding from the temples but that enigmatic smile and those intensely clear green eyes marked him out to be very sharp. He kept his body in good shape and if not working at the hotel was at the gym, so all round he was a very soft-looking, handsome man.

Paul remained as he had always been, extrovert and good-looking and as he became older never made exceptional efforts to remain the young successful man about town. He had exactly what he wanted on an emotional level and that was fine. But dare someone else publicly move in on Gerald and Guy Fawke's night had nothing on Paul, so from their beautiful terraced house in Richmond everything was, in Paul's mind, just fine.

The same could not exactly be said for Gerald. He enjoyed the living arrangements with Paul and who wouldn't? – dinner parties, everything worked around his work schedule, but he, although formal in social situations, had let his guard down ever so slightly and he now viewed James in a very different way. The fact that he had saved him from what perhaps the others might have thought about him and the theft produced a certain 'knight-on-a-white-charger' effect and he was inwardly proud that he had resolved the problem. But no matter how he looked at this situation, James seemed well and truly off-limits, at least for the moment, he thought to himself.

The architect from Bainsdale had gone ahead and finished all the plans of Donegal and it was over a copy of these that Catherine and the others, before a Sunday lunch, discussed the possible developments and changes to turn this very rundown house into what James saw in his mind as a finished country house. It was Paul who inevitably decided the overall plan and the room usage.

'How odd they demolished the top sections of the chimneys,' commented Catherine.

'Oh, don't worry. We can have them all back in a flash,' laughed Paul. 'We shall annexe the detached back section with a wide glazed corridor, something smart, I think, but completely in keeping with the rest of the house and that ghastly skillion section is to go at once. We shall just simply wrap the house in verandas. Oh yes, how smart! I can see it all.'

On the dining room table, with a fine-line red pen and a ruler, he began the final design with everyone watching and making suggestions.

'Oh, the kitchen is too small,' Gerald insisted.

'It's not exactly an international hotel,' Paul snapped back, 'but if you and Mark want to spend your time cooking while the rest of us are having a drink that's fine. I can make it larger.'

'Good idea,' Mark heard himself saying.

'Oh, talking of food, I'm starving,' James butted in, and while Paul made yet another change to the floor plan the others moved to the informal dining room/kitchen area to a marvellous aroma of cooking smells from Mark and Gerald's talents.

'It will have to be totally re-plastered,' Paul warned, coming into the room,' and, by the way, where is my glass?'

'Coming up!' laughed James, and the noisy lunch continued until well after four o'clock, with hundreds of ideas thrown back and forth about Donegal.

'We must get a good garden designer in,' said Catherine. 'I am sure we may need windbreaks planted at once, as the wind sweeping right across the lake from the ocean in winter will be freezing.'

'I know a couple of garden designers. I will have a look at their work and then we can decide, but the first thing we must have is the electricity re-connected, underground, of course, and that damn road repaired. It's shocking. I'll speak to the architect on Monday.'

On their way home from Catherine's, Gerald asked Paul whether he was interested in the other house nearby Donegal. Paul was very non-committal. 'It's just so far away – three hours every time and three hours back. Oh, I don't know. I'll just have to think about it.'

'I think it would be great to have a house near Catherine and the boys, even if we bought it as an investment and let it out and eventually used it as a retirement idea.'

'Oh, Gerald! Keep a property for twenty years or so? I don't think so.' And so Gerald let the subject pass, but thought that a house so close to where James was living was not a bad idea at all.

With the floor plans now completely worked out, Catherine more than any of them threw herself into the idea of furnishing the property. She and James spent hours working out what furniture they needed and where it would all go. It was on one of these planning evenings that Mark arrived home to shouts of laughter from the kitchen zone and moved down.

'Well hi! What's so funny?' He kissed Catherine and then James, as this was his now accepted method of greeting.

'Look. What do you think?' Catherine laughed as James poured Mark a drink. He leaned over to look at an auction catalogue with an enormous chandelier for sale.

'It's great, but I honestly think if we had it fitted at Donegal we should have to walk around it.'

'That's what we thought,' Catherine said, 'but it is nice!'

Mark had not sat down. He narrowed his eyes a little and glanced from Catherine to James, so that James asked him what was wrong.

'I was just thinking, and this is only an 'if'. As I'm now resident here at East Melbourne, my terrace house is vacant. I spoke to Maggie today about it, but she has said that to let it fully furnished would be tantamount to losing a great deal of the contents over time, so what do you think about transferring the contents from the terrace to Donegal and then letting the house? The rent from the terrace should pay a gardener full time.'

'What a fabulous idea,' Catherine answered. 'But Mark, you have a marvellous collection of things. Won't you feel a little lost with them all at Donegal?'

'It's strange. I have been here since Dermit passed on and I can honestly say I haven't missed one piece. And perhaps when Paul rearranges them all at Donegal it will be like a new experience.'

'Sounds good to me,' James agreed.

'And me too,' said Catherine. 'Well, Paul has a fully decorated house to relocate, so James and I will look for a smaller chandelier. And don't worry about dinner this evening. I am taking you both to a little restaurant in Richmond that Gerald recommended, so, Mr Barman, how about another drink?' James did his duty.

'How was work today?' she asked, when they were seated in the restaurant and orders taken.

'Fine. Maggie keeps us all in line.'

'And Estelle?'

'Well, the figures are better than Rodney's were but she's really is a tough manager. I don't think that the staff will be dipping in for a Christmas present this year. Rodney has settled in Head Office and is quite efficient, so everything for the moment is fine.'

They chatted on but inevitably when together the subject reverted to Donegal. The relationship between Mark and James was just growing stronger and it was James, after this evening at the restaurant, who simply never used his own bedroom again.

'Hello,' said Mark, in a very business-like way. 'Oh, Gerald, sorry, I didn't recognise your voice over the phone. Can I help you?'

Gerald explained he needed a favour; when Mark replied, 'Anything,' Gerald laughed and said it was a dangerous offer. 'But, listen, I want you to keep this a secret. I am seeing you for drinks and dinner this evening, I believe. Could you find out the exact situation with that house that's for sale next to Donegal, but not a word to anybody.'

'Of course. I'll get on to it now. Looking forwarding to seeing you this evening.' Mark hung up and called Rodney Taylor into his office, asking if he could have all the information Gerald required in an envelope on his desk before he left that evening.

'Hi! Come in!' cried Catherine, as Faith handed her a beautiful bunch of roses. 'Darling, you shouldn't have.' They walked down the gracious corridor to the kitchen area where the flowers were taken care of.

'I'm home!' came a yell as James moved quickly down to the kitchen. 'Hello, Faith,' he greeted her and kissed Catherine.

'Oh, I see,' said Faith. 'Don't I merit a kiss as well?' so he moved across and kissed her also.

'That's more like it, beautiful!' she laughed. 'Where is Mark?'

'On his way. Would you like a drink?' She said she'd love one, and they moved to the drawing room, chatting on about Donegal. 'I'm so curious to see it,' Faith said.

'Wait a minute. Catherine took hundreds of photos of it. They have all been downloaded. I'll get the laptop.' He disappeared.

Faith glanced at Catherine and noticed a calm look about her. 'You're a lucky woman, Catherine. James is so sweet.' Catherine agreed with a smile, as she looked at Faith, and said that in that stage of her life, to be supported by Mark and James made her very aware of how fortunate she was.

'Half your luck! The problems and tensions at home are starting to get me down a bit. Keven's fine, but Terry is a real handful. He brought home the other night a man that was tattooed everywhere. He removed his shirt to show Terry a particular design. Can you imagine! Richard came through the doorway and sarcastically asked this young man was he just out of prison or a sideshow act! Need I say anymore? Terry began the shouting and Richard replied. It really is awful. I just hate these situations and they are now almost every night.'

'Terry can be difficult,' Catherine agreed and Faith turned her head to stare at her.

'Here it is!' and James bounded into the drawing room with the laptop.

'Well, it's a bit run down, I must say,' was Faith's surprised comment. 'I wasn't sure what to expect, but there's more work to do than I thought.'

'It will be finished in a flash,' James insisted with a smile. 'It's being re-stumped this week and then the builders are to start work. Won't that be great?'

'It certainly will, darling,' Faith assured him, glancing at the photos again.

The front door opened with Mark's voice chatting on to Gerald and Paul. After greetings had been passed around it was Gerald who noticed that in the holding of James's shoulder by Mark and then kissing him that this relationship had moved well beyond the friendship level.

Mark went into the kitchen to begin the meal with Gerald joining him. Mark noticed Gerald's movement in the kitchen. They were smooth and calculated, never any waste of energy at all. Those strong muscular arms and large hands seemed his professional trademark, whether on the tennis court or in the kitchen.

'Here is the information you wanted,' Mark told him, handing over the envelope and smiling. 'Our secret, but I don't think you are going to be very happy at all.'

When Gerald asked why, Mark looked around behind him to see if anyone was there. 'It was sold this morning.'

'What?' and just at that moment Paul swept into the cooking zone. 'Well, Gerald, I see Catherine gets roses and we get nothing!'

'I'll get you a drink,' Mark said. 'Come with me,' noticing that the very good-looking chef had become quite rigid and had narrowed his beautiful green eyes. There was no further discussion of the real estate as now everyone moved back to the informal dining area, chatting and exchanging gossip. A great deal of it James did not understand, as they spoke about or trashed people they had known for a long time. As the meal progressed, Gerald excused himself and disappeared but when he returned it was easy to see he was furious. In the most sarcastic voice possible he said to Paul, 'I believe this is for you,' and thrust the envelope Mark had handed to him earlier into Paul's hand. Paul glanced up at him in surprise and the conversation stopped.

'What's wrong?' he asked.

'Open it and read it, especially the second last page.'

Paul did as bidden. 'But this is the house near Donegal.'

'Oh, you're a genius,' said Gerald with narrowed eyes.

Paul turned to the second last page, and then screamed, 'I don't believe it! How on earth has this happened?'

'Why don't you think about it for a moment? Gerald snarled sarcastically.

'Lost the plot, boys,' interrupted Faith. 'What's all this about?'

'It's about Paul being slow off the mark. The house next to Donegal has been sold lock, stock and barrel for a very reasonable price, but who do you think has purchased it? Only one guess!'

James had never seen Gerald like this. He was exceptionally agitated.

'I don't believe it,' Paul reiterated. 'Jenny Walls has purchased it. I suppose that means there will be a Greek flag in the front yard.' His voice was bitter.

'What?' exclaimed Catherine in sheer horror. 'Jenny Walls! Good heavens, I can't bear her.'

'Who can?' asked Gerald, still in fighting mood.

'Well, I must say,' said Paul in a bitchy manner, 'at least the horizontal striped house and her stretch outfits with the same horizontal stripes should co-ordinate perfectly.' He now took the line that Jenny Walls had taken the house he desperately wanted and vented his spleen. Gerald remained virtually silent for the rest of the evening, with 'yes' and 'no' being the extent of his conversation.

The next few days for Gerald and Paul were frosty, with Gerald still furious that Paul's dithering had lost them the country house he wanted, and it was well over a week before things returned to a sort of normality. Paul was now being very careful in the conversations he had with Gerald and the subject of country houses was taboo.

Work began in earnest at Donegal and as summer was on the way everyone had high hopes for progress. The electricity was easy, this being due to its being re-directed underground from the house that Jenny Walls had purchased to Donegal. It was all completed within a week but the access road was another story. The council was anything but co-operative and delayed repairs, to the workmen's annoyance.

Paul found a garden designer. After a great deal of trouble he located a very effervescent man called Sammy. He was average height with brown hair and eyes and carried a little too much weight though not an excessive amount. He had a way with words which could only be described as hysterical. After ten minutes in Sammy's company everyone was laughing, but although he dressed in a conservative manner it was his shoes that were odd. It didn't matter what he was wearing, he always wore brightly coloured sand shoes, reds, orange, electric yellow, sea green, leaf green – the list of colours went on indefinitely and James said to Mark that he must have had at least thirty pairs of these sand shoes and all in the most pristine condition. If one saw him in a blazer, collar and tie, to be sure as one's eyes moved down he would be wearing a pair of scarlet sand shoes.

Catherine thought it extremely odd. He was not a trained garden designed, Sammy Sillcock, he was virtually, if one listened to him, a master of all trades, but, as Paul had recommended him, the three of them accepted the arrangement. So, armed with sketch pad and multi-coloured felt pens they all set off one Sunday morning for Donegal. It was a pair of legs trimmed with saffron runners that stalked about the site, not talking to anybody, while Paul took the others to have a look at the progress of the building. They were delighted that so much had been achieved in such a short time and the skillion section attached to the front of the house had been demolished. This gave the whole structure a much more architectural look, without the tacked-on bits that had nothing to do with the façade. The two sections of the house had now been joined together but the glazing was not finished, and Catherine, like the boys, was very surprised at how large the spaces were. After a thorough inspection with Paul going over details again and again, they moved out to see Sammy walking about and then standing very still and turning and stepping out distances and returning and sketching or writing in coloured felt pens everything he considered necessary for the garden. But what everyone felt strange about it was that they had no input into the design. Even Paul thought this highly irregular and said so.

'Don't worry, darling,' Sammy said, in his quaint colourful way of speaking. 'You will absolutely adore it. I shall begin Monday morning,' and that was that. No matter how Paul attempted to bring the garden into conversation, Sammy told yet another hysterical story and quite often they were at his own expense and so the subject of the garden was evaded yet again.

Catherine was concerned and the following week sat down with Paul to discuss the situation. 'But, Paul, we don't even have a cost for this garden layout.'

'Yes, I know. It's strange, but he is brilliant,' he said, weakly.

'Well, I will give you a maximum and I shall not pay one cent more. So you can explain that to Sammy and insist he works to budget.'

Although Sammy seemed flighty, when it came to work he turned into another person, aggressive and, it seemed, according to the team working with him, without any patience at all. So with teams of workers, Donegal was becoming a reality.

However, works at Donegal were not the only project under way, as the thirty day settlement for Jenny Wall came through and she also began a vast re-building project, demolishing and re-designing the whole of her new property, which went by the name of 'Bona Vista'. Although they were often at the building sites at the same time, no one ever made a move to communicate one with the other. Jenny had used a very young, avant-garde architect and the stripe concept that already existed on the original house was carried through and repeated on out-buildings and inside the house itself. As Paul said, having had a look, 'It's just so Jenny. It's hideous and the colours are electric, just so her.'

But in Jenny' mind this exceptionally 'modern' look was just what she wanted as a smart hideaway with the impressionable young Greek lover who went by the name of George.

But in all this work at Donegal, with one of them or all four, backwards and forwards, it was Gerald who felt a little out of it and James sensed this. He spoke to Mark about it in bed one evening. 'I am sure Gerald thinks with all the happenings at Donegal that he is just left out. What do you think if when he has a day off Catherine and I take him for a picnic there?'

'I think it's a great idea,' Mark replied with a smile, 'providing it's just for a picnic.'

James looked at Mark and turned his head a little to the right. 'Mark, what are you implying?'

'Nothing.'

'Surely you're not jealous of Gerald, are you?'

Mark said of course not and with that James rolled over on top of him and kissed him. 'You know, for a smart guy, sometimes you are a bit silly. I love you, don't you understand that?'

Mark swung his strong arms around James and held him tightly. 'Yes, I do understand that. I love you so much that sometimes I can hardly breathe. I can't imagine what I ever did in the past without you.'

'Mark, you have to learn to trust me. I will never be with another person. Only you. And hopefully you know this by now.'

'I do.'

It was interesting that in this love affair between Mark and James it was James who was the more vocal. Mark, being Mark, assumed that just being there was sufficient for him: to vocalise his thoughts on love was extremely difficult and he felt slightly embarrassed and vulnerable, so it became James, his junior, who became the power in this relationship and the ever debonair Mark in private moments waited patiently for James to tell him the things he wanted to hear but to respond in the same vein was for him extraordinarily difficult. His 'yes' and 'no' for the moment James accepted but as time progressed he began to demand a more positive and vocal response to their love.

Whereas at Donegal, with Paul playing 'Madam Lash' the progress was orderly (though, as Catherine said to Mark and James one evening, just so slow) the great changes at Bona Vista were not without great drama, as was to be seen when a section of the side of a veranda was demolished, which had everything to do with incompetent workmen and Jenny taking a hand in things. A century old cypress tree was felled, and it collapsed across the side of the house and took with it a section of the veranda roofing. Jenny's extraordinary use of expletives as she adjusted her over-obvious 'Jackie O' glasses with red frames, had even the hardest workman spin around in surprise. Whereas at Donegal it was all about planting trees, at Bona Vista Jenny saw the reverse 'to tree'd in I need a view', so the result was a denuding of vegetation. Fences out, buildings all 'au naturelle was Jenny's cry and an enormous eighteen metre swimming pool, with a bright orange lining offered very little respite for the eye. The look Jenny sought to create was Mexican – bright colours, clear views.

The problem was with a traditional Australian house built in 1902. There were aesthetic problems and real ones. The house might have, for one reason or another, the weatherboards painted in alternate colours and this most certainly was not what one would have considered the fashion at any time, but to take this quaint idea and use it around and over the out-buildings produced an effect that was more like a circus than old Mexico. Being a lath and plaster construction, inside Bona Vista was not going to take rough handling, so walls cracked as a result of opening spaces and two of the bigger parts of two ceilings collapsed, leaving Jenny all the more distressed and angry. Bona Vista still had a long way to go.

Sammy Sillcock, from appearing to have done very little, suddenly, in less than a month, seemed to have become magic. Empty spaces around the house became avenues of plane trees and the cypress wind breaks appeared. The small swimming pool looked like a decorative pond at Versailles, with four pedestals with covered urns at each corner. Each part of this now divided garden took on a different character. The large space was broken up into garden rooms, each grand, and if Catherine thought it just a little pompous, James adored it.

There was a large use of decorative urns but only one statue. 'They are used far too often for such poor effect,' explained Sammy to Catherine, today wearing a pair of hibiscus pink sand shoes with the cleanest white laces. Catherine and Mark were absolutely sure that Sammy was going to have a great deal of trouble staying within the budget but this was not to be. But trouble was to come, though from of all people it was James, who verbally took our effervescent Sammy on.

This explosive afternoon took place in Melbourne during a quiet – or so it should have been – Saturday lunch, when he was decked out in apple green sand shoes and matching jumper. Sammy was in high spirits and as Gerald did not have to work until the evening he and Mark had produced a late lunch with everyone in high spirits, and Sammy yet again telling another extraordinarily funny story. Faith thought him splendid but at this time she was aware that although she was, as usual, always invited either to lunch or dinner, Terry now was most certainly not. Catherine's excuse was always the same. 'Darling, we don't want the boys being worried by Terry,' and Faith, realising the situation, but not about the theft, just accepted it.

The row started out simply as an extension to garden talk at Donegal, nothing more, with Sammy the star as usual. He handed Mark a sheet of paper stating that the name underlined in red felt pen was the local person he had taken on as their new permanent gardener, saying he had interviewed eight people and this was the one for Donegal. It was only when James ran his eyes lazily across the sheet and saw the underlined name that fireworks began. James picked the sheet up slowly and glanced at the name underlined in red felt pen. He swung around in front of both Mark and Sammy and, to everyone's surprise, said sarcastically to Sammy, 'If you want him, you have him,' and then began to raise his voice, 'but we will not under any circumstances employ this bastard.' The room fell into silence and Mark instantly moved and put his arm on his shoulder.

'It's fine, James. There are eight names on the sheet. Sammy can pick another,' and was aware James was exceptionally rigid. Instead of letting it pass, Sammy continued, 'Let's not play the prima donna, James. He is great for the job.'

It was a slow movement that everyone watched, especially Gerald, like a picador that is calm, determined and then makes the thrust.

'If you think he is 'great',' James virtually spat at Sammy, 'then make sure you are not with him and his feral friend when it's dark because I promise you, you will not hold the same opinion afterwards about this bastard.'

Catherine immediately attempted to change the subject but James was very upset and left the room. Everyone looked at one another, not sure what to say. Even Sammy's smart one-liners took a nose dive.

'Gerald, would you look after the kitchen for a moment?' and Mark left to go upstairs to their bedroom. He walked into the room to see James standing like a silhouette against the window, looking out into the street yet seeing nothing. Mark walked slowly up behind him. 'James,' he said, softly, but James did not look round. Mark at this point, became confused whether to hold him in his arms or just to let him decide what to do. For once in his life Mark emotionally took a stand and placed his arms around a very rigid James and just held him without saying anything, until James slowly moved around, embraced Mark and began to cry. The helplessness Mark felt was overwhelming. 'I'm here, James, and I always will be,' Mark heard himself saying as James's body convulsed with tears. Mark wasn't sure how long he held him like this but finally James drew himself apart.

'You go and have lunch. I am not hungry. I'll tell you about it later.'

Mark went back downstairs to say James would not be joining them and so they should begin lunch - but not before Sammy had found an alternative gardener on his sheet.

Everyone was most concerned, especially Gerald, who had only seen a buoyant nineteen year old called James but today he had witnessed a very different young man and his suffering and anger had surprised him greatly as it had the other members of the lunch party. Clearing the plates, he was surprised to find, when he went into the kitchen, James sitting by himself eating a piece of the corned beef with his hands.

'It's not bad, the beef,' smiled Gerald and waited for the response.,

'It's great,' was James soft reply. Never in Gerald's life had he ever wanted to round the table and hold James in his arms. James thanked him and Gerald placed the plates in the dishwasher and attempted 'normal' conversation. At one point he leaned back against the kitchen bench and looked at James. 'We have all had difficult periods in our lives but it seems you are the survivor. Most don't make it.' He stopped and looked at his feet. 'Will you join us for dessert?'

James said he would. 'You are very good to me, Gerald. I like you very much.'

At that point Mark entered the kitchen with another stack of crockery. 'How do you feel?' he asked with a frown,' and when James just said he felt OK the conversation stopped.

When he went back into the dining room and took his place, Gerald put in front of him a light selection of what they had already eaten, and it was noted by more than one of the guests that the presentation was very smart. Conversation continued but the subject of gardeners was taboo. At the end of the afternoon, the guests left apart from Gerald, who was to go directly to work at the hotel. He remained for a while and with a glass in hand James started to explain why they were not going to employ the man Sammy had suggested. He took a deep breath and looked at the three of them, each of them so different but each of them in their own way totally supportive of him. This gave him the courage to tell a small but terrible part of his past.

'My father got drunk as usual and he attacked me one night. I ran out of the house and up the street to a small park that overlooks the lake behind the ocean. I sat on a bench and cried.'

'James, you don't have to tell us this if you don't want to,' Catherine interrupted softly. He looked at her in an odd way as if to say she would not understand even if he told her, and carried on with the rest of his sad tale.

'There were two of them, the person whose name Sammy had on the sheet for work and another.' He put his hands up to his head as if to shield himself from a past danger. 'Call it what you like – forced sex, rape – it's the same.' He looked at the floor. Mark instantly rose and sat beside him on the settee and put his arm around him.

'How old were you when this happened,' Gerald asked.

'Not quite fourteen.'

'The fucking bastards,' Gerald exclaimed. 'What did you do?'

'It was the time I met Miss O'Brien. I told her what had happened with my father and these two bastards –'here he stopped and Gerald refilled everyone's glasses.

Catherine felt a sensation of anger inside her that she had never felt in her life. He was a child with a father that beat and raped him, and here he was sitting opposite her in her drawing room. A great sense of sadness tinged with hopelessness swept over her.

Mark's response was more positive. He could take his lover and hold him and kiss him – all these things he saw in his own limited way as positive thoughts to help James, but the one who summed up the situation without any sentimental thoughts was Gerald. A certain part of his system that was logical and ordered turned upside down and for one reason or another he thought only of revenge to make them pay. Sammy had the address and telephone number of one of these vile louts and the other would be simple to locate but this information for the moment he decided to store. But as fate would have it, not for long.

We are told that life goes around in cycles. Well be that as it may, the strangest situation was to occur as a result of a screaming match in Faith's house one Thursday evening. Richard and Terry began the evening relatively quietly, with the usual sarcastic comments, but all seemed calm until a comment of Richard's which now no-one remembers set off a violent argument and for the first time a punch was thrown, which Richard dodged. Faith at this point just took over and ordered both of them to leave the room in opposite directions. An hour later she called Terry in to say that as from Monday he had to find a job and lodgings as she had just had it. She said she was prepared to organise a flat and pay the first six months' rent. Nothing more! To Richard, she was just as determined : pack and leave. If both of them was very surprised, so was Faith. This had been the straw that had broken the camel's back. As she later said to Catherine, after ordering them out she felt strangely free.

Terry never assumed the sun would ever set. He had lived his life without responsibility. Now things looked very different, but not to be deterred he telephoned Mark for a position. Mark was still anything but happy with him about the theft and thought twice before making a decision, then it came to him. He gave Terry a telephone number and wished him luck. Then he hung up, just as Maggie came into his office. She noticed a broad grin which was most unusual for him.

'Yes?' came a sharp reply and Terry explained what he wanted over the telephone on Friday morning.

'What are your credentials?' asked Estelle, pretentiously.

'Better than yours!' was the flippant reply. 'I spoke to Mark about you.'

'Oh, did you? Estelle replied. 'I can see you in an hour's time.'

'Make it an hour and a half,' and with that he hung up.

To say Estelle was surprised was an understatement. No one, but no one, spoke to Estelle in this manner and she was out to give this so-called Terry the lesson of his life but at the same time she was oddly wary of his being so glib as to offer Mark's name as his only reference. She was aware while working at her desk that her left hand was adjusting her hair.

'I'm here to see the manager,' Terry announced to Kylie, and was very aware of Christian Hall, who had arrived at the same time, as they had entered the door together. Terry thought a night with the handsome Christian might be just what he needed. Kylie put a call through to Estelle to say that Terry was there and had an appointment with her. She stood up and ushered him into Estelle's office.

'Who's the gorgeous one?' he asked her.

'Mine!' she snapped. Terry smiled falsely, then said, 'Good morning,' in a chirpy fashion as he glanced at Estelle. 'Good heavens, you must do something about that eye make-up. It's so eighties!'

Estelle's eyes narrowed and her body movements made it quite clear this was not the approach she liked. 'I say, Estelle,' he went on, 'isn't that guy in the outer office cute?'

She found herself asking who he meant, and was told, 'I believe he's the receptionist's boyfriend. What a waste!'

Although she agreed wholeheartedly about the diagnosis, she attempted to keep the conversation on a business level but to no avail.

'Estelle, why are the photographs in the window display all with ghastly red surrounds? It's so primary school! Soft colours, Estelle. You are selling to adults, not sweets to children.'

Estelle just sat there. She had an odd feeling she was being interviewed, not Terry. He chattered on as if he were at a party and every time she attempted to put the interview on the right track Terry interrupted and changed the subject. 'You know, Estelle, why don't we just dump the tart on the telephone and share the hunk?' The smile that crept across Estelle's face was virtually a sign that given the chance that's exactly what she would do, but sharing him with Terry had never been part of her solution. For what reason Estelle never knew, she hired Terry on a month's trial. He went out with the other salesmen to check out if he really liked the work and in his usual assertive manner decided it was just not him and after the second week sat with Estelle, who was still fascinated by this handsome young man who spoke to her as if he had known her all his life. It was precisely at this moment that the long awaited explosion occurred.

Estelle had impatiently asked Kylie for some files and demanded them at once. Instead of waitng for her to bring them in to her office she left Terry sitting there and followed her out. Kylie was not aware Estelle was behind her. 'The fucking old crocodile,' she remarked to a fellow worker whose eyes opened wider than a saucer as he had seen Estelle behind her. The slap delivered to Kyle by an outraged Estelle was returned just as sharply.

'You're fired!' Estelle screamed.

'Thank God! I won't have to put up with you every day, you bitch!' yelled Kylie, and grabbed her handbag. The slamming of the real estate office door made it quite clear Kylie had left for good. Terry, who had witnessed this dramatic scene from the doorway gave a round of applause, the only sound in a shocked office.

'Well done, Estelle. Come and have a drink.' He moved back into her office, opened her bar fridge and poured himself and her a drink. 'Now, darling,' he said, with slightly narrowed eyes. 'The job as receptionist is mine. Cheers!' They clinked glasses.

'Can you believe it?' asked Maggie, as she related the hijinks at Estelle's branch as the news had come via one of the employees who had witnessed the slaps. 'Well, well,' she went on, laughing as she looked at Mark, 'and this new chap seems to have Estelle eating out of his hand. Do you know him well?'

'Unfortunately, yes. He's a friend of Catherine's but I do find it all very odd, Terry working as Estelle's receptionist, very odd indeed.'

'I'll say! I am told he speaks to Estelle in a very equal way and she takes it. The rest of the staff are terrified of her. Oh, well, they seem an oddly assorted pair but you know what they say "opposites attract".' She collected the file from Mark's desk and headed for the door, leaving a very bemused Mark considering Estelle and Terry working together.

'Really?' said Catherine, having a drink with Mark and James before dinner. 'Not a combination I would have thought would have worked.' And then she looked at Mark. 'And yet they are actually quite similar in their determined ways,' which was the opposite diagnosis from what Maggie had made.

If Sammy Sillcock had been working furiously to have Donegal finished before late autumn, yelling and screaming at the workers, his nights cannot be said to have been dull. He had taken the liberty of going to Bona Vista to see what Jenny Walls was doing, but as she wasn't always there it left George, her gentleman friend, in charge and Sammy, being Sammy, took advantage of Jenny's absence. The two of them found they had much more in common than gardening, so Sammy's continual absence from Melbourne, although he had the perfect excuse, work, the night-time activities with George were much to his satisfaction. It goes without saying that our Jenny was not aware of George's nocturnal adventures with Sammy. He was good-looking, was George, tall, with a very good set of shoulders, a strong face with a pronounced nose and full lips, a very dark beard line and shiny, black, wavy hair – 'absolutely available' in Sammy's words and 'more than adequate'.

Gerald was at the top in his field and the management held him in high esteem but this hotel chain had a major hotel in every capital city and a secondary range of hotels in seaside towns, which in the holiday seasons did very well. One evening Gerald was overseeing the kitchens when an extremely odd situation occurred that was to change his life completely. The evening meal was served and so on this Tuesday, with the beginning of the autumn winds, he felt quite free to leave the last of the evening in the other chefs' very capable hands. It was then that a waiter entered the kitchen and said one of the last clients in the dining room wished to speak to the head chef. Gerald removed his hat and followed the waiter to the last client, sitting by himself in the furthest corner of the room.

'How do you do?' was the first greeting. 'My name is David.' He rose and shook hands. He was a man of about sixty or more, with long grey hair that was swept to one side. 'I have been waiting for you.'

'I'm sorry,' Gerald replied. 'It's been a busy night.'

'Oh no, I don't think you understand.' But Gerald, being quick, understood only too well that this older man wanted something from him, and the three-letter little word 'sex' came instantly to his mind.

David sat down. 'You're wrong,' he said with a smile. 'I am here this evening for you. I have a clear message for you but sex is not part of it at all.'

Gerald suddenly felt embarrassed. It also felt odd that this man was virtually reading his thoughts. 'I don't think here would be appropriate,' he smiled yet again. 'You can drop me off on your way home.'

They moved to Gerald's car where he motioned to Gerald to get in. The terrace house was beautiful, one of the very large ones on Richmond Hill and it was exquisitely decorated inside. Strangely, although in all Gerald's life he had never done anything like this he didn't feel afraid. He had picked up good-looking youths or men and the night had been more than pleasurable but to have a much older man direct him like this was an odd but challenging situation.

'Do open the bottle. Don't worry, I haven't put anything into it. The champagne is a very good year.' Gerald took the bottle and glanced at the French label and the year. He wondered what the hell he was doing there and how on earth he was going to explain this to Paul.

'Do sit down.' David motioned to Gerald and they sat opposite one another at a beautiful Georgian card table. David sampled the champagne and declared it to be excellent. Gerald followed suit.

'Well,' said David, 'you are much more adventurous than you think. Just imagine you having a drink with an old man at twelve fifteen in the morning, instead of being with your acquaintance, asleep beside him.'

Gerald felt a shiver run up his spine. Who was this David and why had he so easily followed his instructions to deliver him home and have a drink?

'Relax,' David continued. 'I shall start at once.'

Gerald became quite rigid and hastily consumed his glass of champagne, at which David handed him the bottle to refill his glass. He then reached to a side table and took, wrapped in a square of silk, a pack of tarot cards. He unwrapped them and shuffled them.

'Do please cut them into four.' He made this request after lighting a candle which he placed on the same small card table. Gerald, having done what was asked, watched with real intensity. David's hands were plump, just like his face as well as his whole frame, but his overriding aspect was kindness and a softness that, although he was over-weight, wasn't heavy in an odd way. He dealt the cards out slowly, three by three. 'Well, well,' he murmured, 'he will be with you all your life but not as your lover.' Gerald tensed. 'Do help yourself to a drink.' He turned the cards again. 'You are going to move addresses. Don't be afraid. He is waiting for you – not the first boy, but the second. As for the first boy, you will arise as the avenging angel for all those who have persecuted him and for that you will have him as your closest friend for life.' He then gathered all the cards and re-shuffled them. Gerald was now feeling quite strange. Who was this David and how had he so easily ended up in his beautiful sitting room? 'Please cut the cards again.' He smiled, then dealt and reversed them. 'Oh, I say,' and an intense frown came over his face, 'you have got it all worked out.' He began to laugh. 'Don't worry. A stripe is a stripe.'

It made no sense at all to Gerald. 'You need this change, so take it. In less than fourteen days you will receive the opportunity. Don't see it as lesser than what you have. He is waiting for you.' He smiled again and gathered all the cards together, wrapped them in their silk cloth and said, 'Gerald, it has been so nice to meet you. I am sorry but I now feel quite tired. You know my address. If you ever want me to help you, all you have to do is to ring the doorbell.' He stood up, but Gerald found he had a great deal of difficulty in standing up as his legs felt extremely weak. They said their goodbyes and Gerald wended his way home with only one thing thrashing through his mind, whether to tell Paul or not. And so it was that the next morning Paul noticed Gerald just a little more tense than usual but said nothing.

By this time, Donegal was almost completed. It had been a rushed job but a good standard had been maintained throughout and James, at every opportunity, rushed to check on the progress. It was strange that Sammy being Sammy was particularly formal when alone with James, which suited James perfectly. Donegal was binding the three of them together. They had a common aim or idea and it equalled a chance for an extension of their lives together for the future.

Ten days after Gerald had seen David he began to forget the readings, although every now and again something would jolt his memory.,

'Gerald, may I have a word with you?' asked the manager of the hotel, with a bundle of papers under his arm. 'Could you spare me ten minutes?'

'Sure!' While making conversation about the kitchen, the manager asked Gerald how he found his staff.

'Excellent. Everyone works well together and there is never any confusion.'

'Thanks to you.' The manager smiled, opening the door into his office. 'Sit down, Gerald. I want you to do something for me. As the kitchen staff are so well organised here, I want you to take over the shambles at Lakes Entrance. There has been problem after problem in the kitchens.'

'Hey, Lakes Entrance is not just around the corner, you know.'

'Yes, I realise that. We'll make an apartment available to you.' When Gerald asked how long he would be required to stay there, the manager said he thought it would be no more than three months. In that time he would be able to train up a staff as he had done here, and obviously they would increase his salary to what they would both agree on. 'When you are happy with the situation at Lakes Entrance your position here will be waiting for you. What do you say?'

'May I give you an answer tomorrow morning?' Gerald asked.

'Certainly, but remember you will receive a very generous boost to your salary, and a living-away-from-home allowance,' and he began to laugh.

While driving home from work, it all flooded back to Gerald : the cards, the new work and the advice behind it not to be afraid.

'What?' cried Paul. 'Where?' Lakes Entrance was the reply. 'That's ridiculous. Tell them to find someone else. You can't possibly take that work. It's three hours from Melbourne. It's crazy. Thank goodness you are not considering it.'

'Oh, but I am. The money's almost double what I'm earning now and there are lots of fringe benefits. I'll have to think about it.' He spoke nonchalantly. Paul just stared at him in amazement and suddenly felt very insecure.

'What am I supposed to do?' he exclaimed, 'feed the cat and put the rubbish out and for that matter how long will you be in this God-forsaken place?'

'Probably three months. Anyway, you feed the cat and put the rubbish out now, so I don't see any difference at all if I am here or not.'

A dinner party at Faith's now Terry and Richard were gone was very pleasant, with Faith's other son, Keven, helping her, but it was obvious to all that the air was very frosty between Paul and Gerald. Though Gerald continued as normal, Paul was very sharp.

'Have you ever heard of such a stupid idea? Paul asked Catherine. 'It's ridiculous and so far from home and it's not that we need the money.

Catherine tried to calm the situation down. 'Listen, Gerald, you have a certain flexibility with your work. You can stay at Donegal and Paul can come and stay with you when you both organise yourselves.'

Faith pushed the conversation further. 'Darling,' she said, looking at Paul, 'it's not the South Pole. It's only three hours away. Just think – if you had purchased the house Jenny Walls bought, the arrangement would be just perfect!'

Paul said thank you, though sarcastically.

'Come on, Paul. Three months will pass in a flash.' And, as she said, a part of Donegal would be almost finished or he could stay with Gerald.

But it didn't matter how everyone tried to convince Paul this was not the end of the world: he took the stand that he was hard done by and Gerald was deserting him. This, to Gerald's amazement, was the thing that distressed him less than anything. So plans went ahead for Gerald to move to Lakes Entrance so the hotel's kitchen staff could be trained up ready for the holiday season. Paul was as obstructive as possible, which now put a great deal of pressure on Gerald and he hated it. Living with Paul, for the first time in his life, became difficult. The constant arguments and criticism just never stopped and as Gerald said to Catherine he was so looking forward to getting away from Paul for a while as he had become impossible to live with. This tension was to continue and the stress on the relationship became electric. Paul saw this exit from his life by Gerald for three months as tantamount to the relationship being finished. What he didn't realise was that by exaggerating his performance as the abandoned lover he was in fact bringing it on slowly but surely. Gerald felt a strange sense of adventure and an assurance, due to David's reading of the cards and if he couldn't have the first man the second was waiting and anything was better than the drama he was having to put up with day in day out.

'Sit down,' Faith demanded of Paul, as he had called in for lunch, which she had organised for just the two of them. She poured him a drink and in the most sarcastic tone asked him how did he plan the rest of his life living alone. Paul was shocked and his face showed it.

'Really, Paul, if you want Gerald to leave you for good, you are on the right track. Keep up the bitching and the drama and you may find he will leave well before the end of the winter – and I don't just mean Lakes Entrance. Do you understand me?' She had raised her voice and Paul just stared at her.

'You don't understand,' he began.

'Oh, but I do, sweetie. I have known you and Gerald since school and I happen to love you both, but you are destroying all you have worked for, Gerald's love.'

'Oh, you're a fine one to talk about relationships lasting. A couple of months ago you threw both your husband and your son into the street,' Paul spat at her.

'True, true, and I couldn't have been happier. Do you have any idea what it's like to live in a situation like that, where people argue from morning to night? It eventually gets you to a point where you just can't continue. Do you realise this is what you are doing to Gerald? I had no idea you were so insecure.'

There was a deathly silence.

'Listen, Paul, I can't imagine Gerald without you and vice versa, but think about it. Don't throw everything away. You have a great relationship and it really distresses me to see it falling apart because you don't seem to trust him.'

Paul filled both glasses and realised that what Faith was saying was probably true. He just looked vacantly at her. 'It's as if he doesn't really care about me, he's so eager to dash off to the beach and leave me at home. Three months is a long time.'

'When you consider you have both lived together for years, I don't see how this three months is such a drama and why you're reacting like this.'

'I guess I'm afraid that during the time he will find someone else.'

'Come on, darling. Let's have lunch.' They walked to the dining room arm in arm. 'Darling,' she went on, 'if Gerald was going to find someone else, he would have done so by now, but he hasn't. I think you are over-reacting.'

So the next few months were tense but the verbal attacks stopped, with Paul using all the self-restraint he could muster, hearing in his ears Faith's warnings. But if he had known of David's reading of the Tarot cards he would really have had all the warning bells ringing.

Gerald returned to David for another reading of the cards and was genuinely surprised. They were identical. 'Change is inevitable,' smiled David.

CHAPTER 5

Change

CHAPTER 5

Change

Change occurred within the group in a variety of ways. James had lost his skeletal appearance and was more handsome than ever but he still remained a mystery figure and with time everyone accepted this. But the mystery remained. Whenever he returned to Donegal he did not continue the twenty minute trip to Lakes Entrance. That part of his unhappy youth he closed like an iron door, never having any intention of re-opening it. Of his father, he never spoke and so to Mark and Catherine it was something they respected and so it was never a part of the conversation.

A huge removal van arrived at Mark's terrace house and in three hours had packed up the contents and made its way to the freeway and then on to Donegal. This, for James and Catherine, was fantastic. All the hours they had spent together, planning where it would all be placed was virtually ignored by Paul, who spent four days at Donegal fine-tuning the house, with Sammy still in the area but apparently not working at Donegal, yet always about, smiling. It was in these four days of frantic organisation that Paul realised that this was where Gerald would be staying but he did not say a word about it. After the four days, Catherine, Mark and James made the trip up to see the finished results, having had Paul ban them from going until it was all done.

To say they were surprised was an understatement, with a fledgling garden laid out with large, deciduous trees with their fragile branches moving restlessly in the wind, and the young hedges planted it all looked very precise and that was exactly as Sammy wanted it. They found him wearing orange sand shoes with blue laces.

'Come, let me show you around.' He gave them a tour of the gardens along with a young man in a thick woollen jumper, jeans, coat, a woollen cap and rubber boots, who was introduced as the gardener. He was twenty seven years old, tall and very solid, with a good-looking face with strong features and just a hint of a smile. His face was quite tanned, even though it was now the first week of winter. What Mark noticed was his exceptionally powerful hands.

They entered the house where Paul took over the tour and the smells from the kitchen announced that Sammy was preparing lunch for them all. Catherine had this odd feeling that in a certain sense this house was never going to be a private hideaway : there were always going to be groups of people filling it up. For Mark this was an odd situation, being shown over the house, but most of the contents were his own. In the living room now hung the huge painting that he had purchased at auction with Catherine and Faith. It seemed years ago. The house looked splendid with Mark's collection of fine antiques now in carefully chosen positions. Donegal was larger now, with the extension, and so rather than the cramped over-furnished look Mark had had in Melbourne, everything was positioned more graciously, with modern divans for more comfortable seating.

James took Mark upstairs to show him the guest bedrooms, but it was Paul, despite his anxiety about Gerald, who linked an arm through Catherine's.

'He would have loved it,' he smiled, looking into her eyes.

'Yes, Dermit would have felt very much at home here,' she agreed, and they continued a tour of the kitchen and dining area, one formal and the other informal. It was to the latter, with Sammy, crying instructions, that they all drifted for a splendid lunch. While upstairs inspecting the room, Mark also thought of Dermit, but in a split second he turned and held the young man he loved so desperately, and although he had heard both sides of the story about Gerald and Paul he knew in his heart that he would have sacrificed anything rather than live three months without James.

Gales of laughter, and Sammy holding the floor, guaranteed a successful lunch and as they were staying for the first time there it was quite the adventure. While drinking after lunch in front of the open fire, Sammy excused himself and laughed, saying he had 'fish to fry'. No one doubted his capacity to find himself a companion but they would all of them have been surprised if they had known it was Jenny Walls's boyfriend.

Bona Vista was just liveable and George was resident, with Jenny telephoning two or three times a day to find out the progress though he did not always answer. It depended on what he was doing and with whom. George had assumed the role of manager-controller, a slightly silly move on Jenny's part but she assumed that giving this young man a certain power would automatically guarantee his trusted affection for her. This was the first mistake, the second being he had not the slightest idea of architecture and so error after error was the result. George was totally uninterested: life owed him a bliving and Jenny was the one to pay, literally. So with a plentiful supply of wine and food, not to mention Sammy for extra entertainment, life in the country for this twenty five year old, very-sure-of-himself, Greek was not so bad at all. In fact he found himself much happier with Sammy than he did with an ever-complaining Jenny.

The weekend passed very pleasantly, with Paul leaving on Saturday, so it was just the three of them, and it was Catherine who said to Mark and James that this was just perfect. She gave a deep sigh and stared at the burning logs in the open fireplace.

'I wonder if Jean saw the house finished like this?'

'Not quite like this,' James said, 'but a bit simpler – but just as happy.' He smiled.

Catherine asked what the name of the gardener was. She had missed it with Sammy clowning around.

'His name is Martin,' said James, and when Mark asked if he knew him, he went on.' A little He was in the senior class when I started, but I have forgotten the story. He got mixed up with a girl. I don't remember if they married but it was a bad ending and as he worked for the girl's father he was fired and bad comments were circulated about him. He once helped me when I was young, at school. He must have been in his final year. Someone hit me and he came to the rescue, but that's all I remember about him. I don't suppose today he even recognised me.'

They carried on, elaborating on Sammy's stories and disasters at Bona Vista, but never thought to put the two things together.

Winter continued like this but every time they arrived for the weekend there was Sammy preparing lunch and telling funny stories. It was almost like having a live in-help but as usual the minute lunch was finished he disappeared. It was a situation that was invasive but the minute this went through your mind he was off – quite odd, thought Catherine. The boys were more accepting of it. One weekend both Faith and Gerald came but for one reason or another there was no Paul. With Gerald and Mark in the kitchen on Friday evening, laughing, while the other three were close to the fire with the ever-empty glass in their hands, James, as a result of this company, had become as Catherine described him to Faith, quite a professional drinker. Faith asked had they ever seen anything of Jenny Walls.

'In town, yes, at gallery openings, but although she is probably less than two hundred metres away, never here, thank goodness!'

'Funny,' said Faith. 'She always ingratiates herself at every opportunity.'

Whilst chatting over dinner, Catherine said to Gerald, 'Listen, if the apartment at the hotel is not satisfactory you can stay here. It's only twenty minutes away from work, closer than working in the city. It's up to you.'

Gerald thanked her. 'It's a great offer. Living and working in the same space for three months could be a bit claustrophobic. Let's see how it goes.' And that was it, when Gerald moved to Lakes Entrance and began to overhaul the hotel. He was very pleased to just get away from the intense work programme and relax at Donegal but it would not be long before relaxing alone was a thing of the past.

His day off was Tuesday and the first free day off he walked through the gardens of Donegal and then out of the gate toward the alarming kaleidoscope house that, had Paul been more co-operative, would have been theirs. He was genuinely shocked at the extreme use of colour. It was so aggressive against the environment; the constant stripes everywhere and orange was not his favourite colour. As he walked about with not a soul in sight he imagined it restored and not bastardised as it now was - and why had Paul not been more co-operative about the purchase?

'Hi!' came a voice from the veranda, and Gerald spun around.

'Oh, I hope you don't mind me looking around,' he said.

'Not at all,' came a deep voice. 'Come in and have a drink.'

Gerald was given a tour of the interior of the house. If the outside was aggressive, the interior was just tasteless. Colour was everywhere. There was not one place or one thing for the eye to relax on. Everything just screamed! Gerald sat down on a bright blue settee with orange cushions. 'Seems like Sammy's shoes,' he thought and when the glass was handed to him and the fingers remained locked for a moment he was very aware this good-looking George wanted much more than just a chat. Perhaps if Paul had not over-reacted and continued the drama for most of the autumn, although it had toned down quite considerably after Faith had spoken sharply to him, but it all added up to a new and pleasing avenue. Gerald and Paul had been together for well over twenty years so sex was not part of the game now, but the emotional bond was a strong as ever – or was it? thought Gerald, as he allowed George to rest one arm on his shoulder. And that was all it took.

The next morning, Gerald left Bona Vista early, returned to Donegal, changed and left for work, feeling as if an enormous weight had been lifted off his shoulders. It was from this moment on that Gerald transferred from the hotel accommodation to Donegal permanently and so he took over the complete re-organisation of the kitchen there. He knew of Sammy's dealings with George and the two of them worked around this, but strangely Gerald never invited George to Donegal and George, it seemed, was not even vaguely interested in seeing it. The other odd thing for Gerald was that every now and again either Sammy or Catherine would have a message for Martin the gardener but Gerald had never seen him, due to the Tuesday he did not work, so an envelope with a message was left for him if necessary, which was rare, as he was obviously contactable by cellular phone.

Work for Gerald was another thing altogether. The hotel kitchen was extremely badly planned and several phone calls to Melbourne had an architect at Lakes Entrance attempting to solve the problems but it was not just logistics that were a problem. It was the staff, and Gerald was forced to begin to work within this situation. But not for long, he thought. The previous head chef was still present and anything but pleased that Gerald had arrived. The implication was crystal clear, that he was not up to the job and so he was obstructive in every way. By the end of the first week a call to Administration in Melbourne confirmed him in his position as head chef to hire and fire as he saw fit. Armed with this information, transformation within the kitchen took place.

John Williams had been in charge of it ever since the hotel had been totally revamped. He was thirty years old, thin as a rake, with the narrowest eyes, that made him look slightly oriental but the rest of the look was one hundred per cent Australian country. He had no distinguishing features except his narrow eyes. He was of medium height and had a very smart, chic attitude. Needless to say the other three chefs found him difficult to work with. Mario was in his forties. He must have been handsome once, mused Gerald, but the good life and obviously a liking for his own cooking, saw this cheerful man overweight. The other two staff members were Collen, who had inherited all her Irish background – red blonde hair, a narrow freckled face, watery green eyes. She was extremely thin (but as Gerald found out) someone he worked well with and trusted. But it was the fourth staff member Gerald warmed to on first meeting her. Her name was Mary Winder, but everyone called her Windy. She had an extremely happy face, a mane of auburn coloured hair, a full mouth and twinkling brown eyes. A loss of fifteen kilos, Gerald thought, might not go amiss, but Windy was definitely the star of the kitchen staff, a very ready wit and with a brilliant sense of humour. In the first ten minutes of meeting her Gerald summed her up at once, a loyal and true friend, but a very determined foe if crossed. Her repartee was always of the 'sending up' sort and Gerald was always laughing - but not John. He disliked her intensely and on several occasions had attempted to have her discharged, but as he could bring no concrete charges against her except that he disliked her she stayed as the thorn in his side. So for Windy, Gerald was a breath of fresh air and she leaned over backwards to make his stay as pleasant as possible.

One evening saw what Gerald thought was not something new. John decided he was not going to do as instructed by Gerald and so a showdown loomed up. It was Windy's quick thinking - or bitchy tongue - that saved the situation.

'Now, Johnny,' she teased, 'be a good boy or we shan't let you go and play with the other boys.'

There was a sharp implication as to what Windy was referring to and the four of them watched John with exceptionally bad grace do exactly what Gerald had asked. It was then that Gerald realised there was much more to this skinny man with the narrow eyes and he was certain it wasn't good.

In the kitchen everyone was dressed in uniform but out of it Windy was unbelievable. Where she found the clothes and how she wore them was nothing short of amazing. Every possible colour was put together and she was a big girl : Windy was always recognizable. Gerald then thought that Sammy's sand shoes were tame in comparison.

Whilst all this was going on in Gerald's life, Paul's had slowed down. Watching TV was driving him crazy. The fact that from 12.30 to 1.00 the door was not heard to slam and Gerald arrive home left him with an extremely empty feeling. He really didn't know what to do with his spare time as it had always revolved around Gerald. Both Catherine and Faith came to his aid and this was fine but the trouble was when he was at home, all alone. It wasn't that this was so different from the past: Gerald worked late at the hotel. It was the fact that there was never going to be the door opening and closing late at night, which signalled that someone was there and it was this loneliness which in a strange way began to frighten him. He had never ever been alone in his entire life and things he had just taken for granted in the past changed. A cat that had knocked over a rubbish bin lid which crashed to the ground saw Paul now genuinely concerned, whereas once he would just have used a string of expletives aimed at the cat. He had the security on the terrace house upgraded as he was not sleeping well and wondered how Gerald was coping all alone in the countryside. He need have had no worries: Gerald was coping very well, thank you!

But coping well could not be said for Jenny Walls. She had an independent financial arrangement but it was being stretched to the limit with Bona Vista and even she now realised that George was not a real asset in finishing the house off, so she halted all the work. George obviously still received his allowance as he remained in residence but oddly Jenny could not understand his attachment to the place as she had virtually ordered him to return to Melbourne. He said, though, that he would stay and look after the place as they didn't want any theft since the place was not finished and vulnerable. Under sufferance, Jenny accepted his demand to remain but she was genuinely surprised at his attention and surveillance of the property. For her the big problem, apart from a young lover three hours way, was money. She had overspent and her trendy young architect had handed her an astronomical account for his work. This all added up to a real problem financially and the bills just kept coming in.

Gerald had telephoned Catherine to ask could he bring someone back to Donegal for lunch. She was genuinely surprised at his attention to protocol. Of course he could, she said, and they would all be up that weekend. Windy thought Donegal a dream. 'It's just beautiful!' she enthused, having a tour around both the gardens and the house. She was in a most amazing red skirt with a yellow shirt and blue jumper but topped off with a dark blue jacket with an enormous amount of (as Gerald said later) 'junk Jewellery' and bright yellow rubber boots. 'Just the thing for winter,' she laughed and sat down in the informal dining room off the kitchen and, with a drink in her hand, began to fill Gerald in on the background of his staff, which is generally called gossip. But of all the funny stories about disasters in the kitchen, Gerald noted her eyes narrowed when she spoke of John Williams.,

'He's basically a second-rate chef. He once worked in the local Pizza Parlour, a smart arse, but dangerous,' she said, refilling her glass. 'He has a side to his nature that is violent and brutal. There have been complaints but no prosecutions, but that will come. He is so sure of himself. I hate him. I would never, never trust him,' and then she went on to say that the other two were good but not adventurous cooks, though totally reliable. Gerald then asked her about her friends about town and all the interesting bits and pieces that form background information and then he asked her if she knew of James O'Donald, obviously baiting her for information.

'Oh, I know the family,' she said, 'but the boy James, he doesn't live there any more. I don't know what happened to him but his feral father is there. He's vile, always drunk and very aggressive.'

'Tell me about him,' Gerald asked.

'Well, he is the town drunk. He is on unemployment benefits, hasn't worked for years. The story is that he used to beat the boy James and also his wife who eventually committed suicide, or that's the story. The boy had a friend in Miss O'Brien and she looked after him after the mother died. I think Miss O'Brien was the only person old O'Donald was afraid of. It was odd. I saw her once in the street dress him down for something to do with James and while he was always really aggressive he just stood there without a word until she walked away. Odd, isn't it? A great feral drunk like that afraid of a little old lady'.

Gerald leaned over and put another two logs on the fire.

'And your love life?'

'Oh, forget it. There is nothing here worthwhile except the guys I employ, Marco and John. I don't think either is what one would describe as the tops.' He laughed as he said it.

'I'd say the absolute bottoms,' and Windy broke into a gale of laughter. 'No, Gerald, not them, your gardener.'

'My gardener? Oh, but I don't employ him. In fact I have never seen him. I have Tuesday off and so does he, and he is here when I am at work, so as I said I have never seen him. What's he like?'

'Delicious,' smiled Windy, wickedly. 'He's another one who has had a shit life. I feel sorry for him, but at least he has work now. No one would employ him for years. It's really a sad story and an indictment of the mentality of this fucking town.' She sounded more than determined.

'What's the story?' asked Gerald, now very curious.

'Oh God, is that the time?' cried Windy. 'I'm supposed to look in on my oldies. Mum and Dad are very senior citizens. Why don't you come to my place next Tuesday for lunch and I'll fill you in on all the gossip, including Martin. Thanks for a great lunch.' And with a kiss she left and ran to her car as a light drizzle commenced.

Gerald cleaned up, only to be interrupted by a phone call. 'I'll see you in half an hour,' he said and closed his cellphone, then smiled as he washed the last of the glasses.

Gerald's life was not the only one changing; so too was Faith's. One evening Terry telephoned and the long and the short of it was a demand for money and a return home as the prodigal son. To both of these requests the sharp reply was 'NO!' Keven had been the quiet one at home. He was eighteen months older than Terry and with the drama in the house and Terry's extrovert character he was virtually invisible, but now, with both his father and Terry out of the house, and as Faith said, sharply 'for good', he began to blossom. Where in the past he had taken no interest in Faith's friends, he was now always invited to dinners with Catherine, Mark and James, as well as the downcast Paul, and strangely he took a liking to James. Or was it strange? At home he made suggestions about the décor of the house, having often seen Catherine's home and one weekend went with Faith to Donegal where he was a great asset to the group. So now, no invitation was issued to Faith that did not include Keven.

In all this time, Sammy Sillcock had taken on another two gardens and as they were not so close much less was seen of him, especially as George's quick reply on the telephone to him was 'Jenny's going to be here,' and Jenny was someone Sammy had met in Melbourne and decided to give a miss to for life. So ever-clever George orchestrated his nights and days as it suited him.

The following week, in the hotel kitchen, yet again tensions were at a certain high and as a result of a returned order Gerald made it quite clear to John than any more examples of not paying attention to order and not looking more carefully at the waiters' dockets would land him in serious trouble.

'You fucking well watch it!' was the curt reply.

'You'll work within this group correctly or I shall fire you. Do you understand me?' Gerald countered.

'If you fire me, you will pay for it for the rest of your life.'

'Don't threaten me,' Gerald said, calmly.

'Or you could go back to making pizzas!' chipped in Windy. 'I'm sure you were much happier.'

The banging down of a saucepan made it quite clear John was anything but a happy employee.

The evening ended on a brittle note and Gerald was now sure that he was going to, at the first opportunity, get rid of John Williams, and Williams had a gut feeling that this was what was going to happen to him.

'Forget him' Windy advised, as the last orders had been sent in to the dining room. 'But be careful. Not only is he feral, but so is his friend, who is all brawn and absolutely no brain, strictly remedial and vicious.' Windy's face had changed. She was not joking as usual. She was offering her new friend genuine advice for his future.

* * * * *

The following Tuesday, as this was the hotel's quietest day, Gerald drove up to the address given for lunch. He got out of the car and duly having had a look around entered a relatively suburban home similar to the one beside the hotel. A press on the button sounded a jaunty jingle inside and the door opened to a kaleidoscopic Windy.

'Come in, sweetie,' Windy knew men very well, and in this town her three best friends were gay men. She consoled them every time the holiday season was over and they were abandoned yet again. 'Another season, boy!' she always replied and their targets, for better or worse, always ended up being married men, with the wife and children at the beach making them an easy pick-up and 'wow, here we go again!' So for Windy, Gerald was part of the fabric of her life.

He entered a conservative interior that surprised him. Given her personality he assumed that it was going to be something like Bona Vista. In fact it was the opposite, elegant as a suburban brick house can be, soft colours, everything co-ordinated, beautiful antique furniture. Gerald was overwhelmed, and his face showed it.

'Don't worry, darling,' Wendy laughed. 'Everyone thinks my house is going to match my clothes.'

'It's great,' he said, being shown into a well-furnished living room. 'One would never guess that from the outside the inside was – how shall I say – discreet.'

Windy again laughed. 'Open the bottle, sweetie,' and she explained that her parents had the matching house next door. 'This one belonged to my aunt, who left it to me, so I simply moved next door when she died. I sent everything to the second-hand shop and started all over again.'

'I'm surprised you still live here,' he said, 'with your dynamic personality I would have thought you would have headed for Melbourne.'

'Big fish in a small pond syndrome,' she told him as she drank from the glass offered her.

'Hey, that's a beautiful credenza,' enthused Gerald, looking about.

'Oh, so you're into antiques, are you?'

'Well, my partner is an interior decorator, so over the years I have picked up a bit.' He smiled broadly. He was handsome, she thought, and not only that he had style. Those broad shoulders and that very masculine face.

'You're friend's very lucky,' she said, as she tried to search his background.

'Well, he doesn't think so.' And when she queried his comment, he went on, 'Well, he hates the fact that I am down here and not at home.'

'And where's home for you?' she asked, looking straight at him. He was quite taken aback and the instant answer was, 'I'm not sure.'

'Good for you. I'm sure you're going to like living here and it will be great for me. Smart men are hard to come by.' She excused herself and went into the kitchen, as Gerald's eyes circled the room, taking in a collection of furniture and paintings that showed an innate sense of taste, but something he would never have thought of as Windy's home.

'Table, darling.' Although she addressed him very informally in a social situation, at work it was very much more formal. 'You won't believe it, but after we were talking last week about O'Donald I saw him the other day, dead drunk on the pavement when I came out of the supermarket. They should just put him down.' Then she dismissed the subject.

Gerald was eager to pick up from the last conversation. 'Well, now we have time, tell me about Martin.'

'Darling, he is divine.' She laughed. 'And it isn't because he is my only handsome cousin.' Gerald exclaimed in surprise at being drawn into this web of local knowledge.

'Do help yourself to avocado dressing,' she went on. 'It's such a sad story and so is Martin. Everything is so sad.' She got up and fitted a CD into the player. Diana Ross suddenly filled the room. 'Don't you just love her? She is the tops!' she said, and with Diana Ross and the Supremes singing love themes she began to weave the tale about Martin to a very interested Gerald.

'He is a year older than me. Martin's mother and mine were sisters; his father has a brain that rates at sub-zero and he has two sisters, nothing brilliant but neither off the bitches when he was in trouble ever helped him. So much for family sentiment. I never speak to them but I get the greatest satisfaction from refusing to acknowledge them when I see them at the supermarket as it's the only place I do see them. I feel really good about it. Oh, just a moment, I must look at the main course. I'd thought of doing a low calorie meal and then forget in the next moment.' She laughed, as usual.

The main course was served, which Gerald thought was excellent, well thought-out and cooked to perfection.

'You can't go wrong with a fillet,' she smiled, but he noticed that everything with this meal was perfectly co-ordinated, a bit like the thought.

'Martin was the bright one at school but his dumb father refused to let him go to university, so he looked for employment here and worked in Ashcrofts' hardware store. What a disaster for an intelligent, handsome boy! Yes, you are right. The owner's birdbrain daughter thought that this would suit her to the ground. Sophie Ashcroft was probably the most vacuous person in the world, heavily made-up and false as can be – a real bitch. Well, he held off for some time and here I am willing to take a bet,' she continued, refilling their glasses, 'that he was interested in a boy, a young boy. I tried to talk to him about it but he started the conversation and then just cried. It was so sad. Why can't men be like you, Gerald? If you like a guy you get on with it, but Martin couldn't. He was shy and vulnerable and Sophie Ashcroft needed a good-looking husband and began to apply the pressure. Personally, had I been Martin, I would have left town or committed suicide.'

This had Gerald in hysterical laughter, as this conversation was accompanied by a great deal of hand waving and straightening of hair, very theatrical, he thought. She was a good story-teller. 'Well, then, what happened?'

'Well, what do you think? He was pressured by her family and his into this most unsavoury marriage. What a fucking disaster!' She shook her head and reached for the bottle. 'Well, apparently the love-making bit after the full over-the-top wedding –' (here Windy burst into full-throated laughter) '– she looked like a Barbie doll on heat.' She threw herself back into her chair, laughing until tears ran down her cheeks. 'She was such a mess! What she couldn't wear she carried!.' Windy fell into helpless laughter. 'She could hardly walk in the bloody frock, it was so over-loaded with decorations and appliqué work, hideous in the worst possible taste. I believe it cost a fortune. I am so glad she was ripped off.'

'Well, what about Martin?' Gerald asked again.

'Poor Martin!' she sighed. 'Apparently he just couldn't do it. Personally I would declare him a saint. Imagine waking in the morning and finding Sophie Ashcroft beside you – Godzilla herself!' This had Gerald in hysterical laughter.

'But the nasty bit is this, as he had no sex with her she then, being a married woman and with a cover, took up with the most feral member in town – yes, you have it in one – John William's best friend. The parents, especially her father, realised all was not well and in an attempt to support this whimpering bitch declared to all that Martin had stolen from his store and was a homosexual to boot. Can you imagine? In this town! It meant no work at all for him and apart from any family no one spoke to him at all except to shout vulgar comments at him. I personally would have had the greatest pleasure in using the largest meat cleaver in the hotel kitchen and dividing her in two.'

Little was Windy to know that the threat to cut someone in two was to become a reality much more quickly than she could ever have imagined.

* * * * *

The season picked up and so Saturday nights at the hotel became quite busy, due to a completely reorganised menu from Gerald, but this Saturday night was extremely busy and as some of the patrons ate early it left the tables available for a second sitting. He looked happy, which was rare and the narrow eyes seemed less tight and John moved about the kitchen without any problems. Gerald and the others worked frantically to organise the orders and it was at this point that Gerald reasoned that if the holiday season continued like this he would have to take on another staff member. As he worked at one end of the kitchen he suddenly heard a yell of 'You bitch!' as John shouted. The rest turned and witnessed Collen, who had taken a swing at John with a large frying pan complete with a pasta and sauce in it, and it had spilt over the front of him. She was now menacing him with the extremely hot pan. He immediately, in a sense of self-defence and arrogance, grasped the largest carving knife and moved toward her. The other three downed utensils and rushed to Collen's aid but it was Windy who was first on the scene. She grasped a large meat cleaver and used the flat side of it to strike John on the left side of his face. He dropped his weapon as he grasped the side of his face which became in an instant bright red.

'Don't you touch her,' Windy screamed, 'or I'll use this cleaver to sever that tiny thing between your legs!'

'You're fired!' shouted Gerald, as he quickly moved down to the fray. 'Get out now or I'll call the police. Now!!'

John, covered in pasta, with a tomato and pork sauce, seemed completely confused. He just looked at the four of them, now armed with kitchen weapons and very quietly left the kitchen, with Collen shaking and crying her eyes out.

'He's on the stuff again,' said Windy. 'Did you see his eyes? He looked like a snake.'

'What happened?' Gerald asked sharply, and as Collen began to explain the story a waiter arrived for the prepared plates.

'Five minutes,' Gerald barked in an assertive voice. 'Get back to it'. The four of them spun back into action, with Collen cleaning up as she prepared another pan of pasta.

'He threatened me with rape. He and his feral friend, after work, this evening,' she said in between preparing the food. 'I hate him.'

'Don't worry,' Mario reassured her. 'I'll follow your car home tonight and make sure that you get inside safely.

Collen thanked him and then said 'I'm sorry, Gerald, but he had slid his hand up under my apron and I guess I over-reacted.'

'No, you didn't. No one has to put up with that sort of behaviour in a work place, or in any other social situation.' He called the manager of the hotel on the intercom and in five minutes everything was explained to him. Then Windy, with the excuse of going to the toilet, telephoned the police and in no uncertain manner explained the situation. As the police had had numerous problems with these two men before, especially John's friend, they were obviously well-prepared.

'You see,' explained Windy, when Mario had escorted Collen home, and addressing her conversation directly to Gerald, 'John has always used drugs, that's why tonight he left without a fight. He was away with it all. The only thing that was real for him was a sexual assault on Collen and you know and I am positive it's not just gossip – yes, fill it up,' she interrupted herself, pushing her glass across the stainless steel bench top. 'You see he only finds sex or he can only raise an erection in a violent situation and as for his friend, I'm not sure whether he is the same, but he aids and abets him. What charming gentlemen!' She spat sarcastically and it struck Gerald like a blow to his face: two men, forced sex, James – these three broken pieces of a sentence shocked him and his face obviously showed it.

'Are you OK?' she asked.

He said yes, narrowing his green eyes and she noticed a frown across his handsome forehead.

'What's wrong?' So he recounted the story of James being raped when he was eighteen years old.

'Did he give you the names of these shits?' she asked, downing her glass.

'I can get the name of one of them from Sammy tomorrow and then let's go from there.'

'The name you get from him is sure to be Barry Whiteall. He is the bastard with John all the time. I am honestly very worried for Collen. I know these pricks and they are very dangerous. For some unknown reason the police are so stupid that they don't do anything about them, so they lead charmed lives but I can tell you, Gerald, you must be very careful. John has been fired and he is going to be out for your bood now and I am not kidding. So watch out!'

Gerald heeded Windy's warning and although he could look after himself physically two louts even he thought realistically could be a real problem, so like Paul in Melbourne Gerald now began a systematic study of the security at Donegal, even if he did spend most of his nights at Bona Vista in George's arms.

And whilst Gerald was in George's arms, Jenny Walls was facing yet another financial disaster. She had invested in a company called 'New Image', which trumpeted a new look fashion-wise, followed up by smart promotions and obviously public relations with Jenny at the helm. It started well. It was new and the ideas came fast but the problem was they did not keep coming, in fact the whole venture slowed down to a halt and again to Jenny's horror the bills kept rolling in. With this fashion venture now losing money and Bona Vista on hold she suddenly began to look at her not-so-bright financial future and obviously the first thing she thought to liquidate was Bona Vista. But this she held off with for a while because of George, though she knew that of all her assets it would go first.

First thing the following morning Gerald telephoned Sammy and true to Windy's prediction the first gardener that James had refused went by the name of Barry Whiteall. He thanked Sammy and sat on the edge of the bed as George attempted to lure him back to paradise. Gerald showered and returned to Donegal and was very aware he was angry, no not just angry, furious, especially to think that he had worked with John Williams and not realised that it was he who had, with Barry Whiteall, viciously raped the young man he thought was exceptionally special, and with this information now stored in his brain he began to hatch a plot to pay the pair of them back for their cowardly attack on James. He spoke only to Windy on this subject and again and again she cautioned him to be exceptionally careful, knowing well these two louts' capabilities.

* * * * *

A busy Friday evening saw everyone moving about the kitchen, attending to their duties, when the door opened. No one looked up, expecting another waiter's docket to be placed on the spike.

'You have all had it,' smirked a very arrogant John Williams. 'I'll fix the lot of you.'

'Get the hell out of here,' shouted Gerald, 'or it will be all of us getting you. Get lost, you loser.'

Williams moved menacingly forward towards Gerald. A sharp crash on the stainless steel work top reverberated through the kitchen and Williams spun around to see Windy with the same meat cleaver that she had dealt him a blow with less than a week before. Even he was bright enough to realise that he might tackle anyone but Windy definitely not and as she moved forward he found he was being forced into a corner of the kitchen with, now, the entire staff armed with sharp kitchen knives.

'Listen to me,' snarled Windy in an icy tone. 'I now have evidence that you and your birdbrain friend raped a boy of eighteen and if we can make this stick, and I am dead certain we can, you will get a jail sentence. So it may be wise just to disappear, both of you, because if any of us see you about town we shall have the police in on this immediately.' And with her considerable strength she slammed the flat side of the meat cleaver down on the metal bench top, causing a report like a gunshot. Williams was visibly worried for his safety and wondered why he had beern quite so silly as to come and threaten them.

'Get out!' screamed Windy and he was only too glad to acquiesce.

'OK. Back to work. No harm done,' she said, but it was obvious that she was very upset.

Gerald rounded the work bench and embraced her. 'You were fantastic,' he said, quietly, and with that they returned to a busy Friday night's workload.

Windy and Gerald had become quite close in a very short time and a Tuesday lunch she organised for him the following week was to change his life completely. He arrived as bidden, having completed his shopping, and as he rounded the corner of the parking lot he saw, stretched out on a park bench, a drunk propped up on one arm, drinking from a beer can and wondered if indeed this was James's father. He glanced at a wreck of a man and couldn't even guess at his age. With his unshaven face and glazed eyes with the beer can clutched in his hand he was indeed a very sorry sight but Gerald felt nothing for him at all and continued to his car.

'Gome in, come in!' greeted Windy. 'Oh, thanks a lot.' She took a large bunch of roses from him. 'They are divine.'

He moved into the well-furnished house with a kaleidoscopic Windy directing him to the living room and he was surprised to see another man sitting down on the divan. As he stood up, Gerald felt a thrill sweep through his entire body.

'How do you do?' Gerald heard himself saying. 'My name's Gerald.

'Mine's Martin,' was the response. The conversation was to say the least stilted but with Windy making constant appearances to see if glasses were full and then dashing back to the kitchen this wasn't always the case. At one point she tiptoed back and glanced between the door jamb and the door to see the two men attempting conversation. She turned and headed yet again to her kitchen with one arm raised and it was evident that two fingers were crossed.

The meal was, as expected, splendid and Windy was genuinely surprised at Martin's input into the conversation. He generally just sat decoratively. He was a handsome man at twenty six. He was, Gerald thought, the most beautiful man in the world. He was a little taller than Gerald and had a very broad chest and shoulders which made him in every sense larger, but it was the face! Gerald had never seen anything like it, tanned, with a good nose, a slightly furrowed brow, full lips and a cleft chin. The thick wavy black hair was offset by the most marvellous pair of green, honey-coloured eyes, fringed by long black lashes. Windy saw it all happening and if Gerald was captivated, so too was Martin. He had had, as Windy explained to Gerald, a 'shit life;' and as such after the separation from Godzilla he lived with his aunt and uncle next door to Window's parents, and no amounte pressure from her would get him to move in with her. He just remained the dormouse next door. But today the dormouse became a much smarter rodent, with the catalyst being Gerald, he became an aggressive social rat with a smile from ear to ear. Gerald tried all the time to engage him in a dialogue where he could if possible make a future engagement with him, but this proved very difficult, as he worked with Windy and to make things awkward for her cousin who was also employed by Catherine and Mark was a very tricky scenario, so as Martin had to leave to collect some supplies for Donegal he said his goodbyes and left.

'Obviously another drink,' Windy quipped.

'Obviously,' came the reply.

'Well?'

'He's stunning,' was all Gerald could muster.

'How divine! I knew it would work,' she said, with a certain confidence. 'I'll have you two married yet.' And burst into hysterical laughter.

When Gerald returned to Donegal he was indeed to grasp the concept of 'hysterical' but in another sense. George was beside himself with rage and thrust into Gerald's hand a real estate evaluation.

'What the fuck is she doing?' was his cry as he opened a bottle of wine for them, but that evening Gerald heard, or understood, little of the drama. All he could think of was a well-built twenty six year-old he had just met with honey-coloured eyes and thick, black, wavy hair.

'She is going to put the fucking house on the market. What a shit!' George screamed, rather hysterically. He realised that with this being the reality he was destined to return to Melbourne and cope with Jenny or make a break to fresher pastures. It was at this moment, just before George decided a night of sex might just save the day – or night. Gerald asked to see the real estate estimate on what Bona Vista in its present condition was worth.

'Look,' exclaimed an excited George, 'they state the place is worth a third less than when we bought it.'

'We' was the only thought that went through Gerald's mind, but he did note carefully the agent's name.

'Will Jenny sell at that price?' he asked, softly.

'Oh, I guess so. She is strapped for cash. What a drag – after all I have done here, she is so ungrateful.'

'Gerald looked about the orange-painted living room and wondered exactly what George's input had been : financially none, but ideas, if there had been any, then this shocking disaster decorator-wise showed him to be lacking in any taste, if not in another direction. To make love with someone when one is thinking of another is basically dishonest and Gerald was very aware this evening that as he made love with George he was thinking only of the possibility of Martin. It is an old saying that the more sex you have the more you need. Be that as it may, for Gerald, after a few dalliances on the side of his and Paul's relationship he was now firmly enjoying George. But a magic had touched him, for the want of a better word, and that magic was called Martin. To think he had been looking after the gardens at Donegal all the time Gerald had been resident and he had never seen him! And yet today there he was probably, thought our good-looking Gerald, the most exotic creature in the world.

If he was having these thoughts, and unfortunately, while in bed with George, Martin was also seeing, after a long and difficult time, an opportunity to break with the past. He thought Gerald extremely handsome but didn't have the courage to say so, especially with Windy at the dining table. Those green eyes, and a professional tennis play as well! This information had come via Windy, who embellished it all in order to lift Martin to a level where he was wanted.

'Oh, I know I can do it,' thought Windy. Two good-looking gay guys. 'I am sure Martin is interested.' nd before she drifted off to sleep on Tuesday evening she ran through her mind a hundred times the possibilities of Gerald and Martin finding one another. 'Oh yes, it's the only way.' And she turned over, certain that today her cousin had met the man of his dreams - and consoled herself that they both played tennis.

CHAPTER 6

A Most Unsettling Time

CHAPTER 6

A Most Unsettling Time

'Hello. May I help you?' came a very professional voice.

'I hope so,' replied Gerald and began the first step in the purchase of Bona Vista.

'Yes, the agent can see you next Tuesday, if that's the time that is most convenient for you. I shall give him your telephone number and he will make arrangements.'

Gerald was not tight with money but he was careful. Having been a professional tennis player he was very aware that the tournaments that paid well were often far apart. So he had always, when time were good, banked well, and continued to do so. His wages at the hotel as Head Chef were excellent and a quick call to his bank and then the hotel administration for a guarantee of future employment all added up to a loan being available if and when he required it. The papers were signed with no-one being aware that Gerald was in thirty days to be the new owner of Bona Vista. He was not exactly sure why he was not telling anybody but his sixth sense told him to sit and wait, and this he did. He knew that by not telling Paul anything about the purchase it was going to put an incredible strain on their relationship to the point where separation might be the case. But for the first time since he had met Paul he had made a completely independent decision and felt very good about it.

The following week he had to collect some hooks for the kitchen at Donegal and so he went to Ashcroft's Hardware store to purchase them. It was then he saw exactly what Windy had attempted to describe. Sophie Ashcroft was, to say the least, odd. It was as if she had stepped out of a Seventies' magazine, but the effect was quite laughable. She was not tall. The upper part of her body was thin but she had broad hips. The denim shirt unbuttoned showed a black bra top underneath and a pink short pleated skirt was amazing. 'Bad drag,' thought Gerald, but it was the face that was alarming. The eyes were extremely made up and her face was plastered in a light beige foundation with the palest pink lipstick on exceptionally large, well-formed lips. But when one looked directly at her the tip of her small nose was so elevated that one tended to see right up the nostrils. And the hair! 'Well,' thought Gerald, 'not even a tacky drag queen would do anything like it.' A long blonde fringe virtually covered the forehead and above this it was all raised up to quite a height and then it fell to the shoulders and was kicked up all around the bottom, and this blonde-white hair was lacquered, so not one hair moved independently when she moved her head: the whole arrangement moved with her as a solid topping to a painted, hard face.

'Yes?' she demanded, and Gerald explained what he wanted. She dutifully located the hooks he was seeking and after paying her a hard voice said, 'See you!' and he thought to himself, 'Not if I can help it.' So this was what Martin had been forced to marry. Gerald couldn't believe it. She was a caricature of a woman. The look screamed 'tough tart'.

It was about twenty days short of settlement for Bona Vista that Jenny Walls put in a sharp call to George. 'You come back at the end of this week or your allowance is finished,' and so, having no intention of working at all, the demand was adhered to, with George none the wiser that Gerald had indeed purchased Bona Vista.

Tuesday lunches at either Windy's or at Donegal became a regular date but now at both residences the table was always set for three. It was here that Gerald found it very difficult to organise anything with Martin and as he was so shy Gerald was treading very carefully, not to make him feel awkward or embarrassed, but a grasp of the arm or a hand on the shoulder generally produced the same effect, a broad smile.

But a broad smile could not be said to be seen on Estelle's face as a client had reneged on signing a very important sale for the company so she was most out of sorts. The following morning, when she arrived at the office, she was amazed to see a group of people all glancing in the front window at the 'For Sale' photographs of Christian Hall and when she gently eased her way to the front, to her utmost surprise she saw a toy possum with his tail supporting him from a branch and with one paw pointing at a house for sale and in his other paw a little card that read 'at last my dream home'. Estelle entered the office, not sure whether she was cross with this type of advertising or not.

'Well, don't you think it's a snappy idea?' chirped Terry, who was early for once. Estelle was obliged to admit although it was not what she considered corporate chic the number of people glancing in the sales window was something that, if it heralded sales, she was all for it. She had modified her approach a little and this was due, obviously, to Terry, who spoke to her as he felt. The other staff were constantly aware that if they did not make their sales perhaps they might not have employment, and in this environment Terry was the only one who led a charmed life, with Estelle every now and again threatening him if he did something she did not approve of, but oddly both of them realising that for the strangest reason they supported one another's needs. It was not unusual that after a busy day the two of them would head off to a wine bar together, with Christian Hall generally the subject of desire and laughter.

And desire and laughter could now be used to describe Mark and James's relationship. Mark had relaxed his tense exterior pose and even at work Maggie noticed a happier head of the firm. He had grasped the rudiments of the real estate world and had made great advances with Maggie's constant support, so in a position where he was the manager and controlled all and now with a twenty year old adoring love he could well afford to laugh happily as Catherine poured them both another drunk, and they planned yet another weekend together at Donegal.

After their usual Tuesday lunch Windy left Donegal in a rush as she had forgotten to collect a prescription for her mother at the chemist's, so left alone for the first time together Gerald sought to engage Martin in more intimate conversation but this was not so easy as Martin tended to change the subject or just ignore Gerald's intentions. In desperation,

Gerald suggested a walk to Bona Vista, as it was now uninhabited as George had returned to Melbourne. On walking down the road to Bona Vista it was Martin who said, softly, 'It's all right, Gerald. Don't push. Everything is fine.' Gerald smiled at him, realising he had made a great error. He had assumed that Martin would be grateful to him for his attention, not realising that if a relationship was going to function the inputs must be equal.

'It's worse than I remember,' Martin commented. 'I saw it some months ago. They really have made a mess of it, haven't they?'

'Yes. I am afraid they have, but it's nothing that can't be repaired. What do you think?'

Martin frowned and looked at Gerald quite intently. 'Yes. I don't see why it can't be put back in order. It's a nice house.'

They had a look around with Gerald still remaining silent about his ownership of it. An inspection inside showed that a great deal of work was necessary to undo Jenny Wall's decorating scheme. They slowly walked back to Donegal, where Gerald, mustering up all the courage he had, asked Martin if he would like to stay for dinner.

'Yes, for dinner,' he said, with a straight face and then the corners of his mouth gave him away and a broad smile swept across his handsome face. Arm in arm they walked through the garden at Donegal and went inside, out of what was now becoming a cool, late afternoon. But if Gerald thought that Martin would just fit into the gap that George's exit had left he was in for a surprise, for although the relationship between them had been formed, it was one where Gerald was going to have to wait for a time before he had Martin as a lover.

Martin had lost very badly in the field of love, forced to marry someone he didn't at all like. The repercussions of separation and the public ridicule of being branded gay did very little to make him think that relationships were easy, so being naturally shy he was very careful about entering a relationship with Gerald. He knew that in the town tongues wagged and he didn't want any more trouble than he had to cope with as he remembered only too well the problems with Sophie Ashcroft. As

Gerald that evening, after dinner, said goodbye to him, a warm embrace was all that was offered.

Gerald tidied up and went to bed with his brain spinning. He suddenly realised that no matter what he said Paul was not going to receive the news of Bona Vista well. If he decided to let Paul in on the secret of his purchase in order to organise the repair and renovation of what Jenny Wall had done, it was tantamount to offering to share the house with him and he knew in his heart the only person he wanted to share the house with was Martin. So now what was he to do? He knew he couldn't do the work. He was not an architect. And if he found an architect to do the work the word 'Divorce' with a capital 'D' loomed up in front of him. He had only a week ago, with the manager of the hotel in Lakes Entrance, spoken about remaining there and not returning to Melbourne. There had been several brisk conversations between the manager and the hotel management in Melbourne and in the end, considering Gerald's ability to lift a second rate hotel kitchen to the situation where now you had to book ahead for a table in the restaurant dining room. All parties decided that when the three months were up the final decision should be Gerald's. Never in his life had he so many independent choices; everything in the past had been resolved, and resolved well, by Paul; now, for the first time, he was on his own. Although he saw major problems he was not afraid of them, though he knew deep down that Paul was the past and the future beckoned ahead.

Then it came to him about the old man called David: 'Don't be afraid. He is waiting for you, not the first boy but the second.' Yes, he remembered what David had seen in the cards, even when he had laughed, 'Don't worry, a stripe is a stripe.' All this information spilled back over him and now it all made sense. But how the hell did this David know or have the capacity to read it in what seemed to Gerald only a pack of decorative cards? The first boy was James, taken by Mark. This he knew. The second was Martin, not George, and stripes, well he had just purchased Bona Vista and in one way or another the stripes were to go.

While working the next day with everything in order, he felt something, almost as if it were someone else's thought, vague, but definitely something he should have noticed before. He couldn't work out what it was and he glanced at the staff. What was it, he thought? Colleen, hard-working, honest; Windy he knew as she moved effortlessly between the stoves and preparation benches; and Mario, reliable and expert on cooking fish, good-looking but overweight: which one of these three had moved differently tonight that had affected his senses. Then he went to the spike to withdraw another order.

The original painters who had had to suffer Jenny and then George, quoted an astronomical fee to paint out their hard work, and walking about inside Bona Vista early one morning before going to work Gerald realised he now needed help and he was going to have to confide in someone in order to see some sort of progress at Bona Vista as he just could not see what to do with the interior, as so much of the original structure inside had been demolished. It took him days before he finally decided who it was going to be to help him, and as he and Martin walked through the house again and again their ideas began to knit together as they saw in their minds the finished interior. And so with this decision Gerald changed his life completely, exactly as David had seen it in the Tarot cards. Gerald was really surprised at Martin's ability to organise the resurrection of the house and at prices that were reasonable, so the two of them kept this a secret even from Windy, although she had a feeling something was definitely 'up' and she couldn't have been happier.

So eventually, the three months were completed and two very different men were waiting patiently for it. John Williams never doubted that the moment Gerald returned to Melbourne he would be offered his old job back again. He had experience in the hotel and he was sure he could persuade or con the management into re-hiring him. He was in for a very nasty surprise when he paid a visit to the hotel manager to be told that as Gerald had decided to stay on there was no likelihood of his ever working there again. The slamming of the manager's door made it very clear he was not happy. In fact he was irate. He had assumed he would have been welcomed back but now things were very different. No job equals no money and his habit was expensive, so he blamed everyone for his dilemma without ever thinking to look into a mirror. And the person he hated the most was Gerald; he had won and Williams had lost. 'Fuck him!' he cried, as he made the bottom step of the hotel foyer, which had hotel guests glancing at him as he stormed toward the car park.

Later he commiserated with his friend Barry Whiteall, who was Sophie Ashcroft's companion, and lived together with her, although Sophie and Martin were not divorced. Whiteall was the complete opposite of Williams. Whereas Williams was thin, Whiteall was very overweight, with a large round face that seemed to glare at one but not see anything. He had a shaved head and it only made his bulging eyes more obvious. From his chin his neck cascaded to his chest and at first glance, if one had made an objective assessment of him, it would be without a doubt 'thug'! His body language supported this one hundred per cent, but it was Williams who was the slyer of the two and, as a result, one thug orchestrated by another and out for revenge equals a nasty situation.

When Windy heard the news of Gerald remaining at Lakes Entrance she was elated but in a few moments, having heard from the hotel manager that Williams had expected his position as head chef back, she took it upon herself to telephone the police to warn them there was going to be trouble and in order to avoid a problem it would be very wise to pass by the hotel parking lot when the staff were leaving for the night.

It happens one day once a year for everyone, and this year Brenda White as usual went all out to make the annual event more special than ever. This year she was fifty three years old and from a regular outdoor life, namely the golf course, looked it. She had an angular figure, quite solid and hard, and an 'I-know-it-all' face. The hair was lacquered with two curls right and left of the forehead and the whole look said 'Be careful'! Every year Brenda's birthday party was something to be invited to and it gave her the utmost pleasure to invite some friends and leave others off the list. Her home was not exceptionally special, in fact it was exceptionally suburban, but in Brenda's mind it was a place people craved to see. The main living space which opened onto the diner-kitchen was, to say the least, drab, with not one piece of furniture to note. The paintings - and there were many - were done by Brenda herself. Enough said. So this year the invitation that had been sent to Windy's mother and had been duly handed on to Windy. It said 'and friend' so Windy took this as a mere gesture. One or two, what's the difference? So the Tuesday before this party, she informed both Gerald and Martin that they were escorting her to Brenda's 'do', as she put it. Martin immediately said he would not go and Gerald really was not all that interested but Windy's insistence saw the three of them on Saturday night, after work, change quickly and collect Martin to make for Brenda's ever-so-smart birthday reception. The door was opened by Brenda herself, who was a little confused at having a large bunch of roses thrust into her arms and receiving a birthday kiss from Windy. 'Twenty one again!' she laughed, as Brenda looked sharply at her escorts.

'This is Brenda,' Windy introduced them. A birthday wish and a shake of the hands saw the three of them in her very crowded living room. Windy signalled a waitress she knew and soon, in this cramped environment, they began to look about at the other guests. This was the first time for Martin since he and Sophie had separated, now almost two years earlier, that he had been to a local gathering and he was generally surprised when people said hello to him. He still, in a way, saw himself as an outcast. Brenda pushed herself through the crowd and glanced at Windy with her two escorts laughing, not at all sure that he invitation was sent as such but decided to leave it be.

Brenda had invited everyone she thought was her social equal, which obviously produced a wide range of people, but all in her mind 'socially and financially well-off'. Then Martin grasped Gerald's arm firmly. 'Oh God!' he exclaimed, and both Gerald and Windy turned to see Sophie Ashcroft's parents holding court at the end of the room.

'Let's get out of here,' urged Martin nervously.

'Not on your life!' came Windy's reply. 'You happen to be my guest and you are with your special friend, and that gives you as much right to be here as those two old bigots.' They saw that Martin finished his glass of wine rather quickly.

The evening was, as Gerald said, relatively tame, until the waiter and waitress began to hand around the second lot of food on trays. By this stage it must have been almost one o'clock. It was at this point that, since the noise was loud no-one, including Brenda, heard her back door open and slam shut, announcing Sophie and Barry Whiteall, both obviously having had a lot to drink. Brenda was prepared to put up with Sophie's parents, well-off locals, but she particularly loathed Sophie, so this gate-crashing at one o'clock had her in quite a state and from this point on everything went wrong. It wasn't only the alcohol that Barry had consumed; another substance had an effect on him, though to begin with his behaviour was loud but just acceptable.

Words could not be found to described Sophie's appearance, but as Windy said, 'Bad taste will do.' As Barry lurched toward a drink tray, he knocked someone's hand and drink spilled over his friend's frock. The man spoke sharply to Barry about his clumsiness. 'Get fucked!' was the reply, loud and clear. It had the immediate effect of silencing the room as everyone looked in Barry's direction as he snatched a full glass from the waiter.

'You have not been invited,' stated an irate Brenda.

'Who the hell are you?' was the reply, while Sophie tried to calm the situation down.

'I just happen to be the hostess and this is my house,' Brenda exclaimed, forgetting that she had a husband, 'and you can leave.'

'When I'm ready,' was the arrogant reply and then Barry noticed Windy, Gerald and, to his surprise, Martin. He pushed his way across the room with people stepping clear of him, with Brenda in hot pursuit as well as Sophie. This large, over-weight thug decided that if anyone left this birthday party it was most definitely going to be the poof Martin and he went to push him.

'I wouldn't even think about it,' said Gerald, sharply.

Barry glanced at a well-built sporting figure. 'Fuck you!' was his response.

'I'm fine, thank you. I haven't reached desperation point yet.' This had a few of the guests with smiles on their faces.

If Barry had been wise, he would have collected Sophie and left but wisdom and Barry were not acquainted. So the first punch he threw missed by half a metre and brought gasps from the birthday crowd. Windy quickly looked for a weapon but found nothing. The second punch nearly connected with Gerald's chin. Then there was a crashing sound and a large silver tray, now denuded of glasses, crashed down on

Barry's shaven head. He stood confused for a moment before slumping in a large heap to the floor. Martin calmly handed the tray back to the waiter, who scampered back into the kitchen to gather a broom and shovel to clean up the broken glass.

'You,' screamed Brenda at Sophie, 'can take this feral mess out of my living room now or I shall call the police!'

Sophie looked quite out of it and sped back to her parents for help. At that Brenda, with a great deal of satisfaction, called the police, as a half-groggy Barry attempted to stand.

'Stay where you are!' Windy shouted.

'How dare you speak to my fiancé like that?' screamed a defiant Sophie, who disliked Windy intensely.

'Fiancé! What a laugh! You aren't even divorced, you tart!' With this, the crowd moved closer, realising that this debacle was going to be fun.

'You fat freak!' yelled Sophie, as she moved menacingly toward a confident Windy. The push was to say the least sharp: Windy had waited until Sophie was between her and the large lump on the floor, completely dazed. The push was well thought-out and as Sophie tottered backward she tripped over Barry and fell on top of him.

'Get off, you stupid bitch!' This had everyone laughing.

'How dare you!' Sophie screamed, as her parents pushed through the crowded living room, attempting to save the evening, and in her anger and impatience to get onto her feet she slipped again and fell on top of him once more. The slap he delivered to her made her reel backwards into a 'whatnot' which collapsed and fell, upsetting all the china ornaments that had belonged to Brenda's mother. It crashed to the floor.

Police or no police, Brenda now took matters into her own hands and armed with a golf club she seized Sophie by her well-lacquered hair. To her surprise, a whole section of this coiffure came away. Sophie, in order to maintain her hair style as tall as possible had had recourse to a wiglet! Gales of laughter followed, as a bright spark asked Brenda if it were alive. Again, laughter was heard through the living room. Brenda roughly dragged a very bedraggled Sophie to her feet and demanded that her parents remove their delinquent daughter. In less than ten minutes the police arrived and removed Barry, who still wasn't sure what had happened, except he had a large bump on his scalp and a thrashing headache. Brenda saw them to the door, holding her golf stick in a very menacing way.

'Thank you, Martin, for saving the evening,' said Brenda, and moved back amongst the crowd, who just thought they might have another drink before they left, even though it was late.

'You were great,' Gerald congratulated him. 'Indiana Jones himself!' and he squeezed Martin's arm. Windy gave him a kiss. 'Great going, Martin. This is just the start of your new life.'

The following day saw Barry collecting his belonging from Sophie's apartment as she was sporting, as a result of the violent slap from Barry, a black eye.

This social evening at Brenda's had a galvanising effect on Gerald and Martin. For the latter it had been Gerald who had come immediately forward when Barry had threatened him and he now felt strangely secure in Gerald's company, a sensation he had never felt with anyone before, and he liked it immensely. So, as the Tuesday lunches continued, it became understood that Martin was having dinner with Gerald in the evening.

The following weekend after Brenda's birthday party, while most of Lakes Entrance was talking about the Golf club, Catherine and the boys arrived for the weekend with Faith and Paul and Keven. As they were arriving on Friday afternoon, lo and behold Sammy Sillcock appeared as if a genie out of a bottle and simply took over the kitchen; it was late on Friday evening, after they had eaten and were joking, that Gerald arrived after work.

The door closed with a bang. 'Hi, everyone!' he cried, and as they all greeted him he said he was fine, while looking around the room at them all.

'Like a drink?' asked James.

'Well, perhaps,' he smiled, having kissed both Faith and Catherine.

'How was the trip up?' he began, and Mark told him it had not been bad, an easy drive as now they took it in threes. Gerald said he thought that sounded really intelligent. And then realised that there was a tension in the room, and it came exactly from where Paul was sitting.

'How's the cat?' asked Gerald jauntily in the direction the question to Paul.

'Oh, as if you would be interested.' Everyone picked up the electric response and realised that this was not going to be a quiet weekend. Gerald ignored Paul's comment and in a moment conversation returned to normal, until Faith said she had heard that Jenny Walls had sold the striped house.

'Really?' said Catherine. 'Who is going to be our new neighbour?'

'No idea, but our Jenny is really strapped for cash. Did you ever meet the boyfriend, Gerald?' Faith enquired.

'Yes, I did, but I don't think he could be called an architect,' hoping this was going to be the last reference to George.

One by one they made their excuses and headed to their respective bedrooms, which left only Mark, James and Gerald taking the last drop.

'James,' said Gerald in a very business-like tone, 'I want to ask you something, with Mark beside you.'

'Anything. Any time,' laughed James.

'Will you testify against John Williams and Barry Whiteall?'

'How do you know them?' James queried, very surprised.

'I'm resident here now and as I had to work with Williams for a while, before I discovered the situation. I am sure, having spoken to Windy, that we have a case.'

'Who's Windy?' asked Mark, realising that a certain light-heartedness had departed the conversation.

'I work with her. She's great. You will love her.'

'Isn't she the cousin of our gardener?' asked James, slightly but ever-so-slightly, narrowing his eyes.

'Yes, she is. She is great fun.' Then he went on to describe the debacle at Brenda's birthday party.

'It's so long ago,' said James, conscious that he had laid his arm across Mark's shoulders. 'What's the point?'

'The point is, James, that these two bastards are continuing their feral habits and, as the police say, until someone comes forward they can't do anything.'

But someone had come forward and the next day after her now talked about birthday party Brenda went at nine o'clock sharp to the police station and pressed a charge, of Barry Whiteall forcibly entering her home, uninvited, attacking her closest friend (even Martin would have been very surprised to know he had been elevated to this dizzy social height), breaking priceless heirlooms and on and on she went, putting all her guests' safety in peril. She could not be stopped. For the police this was the first time anyone had actually laid a charge and so, armed legally with this, Barry was charged. And it was with this information behind him that Gerald tried to persuade James to make a charge at the police station with him that weekend. But James was of the opinion it was in the past and he only wanted to forget about it. So Gerald was thwarted. There was no way he could force James to go to the police and so he saw an opportunity to nail these two thugs straight away.

The next morning he did not have to be at work until eleven o'clock so the pleasant Saturday morning was spent catching up with all the news from Melbourne. 'So they want you here for a bit longer, do they?' Faith said, in all innocence.

'Yes, it seems so,' Gerald told her, happily, but everyone was aware that Paul was not smiling with him. After a hearty breakfast, with all enjoying one another's company, with the exception of Paul and Gerald, James noticed that, despite the tension Paul was creating, Gerald seemed as light as a feather. He moved more nimbly, it seemed to James, and there was, it seemed, a light shining out of his strong, green eyes that indicated contentment or happiness, he wasn't sure, but of one thing he was, being close to Gerald, that he was absolutely not suffering being estranged from Paul.

* * * * *

The weekend saw Paul take a stride down to Bona Vista to have a look at Jenny's disaster and he was very surprised, as he had gone with Faith and Keven, that there was work in progress yet again on this big weather-boarded house. When they went in, as a door of the veranda was unlocked, they noticed a great change, with ensuite bathrooms being in, while all the multi-coloured toilet fixtures were in a heap just to the side of the veranda.

'Well, it seems someone has taken the house in hand,' said a slightly sarcastic Paul. If only he knew that Martin and Gerald every morning went over detail after detail to try to hone the house into a fine residence for the future, perhaps for both of them. But still, nothing was resolved between Martin and Gerald. The latter was becoming worried, as he confessed to Windy that without Martin this house they were working on was just useless to him. Windy was also concerned that Martin had not taken the initiative and made a move with Gerald, and she decided to take matters into her own hands, dangerous as it might be.

The weekend passed pleasantly and only too soon on Monday morning they were all seen heading off to Melbourne. Paul knew all was not well in their relationship and this weekend had confirmed that what with the distant conversation to one another, Gerald speaking to the others but never to him, it didn't take long, having been in a relationship for some length of time, to realise that the flame was out, or worse, there was somebody else. This inevitably called up the green dragon of jealousy, as well as a feeling of rejection and these two sensations were thrashing about in Paul's mind as they drove to Melbourne. He felt anything but fine.

Windy decided that Martin needed a decent shove forward. This pussy-footing around, she decided, was a waste of time, but how to orchestrate it? And then it dawned on her: jealousy, that was it, and so one afternoon, between shifts, as she and Martin were in the supermarket she began her ploy.

'Well, what's happening at Donegal?' she began.

'Oh, the garden's great,' Martin replied, unaware that the conversation at its completion was going to see him a different man. Gerald had told her about Mark and James and in the following chat Windy decided to leave Mark out of the equation. 'It must have been great for Gerald to see James again,' she said, as casually as she could, and to her annoyance Martin made no response. 'A young chap like that, that Gerald helped - he is twenty years old now. Do you remember him? He lived here. His father is that ghastly drunk. Miss O'Brien looked after him.'

'I'm aware of that,' came a most frosty reply, which gave Windy great satisfaction.

'I believe he has grown into a fine young man. Good for him! He just needs a great man to look after him.'

If she had been wanting to upset Martin or put him in a situation where he felt the most important person in his life was about to slip through his fingers, she had done it. And so, for the next two days Martin genuinely suffered the fantasy of Bona Vista together. He saw everything turning upside down and instead of a future, fantasy or not, with Gerald, the spare bedroom in Windy's parents' home next door to her did not seem at this point although it had been a safe haven, what or where he wished to be for the rest of his life. So it was a most determined Martin who waited in the car park while Gerald finished work on Thursday evening and to say Gerald was surprised to have Martin accompany him to Donegal wasn't all quite so easy, but with his handling, Martin, for the first time in his life, undressed with another man and went to bed. Gerald was very aware Martin was without experience sexually and, he guessed correctly, with either a women or a man, so he began the soft, sensitive exercise of love making careful not to make things embarrassing or awkward for the other. He was quite surprised that, given a certain impulse, Martin entered into this love-making with as much enthusiasm as Gerald and later, lying in one another's arms, it was Martin who did much of the soft talking and the plans for the future of Bona Vista suddenly made sense to both of them. Martin slept well, as Gerald had replied to one of his questions – that James and Mark were lovers and deeply in love with one another.

'Well?' Windy asked next day at work,

'Well what?' replied Gerald, with a smile from ear to ear.

'Mum said this morning Martin hadn't come home last night. I assured her it was something that was to become regular. Am I wrong?' Windy was slightly holding her breath.

'No, you're not wrong.'

Windy, with an exclamation, grabbed Gerald and they began to waltz around the kitchen, with Coleen and Mario to say the least surprised, if not entertained.

Wednesday morning, early, had Keven responding to Terry on the telephone and in reply to his question found out that Faith was not in. In general small talk Terry managed to glean that as Faith and Keven had returned from Donegal that weekend that Gerald was not returning but staying on and for how long no-one knew. Armed with this information and as sharp as ever, Gerry telephoned Paul to say he would be around for a drink after work and was looking forward to seeing him. He hung up, feeling very sure of himself as usual.

'Come in,' was the response to the brass knocker summoning Paul to the door, and Terry handed him a bottle of champagne. He was ushred into the elegant living room, which opened through large folding doors to a very smart dining room, all, as Terry was to say, perfectly co-ordinated.

'Well,' Terry began, 'I heard that Gerald is remaining resident at Lakes Entrance.'

'So it appears,' was the terse reply and this was the response Terry was waiting for.

'Well, where does that leave you?' he asked, coming straight to the point.

'Financially secure,' countered Paul, keeping up with the repartee.

'Well, if he is in Lakes Entrance and not returning there is obviously a good reason, and who is it?'

Paul was not sure that this company this evening was everything he wanted. 'I haven't a clue. Gerald's life is his own.'

'Oh, really? How silly of me! I always assumed you would both be together forever.' Terry smiled viciously.

'Yes, silly you,' Paul replied.

'It's your fault, you know. Had you bought the house next to Donegal, you might now be having a second honeymoon.'

Now, Paul was beginning to become angry for he knew that behind this flippant comment was a grain of truth. 'It couldn't be done. Jenny Walls beat us to it.'

'Not only that,' smiled Terry, helping himself to another drink. 'Shall we eat here tonight or find a restaurant?'

'Please yourself,' was Paul's only reply.

'Good. Let's talk about the dirt in the kitchen.' With that, the two of them gathered their glasses and made for the kitchen/dining room.

'Do you remember Sammy Sillcock? Terry asked.

'Of course I do. I hired him to lay out the gardens at Donegal.'

'Oh, so you did,' Terry said in a false way.

'OK, Terry, out with it! What exactly do you wish to say and I suppose it is at my expense.'

'Oh, how defensive you have become! It must be the result of living alone.'

'Watch it, or you may just be eating Kitkat in the courtyard.'

'Darling, how could you say such a thing to me?'

'Easily,' snapped Paul, as he busied himself in the kitchen.

Terry opened another bottle of wine.

'Well, what's the gossip from Sammy?' asked a very curious Paul.

'You know the situation of the sale of the house near Donegal.'

'You mean Bona Vista, Jenny Wall's disaster.'

'Yes,' said Terry. 'It appears, according to Sammy, that he and George were more than just passing acquaintances, so to speak.'

'Oh,' replied Paul, attempting to remain uninterested. 'So what?'

'How can I say this?' murmured Terry, with a false look of despair.

'Just try,' was the dry reply.

'Well, according to our man with the colourful footware, it wasn't just Sammy that was – how should I say? – sleeping with him –'

It was at this point that the crash of a saucepan on the bench alerted Terry to the fact that perhaps it might have been wiser to eat out after all. 'What exactly are you inferring?' Paul demanded, helping himself to another glass of white wine.

'I have to confess,' Terry started, 'I am confused about the details.'

'First time for everything!'

'Listen, if Sammy was having sex with George, and, according to Sammy, Gerald was having sex with George, now that George is in the iron arms of Ms Walls here in Melbourne what on earth is Gerald doing remaining in Lakes entrance? It all doesn't make sense.'

'Let's eat out,' was Paul's reply, as he thrust everything back into the fridge.

Seated in a restaurant less than a hundred metres from the front door, Paul began to wonder what on earth was happening. Here was Terry, and he knew his capacity to connive to suit himself, but if what he said was true then like Terry he wondered why Gerald hadn't, at the first opportunity, returned to Melbourne, if for nothing else than to be with George.

'I just don't know what to make of it all,' admitted Terry, feigning he was truly interested in Gerald and Paul's future. The fact that Gerald had had sex or was supposed to have had sex with George took a secondary position: the oddest thing that confronted both of them was why Gerald was not now in Melbourne. The three months were well past.

'Do you think he has another lover?' Terry asked, tactlessly.

'No idea. It looks as if in the last few month's he's changed radically.'

'Oh, a bit of sex here and there doesn't hurt anybody,' said Terry, in a blasé way.

'Oh, I'm so happy you are finally resolved to the fact that Mark and James are so happy together.' Paul smiled falsely. Terry's response was a false laugh.

'Well, it appears we have both been out-foxed,' Paul commented and Terry, sharply, had to agree. This was the first time during the evening that Paul felt his feet had touched the ground and his stomach had stopped shaking.

'What about your love life now that you are out in the world all alone,' Paul asked, rather viciously.

'Much the same,' came the casual reply.

'Liar! If your social life is so great – and I know for a fact that Faith is not going to have you back home – what the hell are you doing out with me this evening? You are not just here to shock me about Gerald's love-life. I know you very well, Terry. What exactly do you want?'

There was a silence as Terry emptied his glass and signalled the waiter for another bottle.

'You are alone and in a certain way so am I. Why don't we combine forces, so to speak?'

'I presume that that comment has a great deal to do with your accommodation. Am I wrong?' Paul smiled as he suddenly pulled himself back into the social fray.

'Well, why not? Gerald's hardly likely to return.'

'How can you be so sure?' Paul narrowed his eyes, at the same time seeing his life without Gerald leaving a gaping hole in his social existence. 'Easy,' said a nonchalant Terry. 'Look, if I was with somebody and had the opportunity to be with them, there I would be.'

'Pity you can't manage it with Mark,' responded Paul, sarcastically.

'Yes, pity,' was the reply, 'but I haven't noticed Gerald on your doorstep either.' Terry smiled at his retort. Another drink, sweetie?' Paul said yes. 'Look,' Terry went on, 'Gerald may have met someone in the hotel world and they are swinging from the light fixture.'

'I'm not interested in Gerald's sex life unless you want me to go into how happy James and Mark are, never without one another.'

'Point taken!' Terry snapped. 'Well, what do you say? By the way, who owns your terrace house?'

'Gerald and me. Why?'

'Well, if he has decided to stay at the seaside, so to speak, he may want his half of it.'

The conversation was now taking another turn and one Paul did not like at all. 'We should come to an agreement,' he said.

'Hopefully in your favour. I don't ever remember Gerald as the man to throw money about, do you?'

Paul knew very well that Terry had made a very calculating statement about Gerald and he was correct. Gerald was very careful with money and for Paul to pay out half the terrace house's value would put him in a very tight situation financially. He had this strong feeling that Terry was enjoying putting him in an awkward situation and twisting the knife. He thought that he would sleep quite well if he was to break the wine bottle over Terry's head but thought better of it. 'I'll speak to Gerald and let you know,' he said, having paid the bill and stood up.

'Well, let's hope it works out in our favour.' Terry grinned.

'In your favour I think is what you mean,' and saying goodbye Paul walked back to his terrace house with now a new dilemma forming in his mind: how to raise the money for half the house if Gerald demanded it. The other thought that Terry had implanted in his mind was why the hell was Gerald not back in Melbourne?

The repairs at Bona Vista were going ahead very rapidly and the moment a new group of painters began to remove the stripes on the house and out-buildings the circus-look started to disappear. Gerald and Martin saw in front of them the house that with all their planning was developing in front of them. The only unnecessary expense, as Gerald saw it, was the necessity of removing the orange liner from the swimming pool and replacing it with one the colour of sand. This cost more than Gerald had expected but together they worked and planned for their future together. This left them with an almost finished house and not even a chair to sit on as Jenny had removed all her furnishings.

It was now time, thought Gerald and Martin, to let Windy into the secret of Bona Vista and she was elated at the news. So at every opportunity now the three of them sought out furniture for the house. A great deal of this was done via the internet and the rest was the result of the auction rooms at Barnsdale. Gerald had thought of retrieving some of the furniture from his and Paul's terrace house but then realised it just wasn't worth the drama. And drama it was when, the following weekend, Paul, with Catherine, Mark and James, were at Donegal. It was Gerald who realised immediately on his late return on Friday evening that Paul was extremely agitated and knowing him well he realised there was going to be a showdown but not wishing for this to be in front of the others he asked Paul to go upstairs to his bedroom as he had something to show him – or at least that was the rouse.

'Well,' demanded Paul.

'Sit down,' demanded Gerald and realised at this point there was no point in continuing the façade and so he decided to fight fire with fire. 'I haven't returned to Melbourne for three reasons,' he began.

'I can guess at one,' Paul interrupted sarcastically.'

'If you want me to finish, be quiet or simply get out.' Paul was surprised at Gerald's aggressive attitude. He had never known him like it. 'I happen to be living here and the work in the hotel and the staff are great. The second is that I have a lover and it suits me very well.

'And the third?'

'I now own Bona Vista.'

If Paul was steeling himself for the lover, the news of his purchase of the house caught him completely off-guard. He just glanced at Gerald and felt very uncomfortable.

'Well, you haven't let the grass grow under your feet,' he snapped, sharply. 'So where does this leave me?'

'I am not sure. For the moment you have the terrace house in Melbourne and as I do not at this time need extra money it can remain like that. If and when I need the money, with an arrangement to suit you, you can buy me out, but for now I am fine.'

'Lucky you!' was the reply but wondered how on earth Paul knew about George.

'No,' he said, 'not George,' and smiling falsely he suggested that it was time they joined the others for a drink before they all began to think that they were being anti-social.

'Heaven forbid!' was the sarcastic comment.

Whilst in bed, Gerald felt a large weight removed from his shoulders, having confronted Paul with the facts of his new life and the next day he was planning to explain all of this to Catherine, Mark and James and to give them a tour of the re-vamped house. Oh, yes, he thought, everything is fine and realised he was missing Martin very much that evening.

'Fine' was not an adjective to describe Paul as he also lay in bed across the corridor from Gerald. It was all as Terry had forecast, everything except Bona Vista. Perhaps Terry had been correct: if he had purchased the house when Gerald had wanted to he would not be in this most unsettled state now. Hindsight is easy, he thought, and turned over, wondering how he would raise half the money to pay Gerald out and suddenly this and this alone was his driving thought, to pay him out as quickly as possible, as that would be a complete severing of the umbilical cord and he knew until he did it this problem would be always hanging over his head. The next morning, over breakfast, early, when Paul was not present, Gerald explained his new life style to Catherine and the boys. Catherine said absolutely nothing, knowing full well Paul was upstairs. It was Mark who asked outright if Paul was aware of these developments.

'Yes,' said Gerald. 'We spoke about it last night. The only thing I did not tell him was the name.'

It was at this point that James stood up, walked around the kitchen bench where Gerald was standing, threw his arms around him and kissed him.

'If you are happy, Gerald, then so am I.' He hugged him again. Gerald said thanks in a whisper, releasing James.

'Of course, that goes for us all,' said Catherine coming into the conversation, 'but it does leave us in a slightly awkward situation with Paul, as the thing I do not wish to indulge in is divided loyalties.'

'Thanks, Catherine,' came Paul's voice from the other side of the room. 'I don't think that will be necessary. Gerald and I had a talk last night and I guess the only way for us to get along is to go ahead without any recriminations or bitchiness. It will be a bit difficult for me,' he laughed, 'but we shall see. Well Gerald, don't we deserve a tour of your new home?'

'I would be delighted to show it to all of you,' and when he used the word 'all' he stared straight at Paul, who smiled even if it was weakly. So everyone strode out through the gardens of Donegal and down the road to Bona Vista.

'Well, it's definitely better with a new paint job,' remarked Paul and they all looked through the newly re-organised interior. 'Did you have an architect to help you?' asked Paul curiously, now his confidence had returned somewhat.

'No, we did it ourselves, but I guess I just remember all your decorating hints and put them together here.' Paul said thank you, quietly.

The only piece of information for the moment Gerald withheld was Martin's name. He thought that quite enough had been said this weekend and he would wait for another, more convenient, time, but someone's patience was not to be put on hold. When alone with Gerald, James smiled at him and said,' Well, who is he? Do I know him?'

'From a long time ago, I believe,' at which James frowned. He asked again, directly who it was.

'It's Martin,' Gerald confessed.

'But that's fantastic! He's a nice guy and good-looking, if I remember. Oh, Gerald, I am so happy for you!' James again gave him a hug. 'It's marvellous. We are going to be next-door neighbours. I can't wait to meet him.'

'Well, let's wait until Paul has returned to Melbourne. I don't want any unnecessary drama if I can help it.'

'OK. But Paul said he is going back to Melbourne Sunday afternoon, so why can't we all meet Martin Sunday evening? We aren't returning until Monday. Yeah! What a great idea.'

'We'll see,' replied Gerald, thinking this might be a great opportunity but a very shy Martin might not think so.

So with Windy at the helm, a spontaneous dinner party was held on Sunday evening, very late. The last orders at the hotel were at 10.30 so a quick scamper, a change of clothes, and a nervous Martin was waiting and left in Gerald's car with Windy in pursuit. Before she turned her car out of the car park she was sure she saw a figure lurking in the deep shadows near the exit. However, she just assumed it was a play of light and shade.

'Hi, I'm Windy.' With this introduction everything flowed very smoothly, with lots of laughter but it was Catherine who looked very closely at her gardener, now Gerald's lover, and saw him as a vague reminder of the past; the same sparkling eyes, the soft smile, those large strong hands — and when she went to greet him, she held this tall good-looking man in her arms and something swept back over her. The tears rolled down her cheeks. 'It's fine,' she whispered to Martin, who, despite working for her, she had never met.

'You remind me of someone I miss very much.' Then she released him.

He said thank you, very unsure of what he had been a part of and with that and Gerald's hand on his shoulder, the jokes and laughter continued.

'I remember you at school,' said James. 'You saved me one day in a fight.'

'Did I?' Martin smiled. 'I'm sorry, but I don't remember.

'That's OK. I do, so that's all that is important,' and in fact James was right. They had different links to Martin, be it Catherine's thought that he resembled very closely a young Dermit, or the fact he had forgotten saving James. He was instantly absorbed into this group and fitted in without any difficult. With Windy and Gerald telling funny episodes about the hotel, there was a blend in this group from one extreme to the other and no one was threatened or in competition with any other. Each had a personality and everyone respected that in their own way.

CHAPTER 7

Trouble Ahead

CHAPTER 7

Trouble Ahead

After the initial introduction with Martin, everything began to move smoothly ahead. The late spring saw everyone planning at least a full week's vacation at Donegal, prior to the two to three weeks at Christmas, so everything was positive. Though not for everyone. As fate would have it, an aunt of Paul's died, leaving him her estate. With the sale of it he immediately paid Gerald his share of the terrace house and with the A\$350.00 left after all expenses he took Faith out to dinner and they ate and drank the lot.

Because Catherine had offered Gerald Donegal, Paul was never absolutely sure, even having received Faith's firm reassurance, that behind Gerald's love affair Catherine had not been aiding and abetting. But now Gerald and Martin were resident at Bona Vista and loving it, for both of them to wake in the morning in one another's arms suddenly made life worth living. It took Martin some time to get used to Gerald's working hours: to have someone you haven't seen all day arriving home at eleven thirty and wanting to have a drink and give you the day's news, was, to begin with, difficult for a very conservative man, but with discussion it was seen that a warm body slid in beside Martin and drifting off to sleep without the drink and the news being held over until the morning worked well. Working four days a week at Donegal gave Martin time also for work at Bona Vista, so between maintaining the two properties, of which there had been a keen discussion between Gerald and Martin, who refused to be paid for dealing with Bona Vista, both properties well isolated as a result of the poor road became tiny microcosms of life where everything was good and everything was in order. This ideal existence stopped as soon as one joined the main road.

Paul had decided that as he was now free of the financial tie with Gerald the last thing in the world he wanted was Terry living with him. It was all just too difficult and far too dangerous and he had a discussion with Faith.

'I can't do it,' he declared. 'Terry is just too self-centred and inevitably he will cut everyone's throat socially, including mine.'

Faith let out a deep sigh. 'You're right. He is my son and I adore him but there are limits to every relationship and with me I never want to cope with him in a domestic situation again. It's just far too stressful.

Since Keven and I have been sharing this big house, everything has been easy and that's the way it's going to stay,' Faith spoke determinedly.

'Yes, I know what you mean,' he replied, looking at his glass, 'but you have Keven and in the long run a cat really isn't a substitute for a person, although I must confess it's a damn sight more faithful.' He laughed, even if it was weakly.

'Don't look so hard, Paul. He'll arrive and generally when you don't expect him, so be prepared and just let it happen.'

Brenda White bustled up and down the supermarket isles with the trolley, glancing at the special offers and deciding that they were all over-priced, specials or not, then wheeled her trolley up to the checkout register and a very fey young man called Neil spoke to her as usual. They exchanged pleasantries as he passed her purchases across the computer register. He gave her the bill and as usual she paid and left. She had done this exercise all her life. Nothing much was different, domestic chores, she thought – they never finish. As she left the automatic sliding doors with two supermarket bags, one in each hand, to her horror she was confronted by Barry Whiteall.

'You bitch!' he shouted at her and as her hands were occupied with the shopping bags he had the advantage. The shouting at one another drew a large crowd. Barry, as usual, made the first mistake and pushed her against the glass window. As she fell backwards she dropped one of her bags, scattering its contents all over the pavement. At this stage, assuming he was in a winning situation, he walked close to deal her another blow. No one stopped forward to help her.

'Mrs White! Here!' The cashier thrust a broom into her hand as a weapon as he manfully took a swing at Barry and caught him across his back. Barry spun around and knocked Neil to the pavement. This gave Brenda just the time she needed and using the broom as a croquet mallet she yelled at Barry, who was about to sink a foot into Neil's abdomen. Barry turned to face Brenda and with her not indifferent strength she drove the broom head with all her force straight into Barry's groin. There was a loud yell and he sank to his knees.

'One move and I will slam this broom into your empty head! Neil, telephone the police!'

When they arrived, ten minutes later, with Barry groaning on the pavement, Brenda took it upon herself to address the quite considerable crowd that had watched the spectacle.

'You,' she screamed at them, 'you would just stand by and see an innocent woman knocked to the ground and not one of you stepped in to help me. Don't think for a moment I shall forget that. Let's hope, when your son or daughter or wife is being molested someone helps. If this afternoon is any indication of your courage, then you are all in for trouble.' She turned and looked at two slightly embarrassed police officers

'I shall be down to press charges yet again against this feral piece of work. Thank you, Neil. I do hope you are free this evening and it will be an honour to take you to the hotel for dinner. Is seven o'clock satisfactory?'

'Yes, thank you,' he smiled, helping her collect her scattered purchases, as did many of the others standing nearby, out of sheer embarrassment at Brenda's verbal attack on them.

The word flew around town very quickly about the attack on her and many who had witnessed the drama began to worry about Barry being allowed to rove around town, threatening whoever he saw fit. It had been a local matron and the little queen in the supermarket who had had the courage to deal with him – and win. So now there was some local pressure on the police force to do something about this thug.

'I can't believe it,' Windy commented. 'Neil is so weak-looking and yet he went to save Brenda. Fantastic! She is building up a squad of gay saviours : first Martin, now Neil!'

'I think they are eating here this evening,' said Colleen. 'My sister was in the crowd and said Brenda is bringing Neil here this evening for dinner.'

'Well, I for one am going out to congratulate both of them,' said Windy. 'Me too,' was choroused, and to the waiters' surprise, not to mention the diners, the four chefs decked out in white, strode across the restaurant and congratulated them both on their courage.

'You seem to have hit on the correct recipe for finding the right type of men to save you,' smiled windy.

'Yes, it appears so,' replied Brenda, with Neil turning red with embarrassment. They all shook hands with Neil, who held on to a very strong hand for just a fraction longer than was necessary.

This was the second charge against Barry Whiteall and as he was already arraigned to appear before a magistrate the next week, he was warned severely that one more act like that and they would hold him over in the cells until the following week when he was to go to court.

Early on Tuesday morning, Gerald rolled over to find in an instant Martin in his arms and knowing they had the day to themselves it came as close to perfection as was possible. After an exhilarating exercise in love-making and settling back in one another's arms, it was Gerald who asked, 'Martin, why on earth don't you get divorced? I am sure Sophie won't have any objections.'

Martin rolled slowly over on top of him and kissed him gently, but did not respond to the question. But it was a dynamic thought always in the back of his mind. Why the hell had he been so stupid to have gone through with this public exercise and married Sophie Ashcroft? He couldn't remember a time when he thought she was anything but a 'round of applause' in a certain sense, and stupidly he had basked in it. He had never thought her ugly or unattractive in an odd sense and the social pressure for a good-looking local boy to marry into a well-to-do family was strong, and herein lay the problem. This revealed not a strong man but a weak one, terrified if his sexuality was to be discovered. In small communities, this equalled social death and so he had gone along with this travesty, half hating it but enjoying the round of applause at the same time, proving that in any social situation that to go along for the ride where you think you are going to gain and not consider the after-effects, mainly the sleeping arrangements, proves you are either totally inexperienced or totally stupid. And Martin, now thinking it through, had to admit the latter was his case. Then, rolling over and holding Gerald in his arms, he knew that somehow or other he had managed to save himself before he finished up in a suburban hell where wives and husbands only yelled at one another. If he had been more alert and she, namely Sophie, more honest, this semi-dramatic situation where now Martin wanted a divorce, would not be the problem it was to become. And the problem was to do more with Sophie's parents, rather than her and in particular her father, Graham Ashcroft, who saw himself as the pillar of local society. He was president of the Lions group, he attended the local Anglican church, he played golf as expected and indeed saw himself as the all-round man. He was the type you would pass in the street, sit beside at a concert, see at a gallery, appearing even at home to serve you in his hardware store, and the minute you turned your head he was totally forgotten. But Graham Ashcroft was certain that not only did people remember him, but they were clambering for his attention and thoughts on the most important of local dilemmas. Nothing could have been further from the truth. Because Ashcroft's Hardware was the only store of its kind in town, everyone who needed this or that was obliged to shop there, but Graham's conceit was not only did he supply them with what they wanted, even if it was over-priced, but they came in droves to speak and hear what he had to say.

The marriage of his daughter Sophie to Martin was not exactly what he considered ideal, but he also looked at the situation of Sophie not married and and this in his mind was not socially acceptable. Everyone should be married and, married, they should be happy or otherwise, and so this disastrous union was made with lots of protests about Graham's daughter marrying a Catholic. In all small country towns, things of small account are generally fanned up if there is any advantage for one person or another. He was a very handsome man, Martin, and for the ceremony he was definitely the groom, looking much more beautiful than the bride and with Sophie's plastered face he never thought to wonder why this artificial layer of cosmetics which she used to excess was necessary. If only he had had experience he would never have married her and hopefully he would have been supportive of her. Time was to tell. He was the gentleman and supportive of her.

So when Martin finally, one Saturday morning, walked into Ashcrofts Hardware he walked over to Sophie, who lifted her lacquered coiffure ever higher, making the vision up her nostrils even more evident.

'What do you want?' she asked, slowly narrowing her eyes.

'I need to speak to you about a divorce.' She looked at him and didn't seem to see him at all. There was a long silence. 'Let's not talk about it here,' she murmured as she nervously turned her head to see where her father was. 'What are you doing for lunch?' He told her he had nothing fixed, so she said, 'I'll meet you at the little restaurant take-away on Pearson Street in an hour.' Then she quickly moved away to serve a customer.

Martin left, feeling a trifle bewildered. This did not seem the Sophie he knew, who had made quite a spectacle and had ordered him to leave their house or rather the house that belonged to Sophie's father. At the appointed time he entered the restaurant and took a seat, waiting for Sophie. To his surprise she was exactly on time. This in itself was odd, as she, for one reason or another, was habitually late. The waitress took the order and they sat looking at one another, each waiting for the other to begin.

'Why do you want a divorce?' she asked.

'What's the point of us being married?' he replied.

She moved uncomfortably on her chair and did not reply immediately. 'I don't really care, I suppose,' she said, looking at him. 'Do you have to have a divorce at once?'

'Why?' Malcolm asked. He now knew Sophie wanted something out of this divorce. She took her glass of beer and drank thirstily.

'Are you going to get a decree from the Church?'

'Probably. I hadn't thought about it.'

Sophie glanced straight through him into the middle distance. 'Well, if you want the divorce, you can have it. It's too late for me to get anything out of holding on to it.'

'What are you talking about?' he demanded, and Sophie was genuinely surprised that he had become so assertive. She did not remember him like that.

'I am pregnant and as I am still married to you I thought I would use your surname but it doesn't matter now.'

'Don't tell me that Barry Whiteall is the father!'

'Hardly! He can't even manage an erection. You were both a good cover for me, but with that fool soon to be before the court, I can't or wouldn't even think of using his surname. I guess I'll use my own. It's all the same.' She spoke in a nonchalant manner. 'Who cares, anyway?'

'Hopefully, the father,' said Martin.

'Oh, the father! What a joke! Married men are all shits.' With that she stood up. 'Whenever you want me to sign anything just bring it into the shop. There's no problem. Oh, I must say I don't know who he is but he seems good for you. Good luck!' With that she turned and left, just as the waitress arrived with their meal.

The next morning, over breakfast, he spoke to Gerald about the strange conversation with her and then realised that in a sense the fact that he had never had sex with her was probably ideal from her point of view if she had a lover who was a married man, so why did she put on such a show with her parents and order him out of the house when he was the perfect cover? Nothing made sense, especially when she picked up with the feral Barry Whiteall and it was then that he wondered about Sophie's mental stability. Gerald said it made no sense to him at all but while she was in agreement it was probably wise to file for a divorce at once and as he had not lived with Sophie for nigh on two years there could be no claim on her part for maintenance of a child that was not his, no matter what she said.

* * * * *

The week's holiday at Donegal was great fun. The weather was hot and the swimming pool had been uncovered but they all decided that the water was freezing. The mornings were generally shared with Martin and Gerald, but inevitably at 11 o'clock Gerald departed for work, leaving Martin in their care and it was noted there was not too much work done in the manicured garden, but lots of laughter around the luncheon and dinner table.

On Wednesday, just before lunch, as Catherine and Mark were in the kitchen and Martin and James were having a drink by the pool, Martin asked James if he had seen his father while he was there.

'I don't have a father,' was the sharp reply and the conversation was rapidly changed to the final decorating touches at Bona Vista. This determined statement of James was in great contrast to the day before where they all celebrated the first luncheon party at Bona Vista, with Windy and Gerald in the streamlined kitchen organising a splendid lunch, with James playing the barman and the others talking and joking in the large living room which overlooked a newly laid-out lawn, surrounded by the few old trees Jenny had left standing. The stakes in the ground marked the spots for the new trees which were to be delivered in a week's time, which was meant to see Martin hard at work.

Whilst eating, Windy asked James if he remembered Neil, Brenda's new hero.

'Neil Roberts, you mean? He was in the same form as me at school and I remember he was like a person in miniature, very short and skinny.'

'Well,' Windy went on, 'you'll be surprised to know he is the social lion of Lakes Entrance now.'

'I am surprised,' he agreed.

As the holiday season was picking up and the weather was warmer, the holiday town began to swell with holiday-makers and Windy complained that it might well be good for business but the queues in the supermarket were just impossible. And with all the laughter and serious plans being laid out for Christmas, Gerald and Windy had forgotten – or almost forgotten – John Williams, and shortly his name was to be a household word in this seaside town.

It was the usual Saturday night and the staff were very busy, but Gerald was more than pleased as he had only to work Sunday evening, which would give him most of the day with Martin. As they finished up, having sent the last order off, they relaxed over a glass of wine, laughing about a mix-up of desserts that evening.

'I'll be off now,' said Gerald. 'Do you want me to follow you home, Coleen?'

'No, no, I'm fine.' She and Gerald moved out to the car park and when they were where their cars were parked side by side Gerald exclaimed, 'Oh, damn! I've left my telephone on top of the locker. I'll see you at eleven tomorrow.' He turned and went back inside to get his phone, only to find Windy and Mario deep in conversation, and, when interrupted, apparently embarrassed.

'I left my phone here. See you both tomorrow.'

'We're coming now,' and the three of them headed out to their cars, only to their horror to hear a yell that they recognized was from Colleen. The three of them dashed toward the cry and it was Mario who threw the first punch as John Williams attempted to stand, with his trousers pulled down. Barry Whiteall did not even see Gerald's fist and as he fell backward he hit his head on the car parked beside Colleen's. Windy dashed across to call the hotel security while Mario and Gerald helped Colleen, who was in an extremely distressed state, with blood pouring out of a nasty gash above one eye. The two culprits, regaining their equilibrium, raced for their car and Williams accelerated at an extremely fast rate, crashing into a parked car and scratching the duco on another. He drove at breakneck speed to the opening of the car park and all that was heard was a dull thud and the car sped off into the night.

Colleen was badly cut above the eye and her clothes were torn but thanks to Mario and Gerald appearing that was the only damage except the obvious terror of having been almost raped.

'It happened so quickly,' she gasped. 'I hardly knew what happened.'

The security guard was on the spot in a moment and a call to the police brought them in twenty minutes, but as the police car swept down the road with the blue light flashing it stopped at the entrance and did not come in.

'What the hell are those fools doing?' demanded Windy, who was comforting Colleen, now sitting in her car, very upset and shaking. Mario ran over to the police to find out what was wrong, and why they hadn't come right into the car park, only to discover that there was the body of an elderly man blocking part of the entrance. An ambulance arrived and the body of the man was removed.

During this time, Colleen had been escorted by Windy and Mario to the medical centre and the resident doctor, woken up, who treated Colleen's cuts and bad bruising, gave her some tablets which he said she was to take, as he explained to her that she was in shock and these would help her sleep. Windy drove her home and then with Mario returned to the hotel car park.

'I told you to keep an eye on this car park,' said Windy, very aggressively. 'Now look at the disaster. By the way, who was the man that Williams and Whiteall killed?'

The policeman looked at Windy and took a deep breath. 'It's O'Donnell. He must have, as usual, had too much to drink and didn't see the car coming at him at such a speed as you've told us.'

When all the statements had been taken, everyone left and it was a very exhausted Gerald who slid into bed and felt secure with Martin beside him but it was sometime before he got off to sleep. He thought of Colleen in her present state, and went over this problem again and again. What if she had been the last to leave, which had occurred only the night before. There might have been no-one to help her and the ramifications of this sent a shudder up his spine. He had become very fond of his staff and this brutal, cowardly attack affected him much more than he realised. Then another thought passed through his mind: he would have to cross the garden at Donegal first thing in the morning to inform James that his father was dead. He had spoken to the police and offered to do this rather than have them wake everyone at Donegal at two in the morning. He woke late and felt exceptionally empty and exhausted, as if he had been running for miles and miles but not getting anywhere. He told Martin the sad story about Colleen and said that although they had planned a whole day together it wasn't possible as Colleen, he thought, would not be at work for at least a week so he would have to do lunch at the Hotel.

Gerald and Martin walked across to Donegal and the first person they saw was James.

'I'll just check with Catherine,' said Martin, assuming it would be more appropriate if Gerald had this moment alone with James. He went onto the veranda and then in to Donegal to pass on the sad tidings to those inside.

'I'm glad,' was James's reply to Gerald's news about his father. 'It's fitting that a violent man was killed in a violent way. I am glad and I am sure so is my mother.' He turned and looked at the house. 'Miss O'Brien always said that if you lead a violent and cruel life you will be rewarded with the same and he has been.' He slowly turned and faced Gerald. 'It was his fault my mother killed herself. She just couldn't take any more. He beat her all the time and in the end she just gave up. She took a whole bottle of pills and never woke up – no more pain, no more humiliation, just rest.'

'You must miss her,' said Gerald softly.

'No, I don't, really. The only person I miss is Miss O'Brien. You see, she was the only person before I met you all who helped me. She fed me, bought me clothes and gave me money when I needed it. And this,' he swept his arm about, 'was our dream. We were both going to escape the cruel world, but it didn't happen quite like that.'

'But it has, in a certain way. You see, if she hadn't believed in you and Donegal, you wouldn't be here now with Mark and Catherine, so she has made your and her dream a reality.'

Gerald threw his arms around James's neck and as the others came out of the house, they saw James not emotionally upset but strangely liberated, it seemed.

'Gerald,' said James, 'I am also very happy. I am here with you.'

'Thanks.' Gerald released him.

'Come on, let's have breakfast. I'm starving.' And exactly at that moment Martin's telephone rang.

'Yes, yes, no. Gerald will be in for lunch. What a mess!' After a few minutes he hung up. 'It was Windy. They're dead, both of them.' Gerald and James moved over toward Martin to hear what Windy had said. 'They must have been out of their minds. They took the end off the bridge over the river and the car ended up in five metres of water. Perhaps they were killed with the impact of the bridge pylon or perhaps they drowned. The coroner's report will be out next week.'

Everyone looked at James, who smiled. 'Miss O'Brien knew it all, didn't she?' Then he turned to Gerald. 'What are we having for breakfast?' and walked into the house with the others following in silence. It was as if these two situations had never happened for James. He did not speak about them and when the others did he inevitably ignored the conversation and started another with someone else. If he had to find an adjective to describe his mental state it was simply the word 'free'. The town witnessed three very forlorn funerals at which the churches were virtually empty and James attended none of them.

* * * * *

In four days' time, Colleen presented herself for work. 'I couldn't stay at home,' she laughed. 'Mum is driving me mad!' So the hotel kitchens returned to their normal routine and an extra staff member was sought to cope with the busy holiday season ahead. It was this new staff member that charged up a situation in the kitchen that had not been foreseen by anyone.

Lucy Talbot had experience in hotel work and after an interview by Gerald and a fine recommendation from Windy, who was a good friend of hers and had been at school with her, she was eased into the work routine smoothly and without any problems. Lucy picked up the work rhythm and was considered by all as a great asset to the staff. She was a tall, handsome woman, the same age as Windy but with a very good figure and a striking face, good skin, beautiful, with large brown eyes, sensual lips, all set off bt a mane of auburn hair, always immaculately kept. Out of uniform she was a great contrast to Windy, who believed the more colour the better, and this matched her bright and happy personality. Lucy was the opposite. She was well-dressed and co-ordinated. Whenever one saw her she was in beautifully tailored clothes, with soft colours that set off her mane of dark auburn hair. She was considered in the town as an elegant example of womanhood. She was now divorced but the settlement had been that she got just the house she was living in, so money was a real problem. This good job that paid well at the hotel was perfect for her and she genuinely enjoyed it as there was no person to person contact, as there would have been if she had worked in a shop.

'Where shall we put it?' asked Martin. 'All the places we were going to plant the trees are now wrong.'

'Hm,' muttered Gerald. 'You're right. I haven't any idea. Do you think you could bear Sammy Sillcock ordering us about?'

'Providing it doesn't go on for too long. His layout at Donegal is great and I have no idea where this tennis court would fit.'

'Darling!' cried Sammy. 'You have got it all wrong. Silly you!' Today he had tobacco-coloured sandshoes with peppermint green laces but was as conservatively dressed as usual. 'Oh, the constraint is the swimming pool. I see. We have changed the lining. Such a good idea!' He spoke in the most patronising way.

'I only have a certain budget,' insisted Gerald and told him the amount. Whether Sammy registered it was not clear but having a look at the large tubs of trees that had been delivered he changed the subject and demanded to have the nursery's name and address, stating that they had made a terrible mistake with the selection and yes, even if they hadn't offered, a glass of white wine would be fine. So, he changed his tobacco-coloured sandshoes for a pair of yellow boots, took his pad, a box of coloured felt pens, a long tape measure that Martin held the end of. In complete silence, except to direct Martin (which was very odd as once he began a conversation he never stopped) he began. After an hour's work and half a bottle of white wine, he yet again changed his footware to his sandshoes, deposited his sketch book and rubber boots in his car and, to Martin's surprise, though Gerald had seen this at Donegal, simply took over their kitchen and prepared lunch, telling the most hysterically funny story about one of his clients, a certain Mrs Eddie, a middle-aged matron whom he had re-designed the garden for. He said it was all her fault, as he downed another glass of wine and directed Martin to open another bottle. He was indeed invasive and Martin was quite overwhelmed. Gerald just smiled. He had seen Sammy at Donegal in action.

'Well,' he said, swinging back into the story, 'that Mrs Eddie is such a cretin but a rich one, the only type I can abide.' He laughed as he moved effortlessly about their kitchen. 'You see, after the garden was finished, Marion Eddie threw a party, obviously to impress all the locals and invited who she thought was proper to be there and in this formula lay a little grey area called 'Mother'. Have you ever met Philys Tymes, Marion's mother? Quite divine,' he went on without waiting for their response, 'completely away with it all, but quite divine. Well, Marion was determined to make this party a landmark in her social life and so the invitations were well thought out. The local well-to-do, many retired senior citizens who had been, if you listened to them, all great movers in the world, and just a few others, golf club members, church goers - Anglicans, of course - everyone who would enhance this special evening, where they could all comfortably feel inadequate in her new and oh-so-special garden. And so,' he carried on, 'they arrived in droves, everyone complimenting the other, basically, if I can remember, about nothing. The star of the evening was Marion's mother, who, at 76, she still called 'Mummy', much to Phylis's annoyance. Phylis was divine, but was a girl who couldn't hold her alcohol all that well, so after a few glasses she became what is called 'impossible'. With hired staff and a dining room laid out with great care, Marion was indeed ready for her esteemed guests.' Here he burst out laughing. 'She should have known that mummsy was going to have a good time and as always at Marion's expense, but the word 'expense' was very relevant. Phylis controlled a vast amount of capital and Marion and her husband Ron were always on their toes, with Phylis threatening at 76 to leave it all to the lost dogs' home. The worst of it was she was most capable of doing so. So with Marion dressed most conservatively and Ron in collar and tie, looking as boring as ever, Phylis had brought with her a costume that she thought would be more applicable to this social event. It was a long jersey frock with various horizontal stripes of different thicknesses in hot pink, acid green and electric orange. Phylis had had it for years and at the last moment thought it was just the thing for this special evening.

'We all arrived at the bidden hour and I must say with the lighting I had designed the garden looked marvellous. By the way, I'll have yours looking better.' He continued serving the food and insisting they take their places at the table. Whilst serving the food, he continued his hysterically funny story. 'Well, Phylis was a bit bored with everyone saying sensible things to one another and with a few drinks under her belt decided to liven up the party. 'Well,' she said to a very timid specimen who just happened to be the vicars'wife, 'why are you wearing your mother's old clothes?' The very insecure woman pulled her cardigan tighter and just stared at this amazing woman in multi-coloured horizontal stripes with a well made-up face and an extraordinary blonde hairstyle. 'Take the money from the collection plate and get yourself a new look. You're a mess!' She moved on to the next victim. 'As I was saying, Admiral,' and she chatted on for some time aimlessly to a tall very attractive waiter. 'Why are you carrying this tray around?' and with a sharp elbow into the back of an elderly man she said determinedly, 'Get off your arse! What are you being paid for?' and thrust a silver tray of hors d'oeuvres into his arms. 'Move it, slacker!' and moved off to the piano as she heard the music begin. 'A waste of time,' she said to the young man playing the piano. 'These pensioners are all tone deaf, not one to be saved,' and having given the piano player this wise advice she encountered Brenda White with, of all people, Neil as her companion for the evening. Phylis took one look at the situation and summed it up in a flash. 'Come with me,' and she forcibly took Neil by the arm and introduced him to the piano player. 'He's great in bed,' she smiled wickedly at the piano player, 'the best blow jobs in town.' To say the people close by were shocked was an understatement and with a glass in her hand Phylis was off again.

'Oh, Vicar,' she said, supporting herself on the back of a chair, 'where on earth did you find that crumpled piece you call your wife?'

'Mrs Tymes, please, this is a most unnecessary comment.' Phylis mimicked him: 'Mrs Tymes, please, that is a most unnecessary comment,' which had the people close by laughing discreetly. 'Why don't you give her some money to dress properly? She looks so dull.' The Vicar's wife had returned and was seen to be clutching her cardigan together with white knuckles. 'You need a good uplift bra,' and Phylis staggered toward the drunk waiter.

'Absolutely unnecessary, that woman,' stated the Vicar, sharply, to note that there were a lot of faces that showed grins. But our Phylis was not by any means finished for the evening. At one stage she was seen chatting to a most confused gentleman whom she had mistaken for someone else, and then she lurched off to encounter, of all people, Graham Ashcroft.

'Well,' stated a well-primed Phylis. 'How did you get an invitation? I thought we had vetted them.'

'Oh, how do you do,' mumbled Ashcroft. 'This is my wife, Shirley.'

'Well, you're a mess,' said Phylis. 'I believe your daughter's a prostitute. Mind you, it's a good living in this day and age.' This had Shirley's eyebrows just a little higher than usual and stupidly Graham thought that a good dressing-down to this obviously foolish woman was well warranted, and in his most pretentious manner he began, only to be interrupted by Phylis with hysterical laughter which had the effect of everyone moving close for what Sammy called 'the kill'.

'Shirl,' she said, in a very patronising way, 'they are all the same, lousy in bed and never think we would dare tell the world.'

Shirley turned this odd shade of apricot and looked as if she needed an oxygen tank.

'Oh, he's a dreadful fuck, anyway,' said Phylis with a great deal of conviction. 'He didn't even send me flowers the next day. Oh, I'll get rid of him, Shirl, he's a real shit and besides the dick's the size of my little finger.'

At this stage Marion decided that it would be much better for the evening if Phylis was heavily sedated and in bed and she attempted to convince her of this social alternative.

'Fuck off!' was the sharp response, which had the more enlightened guests in hysterics. Now as Phylis moved across the room, her horizontal, striped outfit was decidedly diagonal as she grasped a chair or a guest for support as she moved into the dining room, exquisitely laid out. Sammy said the party picked up then. While talking to a woman she had never met about dildos she supported herself by placing one hand on the dining table in, as it happened, a sort of paté and at one stage removed the hand and forcefully slapped a woman's back, leaving a vast quantity of this paté dip all over the back of her frock.

As Sammy said to Martin and Gerald, who were in tears of laughter, '"She just kept going. She passed the piano player and asked how the blow job was. He turned scarlet and said, in order to rid himself of this harpy, 'We'll sort it out after the party.' 'Oh, fuck the party,' she said loudly. 'Get it while it's going. Time waits for no piano player,' and again moved on to someone else. 'Don't I know you?' she slurred. 'I hope not,' was the pretentious reply. She frowned and looked at him again, in the company of his wife and another couple. 'I know,' she said, with a devilish look in her eyes, 'You like it up the arse.' The silence was amazing and as she moved away, she said to a woman she encountered, 'Some people have no social acumen at all.' She snatched yet another glass of champagne. Back again in the dining room but well clear of the pate dip most of which was now being scraped off the back of a most distressed matron, Phylis saw what had been the careter's masterpiece, a cooked duck with the head re-applied to it, arranged on a large silver salver and garnished very decoratively. 'I had a duck like that once, she announced to a now quieter dining room. 'His name was Donald. Isn't that funny?' she laughed. 'Depends on your sense of humour,' relied a very dry vicar. 'Get you,' she laughed. 'You have a face like a pig and take it up the arse. Who are you kidding?' This produced an electric silence which it appears, as Sammy said, Phylis was not aware of. She reached over, seized the duck, head and all and threw it across the room. 'Go for it, Donald!' she yelled, and the cooked duck carcass and the head tottered dangerously on the velvet pelmet above the dining room window. By this stage, Phylis was feeling a trifle weary and so she moved to the large terrace outside the living room. Why Maureen had placed a well-upholstered two-seater divan on a slippery travertine surface is now history. But when Phylis flopped down on it, someone was sitting on the arm. 'Move your arse,' cried Phylis and a very surprised gentleman immediately stood up. This action, and with Phylis aboard, had the predictable effect of the divan moving and move it did, straight across the smooth pavement and then it tipped up and ended in a large patch of hydrangeas with Phylis half-trapped under it and half in the bushes. 'Let me help you, Mrs Tyne,' cried the vicar's wife as she was the closest and began the process of pulling her up and out of the garden. But our Phylis," went on Sammy, "was a trifle confused at all this fussing and tugging of the vicar's wife and by this stage everyone was on the terrace watching the spectacle. As Sammy said, at just the right time our Phylis had the parting line, as the tugging and attempting to help her to her feet which at this stage was impossible without aid, due to her vast consumption of alcohol. When finally on her feet, the vicar's wife continued to fuss over her. 'Get off, you tired lesbian!' shouted Phylis, which had a white-faced woman totally shocked at the comment. She let go of her and as a result Phylis fell backwards into the hydrangeas, using the most explicit forms of expletive to describe what she thought of the vicar's wife. But this was not the end of the situation. With a bottle or so inside, Phylis was hysterically funny, providing it wasn't at your expense, but stone-cold sober she was acid itself and an interesting exercise occurred three days after the party in Ashcrofts' Hardware store."

Martin and Gerald were hysterical with laughter at Sammy's story. He was always the same Sammy, invasive but so funny that one tended to forget his invasiveness and as anticipated he just took over the whole garden design at Bona Vista, even having a large out-building re-located as a tennis changing room and bar entertainment space, and having trees of completely opposite types planted in positions that neither Martin nor Gerald would have thought suitable. The effect, well it had to be admitted by all who saw the near-finished work, was splendid, very sophisticated and very showy at the same time.

But as usual, the minute lunch was finished Sammy disappeared. 'Fish to fry' was his parting comment. At Ashcroft's Hardware Store, three days after Marion's disastrous party where quite a few people felt very miffed at being spoken to by Phylis in such as they all agreed was a vulgar way, she popped in to purchase a set of 1.5 cm screws for the gardener. The moment Graham Ashcroft saw her, his eyes narrowed. He had been the laughing stock of the party, especially with the comment Phylis passed about the dimension of his penis, which he was still furious about.

'Yeah?' was Sophie's introductory greeting.

'God! What do you look like?' said Phylis in a haughty manner and the customers in this busy store stopped and decided to watch the performance.

'If you can't be civil, get out!' spat a determined Sophie.

'Oh, what splendid customer service we have here! Such a fine way of addressing clients.'

'You are hardly one to talk,' said Graham arrogantly, 'and it's a pity you don't attend church regularly. The vicar's sermon was on abstinence of alcohol. Obviously it's something you should consider.'

It was indeed foolish of Graham Ashcroft to attempt to discipline Phylis in a crowded shop and she, as usual, rose to the occasion.

'Well, well,' she started, and Graham had the odd feeling he was not going to come out of this conversation winning, 'Mr Goody Twoshoes himself!' She smiled. 'What have you ever done for this town except rip all your clients off? Don't talk to me about what I should and should not do. How the hell you and Shirl' and the 'Shirl' she enunciated sharply, 'even got an invitation to Marion's is quite beyond me. We are generally carefull about inviting upstarts to our home. By the way,' she added, looking at Sophie, who had just looked totally confused and thrust a piece of paper towards her, 'get these.' She turned, as she had a captive audience. 'Look at dear Graham, quite the hypocrite, a mistress on the side. So like him!'

The oddest thing was, without knowing it, she was absolutely correct. Graham did have a secret mistress and Phylis's calculated guess came home. He just opened and shut his mouth like a goldfish.

'You see, Shirl, how many nights a week does he claim to be going to the Lions? They only meet once a month. This I know for a fact, as Marion's husband is a member. Good luck, Shirl, get a solicitor and a life.'

With that she snatched the screws she had been handed by Sophie and her parting shot, after collecting her change, was, 'I am genuinely surprised you can find clients on a street corner looking like that.' She turned and left a full store of smiling clients.

CHAPTER 8

Consolidation

CHAPTER 8

Consolidation

After the death of James's father, the police contacted him to say that he would need a solicitor to sort out his father's house and belongings. This being done, and as he was the only living heir, James inherited the lot, including some debts. Mark went with James to have a look at the house and it seemed even more forlorn than when he had seen it so long ago, when he and Catherine were searching for James. James unlocked the door and went in. Mark expected the interior to be in the same condition as the outside but was very surprised that it was neat and tidy and wondered if James's father had had some home help. It was a modest home but James led him to a room only to find the door locked. From the ring of keys that had been returned to James from the dead body, he inserted a key and the door swung open. It was dark, with a holland blind pulled down and heavy curtains pulled across and it had the oddest smell. James flicked on the light and a naked electric bulb lit up the most unusual room Mark had ever seen. They were everywhere, in frames large and small, hundreds of them crammed into every tiny space available. The most exotic of them were coloured a bright blue, hundreds and hundreds of mounted butterflies in frames.

'Good heavens,' said Mark, 'there are thousands of them.'

'Yes,' was the reply. 'These are the only things he loved in his whole life, dead butterflies.'

They left the room after the light had been turned off and James again locked the door. They walked aimlessly through the next interior but James seemed quite uninterested.

'What will you do with the cottage?' asked Mark.

'I'm not sure – sell it, I suppose, although it could be rented. I'm not sure. What do you think?'

'I'm sure with a certain investment it could be let well for a holiday home but a certain amount of capital would be needed.'

James just grunted in reply and they locked up and drove back to Donegal in relative silence.

The following Saturday everyone had lunch at Bona Vista, obviously without Gerald, then lo and behold Sammy appeared in sky blue sandshoes and all. After a brief discussion about the newly formed garden as usual he just took over the kitchen, prepared lunch and told his usual funny stories, generally at someone's expense.

The conversation was light and brisk until Catherine said to James something to do with his father's house. 'What will you do with the butterflies?' she asked. There was the clatter of a saucepan and Sammy demanded to know what they were talking about. Mark told the story and Sammy nimbly moved over to James.

'Have they got any sentimental value for you?' he asked, in a business-like way.

'None at all. It's all the past.'

'How much do you want for them?' Sammy demanded. Everyone was very surprised at this.

'You can have the keys after lunch and take the lot. I don't want them and I don't care about them.'

'Done!' was the sharp reply and Sammy returned to the kitchen area, chatting on as if the previous conversation about butterflies had never existed. And when the keys were returned to James two days later there was not one of the hundreds of framed butterflies left in the room – just hundreds of small nails all over the walls, like a pin cushion.

* * * * *

A phone call to Maggie from Mark alerted him to the information he was seeking : sell the house and with whtever money James received put it down on a good apartment in a good suburb and let it pay itself off. With that very precise piece of information that is exactly what James did. But the butterflies these remained a mystery as to why Sammy Sillcock was so determined to have them and why. He refused to be drawn into any conversation about them.

Mark returned to work on Tuesday morning and Maggie brought in the monthly balance sheets from the suburban branches and together they studied them.

'Well, I have to say Estelle has definitely pulled this branch up,' said Maggie. 'It's second to only one other – not bad in such a short time.'

'Yes, not bad,' agreed Mark. 'It seems she is well suited to the suburbs,' and laughed as did Maggie.

'What's happening with the staff Christmas Party this year?' Maggie asked.

'I haven't any idea. What happened last year?'

'Oh, it was a disaster. Estelle organised it at the last moment - a dreadful venue and lousy food.'

'I'm sure you can do better,' Mark smiled. 'How about coming to dinner Thursday evening. You and Catherine can sort it all out.'

'Great idea! I'll put my thinking cap on and get some quotes.' With that she left Mark's office with a smile on her face.

Christmas was indeed around the corner and Gerald wondered what exactly to do. This would be the first Christmas in twenty odd years he would not be with Paul, but the thought of inviting him to Bona Vista or having him stay at Donegal was not what he considered a good idea when all he wanted was a calm, happy time with others and especially Martin. Paul also mulled over this social predicament and came to the conclusion that any attempt to hold the traditional Christmas with Gerald's lover, whom he had still not met, and play 'Mister-has-been' was not on, so he searched the internet for a vacation and the more exotic the better.

* * * * *

It was just a spontaneous gesture after a joke: Windy saw Lucy place her arm around Mario's shoulder and laugh. It could not be said that Windy joined in and the cutting of a piece of steak Gerald noted was done particularly viciously. It was then Gerald realised what he had felt now and again in the kitchen. It was the response between Mario and Windy. Why hadn't he thought of it, he wondered? Mario, although overweight, was a very handsome man and Windy also was overweight but a very good-looking woman and all of a sudden, right in the middle, was Lucy, divorced: the alarm bells rang loud and clear. Mario was married and had been for some time and according to Windy had a son of twelve. His wife Windy did not see fit to enlighten Gerald about but the tension that existed when John Williams was working with them returned, not in a conflicting way, as it had been with Gerald, but it was obvious that Windy was not her usual bubbly self.

One evening, when the others had left, and Colleen and Gerald were having a drink prior to him following her car to her home which now one or another of them did in turns, he broached the subject of Mario and Windy and it took the second glass before Colleen decided to give Gerald the information he was seeking.

'They have been together for years,' said Colleen. 'It's a strange relationship that they have kept very secret for one reason or another – perhaps it's because of Mario's son. I don't really know.'

'Have you met Mario's wife?' Gerald asked.

'Yes, several times. She's OK, not very communicative but in public orders Mario about a bit. I have no idea what happens at home. Mario never speaks about his home life and no matter how, over the years, I have brought up the subject he refuses to speak about his son. Odd, isn't it?'

'Yes, it is.' Gerald smiled, weakly. 'But when do Windy and Mario have time together? It must be like living on a tight rope.'

'Yes, it must and I do feel that Windy does not see Lucy as a great asset in the kitchen now.'

'No, nor I. I think she sees Lucy as paying a little too much attention to Mario.'

'I agree. There's going to be trouble, I think. I don't really know if Mario is encouraging it or not, but I do know Windy is anything by happy.'

'Do you think Mario will leave his wife?'

'Definitely not. And I suppose it has to do with his son.'

'Well, now, what do we do? Remember, it was on Windy's recommendation I hired Lucy.'

'I think you are going to have to speak to Windy about this at the right moment, but I am sure you are not going to find her ready to talk about it.'

* * * * *

Thursday evening, Maggie was seen sweeping up the path and ringing Catherine's front door bell.

'Come in!' cried James. 'They look great' and she handed him a large bunch of bright yellow roses. They went into the living room.

'Oh, they are beautiful!' exclaimed Catherine and they all seated themselves with James playing the barman.

'Well,' said Maggie, with a glass in her hand, 'I wouldn't miss this Christmas party for all the tea in China.' She began laughing.

'What's so funny? asked Catherine.

'Well, it appears our dearest Rodney Taylor has made a new conquest.'

'Really?' said Mark. 'Who?'

'The attractive blonde in the Records Section. Can you imagine Estelle's face!' She broke into a joyous laughter. 'Oh, what a scream!'

'Well, I hope the venue this year is better than last year,' Catherine insisted.

'Why, what was wrong last year?' James asked.

'Well, apart from the usual drunken evening, some bright spark - and the signs were everywhere - lit a cigarette and when he saw someone coming stamped it out on the wall and the heat from it activated a heat sensor and half the room was sprayed with water.'

James began laughing. 'Maggie, does the invitation say raincoats and umbrellas a necessity?'

'Hopefully not this year,' she smiled. 'Don't you remember last year's party, Catherine, where Estelle thought a quiet cuddle and kiss with Rodney was a good idea, then saw wifey coming and quickly turned to walk away and walked straight into a glass door. The nosebleed was very dramatic.' She was now bursting with laughter. 'Her nose swelled up like a red ping pong ball - quite the sight for the following week at work.'

Over dinner Maggie went on to say that the venue for this year was very smart and so there would be no problems. Yet this Christmas party was to prove how wrong she could be. But it was Catherine who was to show a determination in this period that cemented everything she thought about Mark and James and her constant awareness that she was a very single woman in this world and she desperately she missed Dermit, but that all in a certain sense was not lost. She had loved Dermit without boundaries. He was the only man she had known that had filled every desire for her and it all went beyond sex. The pair of them had been a couple in every sense of the word and she hoped beyond all expectations that Mark and James would be, or feel the same, that fantastic sensation that the right person was there and he was yours. With this idea behind Mark and James, the relationship - not that it needed a support system - Catherine fitted in to the day to day requirement to support not only them but in a sense also herself, and as Faith had said to her she was probably the most lucky woman in the world. Catherine did not disagree with her. She felt at this time, as Christmas loomed up, that the little things to do with Christmas became strangely very important. This was obviously a loss she was feeling but at the same time it was a gain. Everything, no matter how banal, for Christmas for Catherine took on a momentous meaning. So for Christmas at Donegal she was in a certain sense prepared but she was in for a real shock as this period moved forward.

They were all at Donegal for the long weekend and then in two weeks' time were staying for three consecutive weeks. She received a telephone call from Sammy Sillcock asking would she and the boys mind if he invited Phylis Tymes for lunch on either Saturday or Sunday as she had expressed a desire to meet them. Catherine said she thought Saturday would be fine and left it at that. After driving up on Friday night, they waited with Martin until Gerald arrived home from work to have a night cap together.

'You're kidding,' he laughed and recounted some of the repeated gossip he had heard about Marion's party, where the drunken Phylis had taken over.

'Oh, good heavens, what is Sammy thinking of?' asked Catherine as Gerald burst into laughter saying that the vicar's wife now was terrified of meeting Phylis on the street after her adventure trying to save her and of Phylis's sharp comments.

* * * * *

At exactly noon, a burgundy Mercedes drew up in front of Donegal. Sammy and Phylis alighted and Sammy made all the introducitons.

'Well, you have made progress here. Congratulation!' said a well-tailored Phylis, looking every bit the wealthy conservative matron. So they were all surprised, as they expected a completely different woman from Gerald's description of her party capers. She demanded a tour of both gardens and house and was loud in her praise.

'I remember Donegal when I was a girl,' she smiled. 'You could only arrive here by boat. The property was landlocked. It was quite an adventure. A vague relative of ours lived here but it's so much smarter now. They had goats. We thought them quite exotic.' She laughed as James filled her ever-empty glass. Sammy had obviously filled her in on where everyone fitted and with whom. 'Well,' she said, looking at Martin, 'I think working here is much smarter than Ashcrofts Hardware.'

By this time Sammy had disappeared into the kitchen and Phylis took over. 'So you now live with your friend at Bona Vista? Good idea,' she said, with a happy smile. 'I hope you have got rid of the stripes,' and laughed.

Martin, who was generally quite shy, didn't bat an eyelid. 'Do you know why they originally painted the main part of the house in stripes? Gerald and I haven't a clue.' This was indeed a new Martin. This was someone who was in love and that force gave him a security he had never had before. As he didn't know Phylis well, he saw her as no threat, even if he did realise she had a very strong character.

'Fill up the glass, handsome,' she smiled at James. 'I remember you.' She turned her head and frowned. 'Of course! The little boy with Jean O'Brien! My, haven't you grown up well!' She said this with a wicked smile. 'And did you meet your companion here or in Melbourne?'

'In Melbourne.' James, like the rest of them, realised this lunch was like a game for Phylis and one she loved playing and winning. If she could shock, all the better.

'There were originally three sisters that lived at Bona Vista, very good Catholics, if I remember correctly. There was a car accident and one of them was killed. They drove an old Riley and until they all passed on Kate drove and Nell sat in the back, leaving the off-driver's seat vacant for – oh, isn't that terrible – I can't remember the name of the sister who was killed. Anyway, it was always the same one in the back and one in the front as they left the seat vacant in front for the dead sister and they couldn't decide on the colour for the house. Nell wanted blue and Kate cream so the painters painted one board blue and the next cream and so on. I remember seeing it years ago. I went for afternoon tea. It was the oddest thing that I ever saw in my life.'

'Luncheon places!' called Sammy pretentiously and smiled, today wearing coral pink sandshoes with identical matching laces.

'What was so odd about the afternoon tea?' asked Catherine as they all seated themselves and Sammy began serving with Mark this time in charge of refreshments and very surprised at how often Phylis's glass needed re-filling.

'I went,' she began, 'with my mother and a friend of mine. He had longish blonde hair and for some reason Kate and Nell were sure he was an angel. They played duets on the piano. They were very good - Kate played the organ at St. Brendan's - but after a while they would stop, look at one another and burst into hysterical laughter which no-one understood. Anyway,' she went on with a swing of her hand which showed a very beautiful Bulgari bracelet that matched her earrings. Catherine thought she was out to make an impression this afternoon and not only with her funny reminiscences. 'Well, we sat down after the recital and began to eat a very elaborate afternoon tea and in the centre of the table was one of those late-Victorian centre pieces of twisted silver with leaves attached to it and three silver trumpets that held flowers. A ghastly thing but they were fashionable once.' She was speaking very theatrically. She had the ability to keep everyone entranced, waiting for a punch line or some very dangerous comment. 'It was just as the tea was being poured out - I can remember it as if it were yesterday - and all of a sudden the flowers in one of the trumpets shot straight up into the air. My mother was horrified but no one said a word. Kate and Nell continued as if this was normal – 'Oh, she is so glad you called for afternoon tea. My sister really loves company.' When my mother realised that the sister who loved company had been dead for ten years she paled and then, as the afternoon tea progressed, yet again another bunch of flowers shot into the air. I wasn't frightened myself but I must admit it was extraordinarily odd but the oddest thing was the other two sisters accepting that this was a message sent from one world to another.'

'Could it have been that the three sisters were so close and for so long that perhaps the one who had died was simply waiting for the others to part from this world together?' asked James, as everyone looked at him.

'Perhaps,' replied Phylis. 'I have never thought of it from that angle, but I can tell you the image of these flowers shooting up into the air was something I have never forgotten or seen again.'

'Did they have a large property? We only have twenty hectares,' said Martin, and Phylis smiled kindly as the word 'we' was registered. 'No, I think it was about the same.' And then she went into hysterical laughter and it was infectious.

'What's so funny?" asked Mark.

'Oh, they were so divine!' Phylis was now winding up. 'They went to Rome as they had a private Papal audience. How they managed it I haven't a clue but they did. It left for them a real problem. They had a house cow called Mabel, I think – I don't remember exactly – no, no, I am sure it was Mabel. Anyway, a local farmer was enlisted to milk Mabel by hand every day. Well,' she burst into gales of laughter as she pushed her yet again empty glass in the direction of Mark who instantly refilled it. 'When the farmer arrived to milk the cow it went crazy, kicked over the bucket and put on quite a performance. Well, the lad was at all odds to work out what to do with this hysterical cow, so –' and she began to laugh again, which slowed down the story but not the enthusiasm and curiosity to hear the end of it '– he noted on a peg just inside the back door of the house an old day dress of Kate's. He popped it on with a straw hat with a flower attached to the broad brim and went out again. Mabel gave him the once over and was as certain as can be and so for the three weeks Nell and Kate were in Rome, the young man dressed in Kate's dress and hat and milked Mabel without any problem. Really, animals are so perceptive, aren't they?'

Before they could add anything to the conversation, Phylis launched into another anecdote about Kate and Nell. 'You know it is forbidden to bring fluids or fruit into Australia, so as Kate and Nell had obtained holy water blessed by the Pope they were most perplexed as to how to get it home. So, not to be outsmarted, two old ladies with their belongings went through Customs and home here to Bona Vista with the holy water in their hot water bottles.'

Phylis, with the rest of the happy lunch group screamed with laughter at the thought of two aged sisters beating the Customs authorities. And so stories of locals and local events filled the afternoon with everyone in hysterical laughter. At a certain point, while having coffee, Phylis said, 'Sammy's driving, so I will have another glass. Thanks, Mark.'

The front door opened and Gerald walked in. 'How's the luncheon?' he asked.

'It's been perfect,' replied Phylis, 'just perfect and I take it you are the other half from Bona Vista.'

Gerald looked a little taken aback and it was Martin who said quickly, 'Yes, Gerald is the owner of Bona Vista.'

'Hmm,' murmured a playful Phylis. 'Thank God he's good-looking,' and turning her head in Martin's direction said, 'We are all allowed one mistake in our lives and one only and it appears after the Ashcroft disaster you have landed on your feet. Good for you, Martin. I am proud of you.' She did not add any further explanation to this comment.

'Well, it seems I have missed all the fun,' Gerald said with a smile as he moved over to lay a hand on Martin's shoulder, 'but as I have tomorrow's luncheon off, if you would all like to join us at home you are more than welcome.'

'I should be positively delighted,' said Phylis enthusiastically. 'I am dying of curiosity to see the property after such a long time. I heard via Sammy that that Walls woman destroyed everything.'

'Well, we have it more or less in order now,' said Sammy, grandly. 'Shall we go, Phylis? I shall collect you tomorrow for a re-run,' he added, laughing.

'Careful, Sammy,' came a very quick response from Phylis and after general goodbyes and 'see you tomorrows' Sammy ferried a very content Phylis back home.

'No wonder the vicar's wife is terrified of her,' laughed Catherine. 'She is a very dynamic woman.'

'And a tough one,' added Mark.

He was correct, but Phylis had found what she was looking for, a group of good-looking gay men, quick with repartee and a group that would allow her to be a star as long as she remained on her feet, with a glass in her hand. So to be invited the following day : Phylis saw this as an invitation into the hallowed circle. She was not unaware that Catherine, correct and polite, indirectly controlled all and she noted that she wore very good jewellery.

So the following day Bona Vista for lunch saw the same group plus Gerald and as Sammy escorted Phylis into the house after a good look at his layout of the new garden it was noticed that the scarlet sandshoes matched his handkerchief in his jacket pocket exactly. Phylis was full of compliments and a very similar lunch as had occurred the previous day was repeated, with Phylis yet again relating funny stories about the locals though she steered clear of using James's father or Sophie Ashcroft as social ammunition to keep the afternoon rolling.

But Phylis was well armed, just the same. She had noticed Catherine's jewellery so far today. She set out to outsmart it but, as always, two stars always see the same vision. After a walk in the fledgling gardens, Phyllis did something quite unusual. She linked arms with Catherine rather than as usual with the most attractive man, and as they looked about it was some time before Phylis or Catherine spoke. This was obviously due to Sammy taking over.

'Did you play tennis?' asked Catherine.

'Yes, once,' came the response, 'but I don't think I was destined for great things.' She smiled.

'Me neither. The boys love it. Gerald and Martin are great and they are bringing James and Mark into the game. Personally, I prefer to watch from the side lines.'

'At my age, so do I,' laughed Phylis. 'A good-looking waiter and a fine wine are just the thing, don't you think?' she smiled.

'Yes, you are so right. I have a new life now and it's so supportive, so bring on the tennis balls!'

'Oh, forget that!' said Phylis sharply, 'Bring on the cute waiters!' and they both burst into laughter.

They were opposites in a certain sense but the ground rules were laid : gay men – no problems, and men whom they genuinely loved without the problems of sex, so in this most strange situation for Phylis but not for Catherine, these two women began to discover one another through these wonderful men that neither could think of living without.

Phylis now took a second look at Catherine, the controller of the boys and Donegal and she thought also of Bona Vista, but at the same time she was very vulnerable and also due to Sammy's background information, reforming her life with all the boys. In an odd way, it did affect her when Sammy drove her home: she was very aware she was envious of Catherine, of having her constant coterie about her and then she thought of her situation, of Marion and her dead, dreary husband, and realised that in amongst all this she had been the loser. She had stupidly thought that family and what you have was best, but after this weekend she knew it was or had been false. She had all her life played the matron in this wealthy family, drinking heavily, considering there was not much else in life and all of a sudden, with his brightly coloured shoes Sammy had catapulted her into a world she craved for, funny stories, sharp repartee and laughter.

After this sparkling weekend it became almost obligatory to add Phylis into their weekend festivities, and no one objected. She was able to enliven any dinner party : often the lies were poisonous but never did she ever pitch in on Martin's previous marriage, which would have been so easy as she hated Sophie. She always stepped around this easy mark but with Windy she was very careful : whereas a bejewelled Catherine would allow Phylis any leeway Phylis knew Windy would not. So when in company with the group Phylis became two personas, one when Windy was present and another slightly more hysterical when she was not.

Windy had no real opinion of Phylis. She had known of her for years, someone to be careful of, especially if she had had a drink or two, but that was it. Nothing more. But from Phylis's point of view it was exactly the opposite for one reason or another. Windy unnerved her. She always felt that Windy had the capacity to see into her most hidden recesses and in an odd way she never felt completely at ease with her. Windy profited working this all out socially. So in the future there was never a social function that they were not all together sharing and laughing with one another, depending on the particular group together.

Back in Melbourne the next week Faith telephoned Catherine to say she was going ahead with divorcing Richard and although it was not what she had thought life should have offered her, she was now more than prepared to go through with it and, as she said to Catherine, a husband and a son at the same time is quite a deal. And so it was, with no regrets. Faith managed this in a very business-like manner with Keven always left to sort out the tricky bits and as all the properties and investments were Faith's, Richard backed off, accepting a small settlement and that was that.

'It's just like putting the rubbish out every Thursday evening,' Faith announced to Catherine, 'and nothing more'. But although the separation by law from her husband was one thing, Terry was another. He played the situation through to such a point where the verbal matches between Faith and him became electric. She was determined she was not going to live a life where Terry determined in a certain sense her future and she knew only too well that the moment she let her guard down he would return and all the problems in one form or another would return. So she took an exceptionally strong approach, where she said to the ever-pleading calls now that she was to be divorced, that she was not going to be blackmailed into putting up with him returning and living in what was now and had been her home. Terry, needless to say, did not find this approach much in his favour and so the telephone calls became brisker and shorter. The thing that also annoyed him was that the quieter, older brother seemed to have stepped into a role that should have been his, so for the time being he decided to bide his time, absolutely convinced that Faith, after the divorce, would be much more easily managed.

* * * * *

It was extremely crowded and Terry, in a moment, found himself separated from his friends. The noise at this gallery opening was terrible. He literally forced his way to the bar and took a drink, then battled back to find his friends but half way across the gallery he noticed Jenny Wells, complete with yet another horizontally striped outfit, looking as he said later 'horrific'. It was at exactly this moment that a thought crossed his mind. Jenny Walls and George: now where was this George? Instead of making for the other side of the gallery, his dorsal fin went up and his eyes searched for the good-looking, dark man, and there he was, speaking to someone Terry knew. It took less than ten intense minutes and telephone numbers had been exchanged and a meeting made for the next evening at seven. Well, that was easy, he thought and returned to the bar for another drink and then on to join his friends. It should have been exactly as he organised, a 'one-night-stand' with someone that fitted into that category and George, being just as much the opportunist as Terry sexually, suddenly found himself in a situation he not only enjoyed but found Terry and his attitudes similar to his own, and so they tended to bounce off one another. For the very first time in his life, apart from 'Mark the unobtainable', Terry felt a magnetic attraction to his young Greek and against all the odds George felt the exactly the same, and so now there were several hurdles to cover socially and the largest one was finance.

George lived basically day to day. He had never worked and liked it that way. He had a good body and knew how to work it as regards Jenny Walls, who paid for everything. Now, in an extremely tight financial situation she decided that if she was to survive socially it meant money and if she had to shed something or someone, that was it. And so when George's weekly allowance stopped, so did he, and he installed himself in Terry's apartment, much to Terry's pleasure but money was always a problem, though definitely NOT sex.

When Terry explained all this to Faith one evening over dinner, to say she was surprised was an understatement. She knew well enough the situation as regards Sammy Sillcock and George as Jenny Wall's lover, also Sammy's and Gerald's, so at the most she assumed this was just two ships in the night, nothing more, but as time progressed this appeared not to be the case and as much as Terry protested Faith refused to hand money over to him that she knew was to support this relationship. But oddly they were always at every opening, every show and it crossed Faith's mind that only Terry was working and his salary could not be said, as a receptionist, to be extremely high, although she was very surprised he was still employed, as this was his first and only job in twenty eight years. So the reality dawned on her, that one of them was bringing in an extra salary but from where? And realistically she knew there were only two possibilities, prostitution or drugs and hoped desperately that sex was to be the saving situation.

* * * * *

'Later, Gerald,' was Windy's reply to Gerald about a discussion about the kitchen dynamics which had become electric with Mario always the laughing, jovial person at the centre of it all and so for some time Gerald respected Windy's side-stepping any conversation about the problem of Mario and Lucy. Colleen was correct, he thought. Windy is never going to open up about the problem but at every opportunity sought to resolve it with a heart to heart conversation but each and every time Windy jovially dismissed it.

But one evening, about a week before Christmas, there was an explosive situation in the kitchen and Gerald saw a way of resolving the problem. Lucy indeed saw Mario as someone to fill her emotional needs and if something developed from it all the better. She saw him as good-looking, someone who was very skilled in his occupation and his kind and gentle behaviour all added up, according to Lucy, to a bright spot on what was not exactly a glowing horizon. She was aware that Windy and Mario were old friends and whether she deduced that there was more to it than that was unknown, but what was, on this evening, very clear was that Lucy decided to make a very obvious ploy for Mario in front of everyone. Needless to say, Windy was irate at Lucy's bold approach to Mario, who seemed completely confused. Lucy linked an arm through his and she chatted to him. Gerald, immediately, saw Windy very agitated, using a carving knife to dissect a chicken in a most aggressive way. He tried to calm the moment and said to Lucy that she was employed to work not to waste time arm in arm with Mario. He was genuinely surprised, as were the other staff, at Lucy's vicious reply: 'Oh, it's fine for you guys to be arm in arm and have a good time but not for us. Is this the hypocrisy you practise?' She spat this out, still with her arm through Mario's, who looked extremely embarrassed. Windy was just about to attack verbally when Gerald intervened.

'You will work in this kitchen and work as I direct you. My sexuality has nothing to do with the professional running of this kitchen. Do you understand?' he finished, sharply.

'Go to hell!' Lucy answered, over-reacting.

'That's fine,' said a stony-faced Gerald. 'You're fired.'

Lucy spun around to face Gerald, now directly in front of her but she heard an icy voice. 'I wouldn't even think of it,' warned Windy.

Lucy threw down her chef's hat and stalked to the side door. A sharp slamming of it announced her departure, not a happy woman at all.

'OK. Show's over. Back to work,' announced Gerald and they all returned to their work spaces and continued with the evening meal in relative silence.

At the completion of the evening's work, Mario escorted Coleen home and Gerald and Windy had a drink.

'Thanks,' said Windy, looking at her glass and not at Gerald. 'It's all my fault. If I hadn't recommended her you probably wouldn't have employed her.'

'It's in the past now,' smiled Gerald.

'I suppose I owe you an explanation?'

'It's up to you now that Lucy has gone and taken a certain tension with her.'

Windy sighed and refilled both their glasses, then began to explain slowly to Gerald an extraordinary story that had begun many, many years ago. 'I went to school with Mario. We have virtually been together all our lives. To begin with it was all just marvellous. He is the only man I have ever loved and even now we still see one another privately.' Then she laughed. 'And as you can see, with time, we have become matching elephants!'

'Hopefully, happy laughing elephants,' joked Gerald, trying to break the tension in this confession.

'We were always together. After all these years I guess we still are. The flame never went out.'

'But Mario is married,' Gerald said.

'And how! That mess had to do with Mario's family and his wife' s family and with tight family pressure. Finally Mario gave in. The blackmail was loud and clear and the prepared house ready for the newly-weds was the bait. It wasn't that Mario was weak. It was just one of those awful family situations that neither of us could resolve. I think I cried for a month after the wedding. Needless to say, I refused to go.' She sighed. 'Oh, well, that's part of the sad story.'

'Is there another part?' Gerald asked, curious.

'Yes, unfortunately. You see, Mario and I even though he was married to that crocodile still saw one another regularly and obviously slept together. It's strange but perhaps that's what has kept us together all these years.'

'And Mario has no intention of divorcing his wife?'

'It's impossible for now. Peter is trapped in the middle.'

'Who's Peter,' he asked.

Windy looked at her empty glass and then rapidly refilled it. 'When Mario married Claudia and time passed, both families began to apply pressure in a very nasty way, especially the women, and remember they both came from large extended families so when there were the usual family reunions the subject of children was always brought up and as Claudia could not have children the pressure on her was immense. You see, she and Mauro kept this a secret from the family and then the inevitable thing occurred.' She slowly shook her head. 'Yes, I know. Why didn't we take precautions? Well, I thought we had and to this day I don't know what went wrong but I became pregnant.'

All Gerald could do was to exclaim softly.

'I immediately thought of an abortion as I knew my parents were not going to support me and a child and in those days I was working in the dry cleaners so my salary was pretty small but Mario wanted the child desperately and we spoke of it again and again and finally I agreed to what Mario wanted. It must have been very difficult for Mario to explain to Claudia that he loved another woman who was now pregnant but it was Claudia who oddly took over. This was the child she couldn't have. Mario was the father and if she had this child this extraordinary pressure and snide bitching of her and Mario's family – the women of the families, that is – would be removed and as Mario said that at this point in her life Claudia was not coping at all well with the pressure so she was declared pregnant and kept well clear of her and Mario's relatives and moved about with a cushion strapped to her stomach. She had no problem with money, so I went to a holiday resort, claiming I was studying for six months a cooking course which I actually was, hence my job here. The child was born, Mario was the legal father and I then handed Peter over to Mario and Claudia. As much as I do not like Claudia, she has been an exemplary mother but, you see, the deal was that I was not to see him or explain anything to him until he was twenty one years old. So, you see, Gerald, that's my sad tale: even if Claudia is happy enough for Mario and me to see one another, Peter remains her social armour against that ghastly feminine pressure of her and Mario's families. Peter is very well cared for and Mario loves him dearly, so I guess in a certain sense everything is OK, but a perfect arrangement it is not.'

'It's quite a story,' said Gerald, reaching over and holding her arm. 'Does Martin know?'

'Oh, I guess he has worked a bit of the story out, but you can fill him in if you want to. It's all right with me, but for Peter's sake, please don't tell anyone else.'

'I promise,' and he kissed her on the cheek.

She smiled at him. 'I am so glad that you and Martin have made it work. I think you are both well-suited to each other. Look after him. He is well worth any effort you put into the relationship.'

Driving home, Gerald was well aware that although Windy had opened up her private life to him the one part of it she did not elaborate on was her feelings for. This part of her life she kept completely closed.

CHAPTER 9

All's Well That Ends Well

CHAPTER 9

All's Well That Ends Well

As Christmas drew nearer, it tended to heighten so many situations that probably at any other time of the year would have gone relatively unnoticed. The first of these dramas occurred in Terry's orbit.

He had George as a lover and oddly George was now always had a pocket full of money. Terry realised that, as he worked through the day, George either had clients that paid him for sex or the alternative was someone that he dispatched drugs for. Either way, the situation made their evenings deliciously extravagant and they both enjoyed it immensely, even if Terry was convinced this earning by George was anything but ideal. And Ideal it most certainly was not. George had this conceit that no matter what happened in his life he, like a cork, would always float to the top. Terry's analysis of George's earnings was very accurate. He was good-looking and traded on it. George knew his clients and on his return to Melbourne through the pressure from Jenny Wall he moved effortlessly back to his old clients, having Terry as the man to return to. But in amongst this coterie of people whom George believed firmly could not live without him he had one regret and that was Gerald. Gerald had been able to take him to sexual heights he had never dreamed of. Generally for George sex was sex, but Gerald had awakened something in him that he had never felt before and as a result he demanded more from his usual clients. But it was never the same. So in his usual conceited manner he just assumed that the next would be as good as Gerald, but it never quite happened. It wasn't only sex that George dealt in financially.

He was moving drugs and in the past smart circles of clients was tricky. The problem was people talked so he had to be very careful to whom he dispatched the substances, as there were many in this group who were ever so willing for one reason or another to anonymously telephone the police with a name, and George was well aware of this. But his regular clientele on this front remained discreet and faithful and so George's pocket remained relatively full. He was not stupid. He knew full well that not all of the substances he sold to the smarter group were what they should be. He knew he could make a much bigger profit by 'doctoring' the merchandise and he did so, without any qualms. So when a well-known socialite lawyer died of a 'heart attack' one evening only a few, including the pusher, George, knew exactly what had happened. It did not bother him at all. They were clients and he had the 'stuff' and what happened happened.

But George himself was not beyond sampling the merchandise and a line of cocaine before he went out was quite usual. Terry turned a blind eye to this, as he found that George in this state was both more entertaining socially and infinitely better in bed. But apart from this conceit, George could be totally ruthless.

He had only dealt with one supplier and both were happy, but with his return to Melbourne many of his clients stopped calling for one substance or another. It didn't take him long to work out that someone else had moved in on his territory, obviously while at Lakes Entrance in the arms of either Sammy or Gerald. This was inevitable but on his return and being somewhat unceremoniously ditched by Jenny Wall it was necessary for him to re-enter the old swing of things. Very few of his old clients decided to renew acquaintance partly because they were discreetly supplied by another and frankly because George had an erratic side to his behaviour which kept his old clients slightly nervous. Even Jenny Wall found this aggresive side of his nature unacceptable. He could, at times, for one reason or another, become particularly wilful and spiteful and this led, if it were in a public place, to a very nasty scene, where he was capable of anything he felt like, without consideration for anyone.

It did not take him long, once back in Melbourne, to work out who had taken over from him in supplying his old clients with substances that they wanted and so, ruthlessly, he set out to eliminate the person. He thought carefully about the problem and then decided it was better to let the suppliers remove the person, not that George felt that he couldn't but money was tight and he needed to move back into a social circle as quickly as possible and that demanded money. The person who had taken over from him was a woman in her mid-thirties, an elegant woman who went by the name of Christine Burton. She came from a very well-to-do background and had gone to the better public schools so her social contacts were quite refined. She had married a man her family refused to accept, as he had served a prison sentence and so she was cut off financially from the family. Obviously, with her husband's connections and not having any finance available, she decided that as there was a void following George's exit to Lakes Entrance she would take advantage of the situation, and so it was she moved effortlessly around in these 'smart' circles and discreetly in exchange for cash produced what her clients required. For George to threaten her, he reasoned was stupid, as her husband's friends might well decide to deal with him, so he decided to do as Terry had attempted to do with James, discredit her and let the suppliers finish her off as they saw fit. This he did by sending back to the supplier a 'doctored' version of what he claimed anonymously he had purchased from her and threatened to expose her to the police. This caused a real scurry as the police entering into this situation would see clients dash in all directions and not necessarily when the coast was clear return to the supplier. Gallantly, George stepped in and offered to help out, but it was Christine, without substances to sell or money in pocket for her own now expensive habit who began to work out who had made things difficult for her. When she worked out that George was back on the scene she knew instantly she had been set up and stupidly one evening at a gallery opening threatened him, that unless he backed off and forgot about returning to his old life style he was in real trouble. In the loud noise of the opening, with everyone talking over the top of everyone else, George realised that without Christine his life was going to be easier.

'Hey, let's go out to dinner and talk about it', he said, with a smile, and then left her, having taken her telephone number. He walked toward Terry who had two glasses in his hands.

'Who was that?' he said, in a very off-hand manner.

'I'm not sure,' was the reply and they moved across the gallery and out into the fresh evening air.

'I know this divine restaurant,' suggested George. 'You'll love it.' And that was that; yet again off to a smart address and two very contented men finished up as usual in bed together.

But this was not to be the finish of it. George, with a little detective work, found out exactly what substance Christine was addicted to and to say he was surprised was an understatement. He telephoned Christine a week later and, oh so casually, invited her to lunch to resolve their little problem. Christine was personally aloof, but tough, as one has to be in the world she worked in. The lunch was calm and she was not unaware of George's good looks and charm, so the afternoon began on a very civilised level. After lunch, which George insisted on paying for, they left the restaurant but not before George had very discreetly passed a small package across the table that Christine immediately grasped and put in her handbag.

The coroner's report read that the dose of tampered heroin had been the cause of the death of Christine Burton. The following evening, George and Terry dined at a very expensive restaurant and returned to Terry's apartment in the highest of spirits.

* * * * *

This Christmas Terry realised that he was at a loose end, as George had said he was obliged to have Christmas with his family. Terry thought it odd, as he had never spoken of a family before, but was obliged to accept the arrangement and a call to Faith made it quite clear that she was not in town for Christmas, as she and Keven had been invited to Donegal, but they would be back for New Year, she thought.

'I might just give Catherine a call,' he said, in an offhand way. Faith did not reply. She knew something had occurred between Terry and Catherine but had never been enlightened. Whatever it was, his name was never mentioned nor his wellbeing asked after in Catherine's, Mark's or James's company. But Terry being Terry he telephoned without a moment's hesitation : to say the reply he received from Catherine surprised him was an understatement and the 'NO' was a very final statement. It was at this point even he realised that the plan to alienate Mark from James had backfired completely, so he put his thinking cap on to organise something very much to his advantage for a special Christmas. The only thing that registered, like an old-fashioned cash register, was the photographer Christian Hall. But how to organise it was the pre-Christmas predicament he found himself in. Then he thought again : of course, the staff Christmas Party. Oh, how silly of him! Absolutely! The most perfect opportunity – good looking, drunk, how easy he thought, as he poured himself another drink. But as the staff party was imminent, with so many employees looking forward to a pleasant evening no-one could have guessed its outcome.

* * * * *

Whilst all these preliminary plans were formulating in Melbourne and with now less than a week to go to Christmas Day, the fire sirens shrieked loud and clear and the hotel dining room at the Lakes Entrance Hotel was engulfed in a dense acrid smoke that had all the guests out on the terrace level as the fire brigade extinguished an architectural fault that had resulted in a devastating fire that completely burned out the dining room area. This left Gerald and his staff of four (as he had newly interviewed and appointed a young man without any recommendations to the staff) in a very difficult or awkward situation. The kitchens were unaffected by the fire but the electrical system was not functioning, so with this being the height of the holiday season the hotel management made arrangements with a local restaurant, leaving a fully-paid staff free for the five days up to and over Christmas.

Gerald was elated. He could now organise his own Christmas with Martin. No work, just fun. Indeed his relationship with Martin had gone well beyond just being fledgling lovers to two men enjoying every minute with one another. The swimming pool, where costumes were not necessary, for Gerald was great. It took Martin a little time to get used to the new experience but he did, so the six days, four before Christmas and the two or three after, were for Gerald and Martin nothing short of paradise. This relationship had matured relatively rapidly and as they now lived together – although they never saw one-another on a regular basis due to Gerald's work situation – it was a relationship that was calm, without waves and with developing trust. It began to flower in every sense.

Catherine couldn't wait for the staff Christmas party to be over. As the owner of the prosperous company she was obliged to attend but in her mind the thing she wanted most was to escape to Donegal for two weeks with the boys.

As much as Gerald and Martin had made things happen for themselves the same cheery attitude they constantly showed to the world could not be said to be shown by Paul. As Faith had said to Catherine, she was surprised that he had become so negative about everything and everyone and the evenings Faith often spent with Paul were beginning to wear her down a little. Paul began to feel he was being persecuted because of the comments people passed, which he thought were patronising. Now, with the backstop of his life, Gerald, not around, he began for the first time to look at what the future had to offer him and he did not see a full and happy life stretching ahead. He just saw the thing he was most afraid of, loneliness. So with his booking of a Christmas cruise for ten days to the Pacific islands he began to wonder why had even bothered to book it, as he had now set his mind on having a terrible time with people he knew he wouldn't like and on a ship. He was going to be well and truly trapped with them all.

* * * * *

The party venue was indeed smart, a large, tasteful reception centre right on the banks of the Yarra River. Nothing could have been more appropriate and Maggie, looking suitably glamorous, smiled as she took over as the hostess of the evening, showing people to their tables, feeling suitably superior due to the fact that this year's venue selection was infinitely smarter than the one Estelle had selected last year. This was the only time the entire staff got together, as each branch was totally independent of each other and as Head Office in the city called employees in only when they needed to see them there was never a need to see everyone together. The only exception to this had been Dermit's funeral. So this evening there was was a festal mood, with staff catching up with one another and passing on all the gossip that had occurred in the previous twelve months. The loud din of voices and laughter died down as Catherine entered on Mark's arm, looking chic itself. Estelle was sitting next to Terry and they both looked at one another but the usual bitchy comments were withheld, for the present. Catherine and Mark took their seats at the main table and Estelle straightened her hair with her left hand as she saw Maggie go across and embrace them all, including James. Estelle loathed Maggie. She had been a constant thorn in her side and here she was now, swanning around as the virtual owner of the company and although it was unfair to say she behaved in that way Maggie had taken on an enormous amount of responsibility for O'Brien and Company. For when Catherine wished to spend a few days at Donegal, Mark and James always went with her and that left Maggie in complete charge of the company and all the power that went with it. She now was seen by all the staff as someone to be careful of, and as faithful as she was to Catherine and Mark she could be quite pitiless to a staff member she felt was not pulling his or her weight for the Company.

Terry's eyes searched out among the crowd Christian Hall, and to his, not to mention Estelle's surprise, he had arrived with Kyle on his arm, a fact that did not go unnoticed by either of them. Terry had brought along George for whatever reason it might be, especially as he had planned to move in on Christian Hall, so there were logistic difficulties even before the night began. Estelle had seen Rodney Taylor enter with a young girl beside him, chatting on and on, and it didn't take long for Estelle to work out that they were more than just casual friends, so the evening began on rather a shaky social foundation for both Terry and Estelle.

After the usual greetings formally from Catherine, she was very aware that she was alone but not unsupported. This had always been Dermit's role, to address this Christmas party and to make the usual smart in-jokes but this year it was Catherine's responsibility. Formally, with Maggie on one side and Mark on the other for the first time in her life she assumed Dermit's role. She kept the conversation or address to the minimum and sat down. It was here that Maggie stood up and took over, not Mark, and with a motion of her hands everyone stood up in complete silence.

'We are all here for our annual Christmas Party,' she said, with some authority - not that either Terry or Estelle were swept away by this dramatic beginning. 'But we have now completed another twelve months of work and are all the recipients of the consequences of our genuine input to the O'Brien Company. Let it not be forgotten, apart from your Christmas bonuses, that the only reason we are all together here this evening is because of Catherine.'

There was now total silence in this vast reception room.

'Without her belief in Dermit's ideas and Mark's capacity to work them through, every one of us could have been looking for employment elsewhere. It would have been so easy for Catherine to just sell up everything and live without any problems, but she saw fit to keep O'Brien and Company as it has been, a fine company, totally afloat and this evening I think a round of applause is deserved for someone with the conviction that this large group of people are still together and employed. Well, it is totally thanks to Catherine.'

The applause was deafening. Everyone knew very well that if Catherine had made a quick game for cash they would all have been out looking for work, as there would have been no guarantee that a new owner would continue to retain the existing staff. Catherine stood up and motioned all to sit. She looked around the large group of what were her employees and in an odd second she saw the gardener at Donegal who looked so much like a very young Dermit.

'Thank you,' she said, softly. 'He's not here but all of us will keep working for him,' and she sat down to deafening applause.

George, like Terry, checked the large room for opportunities and there he was, just perfect, the most wonderful young man in the world. The logistical problem was that James sat beside Mark and so there was no confusion about who was with who, but, given the opportunity, George was only too sure he could make James the happiest young man in the world. So with George headed socially in one direction and Terry in another with regard to Christian Hall the night was about to begin.

The dynamic start had to do with the need to smoke : the only thing Estelle and Kylie had in common was the need to find a public space where this was acceptable. They found one another on the large terrace overlooking the Yarra River, both determined to have a cigarette. It was also the beginning of a social disaster. To begin with, neither passed a comment and drew heavily on their cigarettes. Kylie then began the verbal slaughter.

'Forget it, Estelle. He's right off older women.'

'Really?' came the sharp reply. 'I hadn't realised he was into bland, dull receptionists.' She turned away.

'Not getting much, Estelle. Rodney with the cute blonde. Well, don't give up. There must be something, I'm sure.' Kylie spoke with a smirk. Estelle was enraged. 'Well,' she said, in a patronising manner, 'Christian can't be as good as we all had hoped for otherwise you wouldn't be looking as though you needed something more than a cigarette.'

'You bitch!' was the reply. On this balmy night there were also others out on the terrace, not for the view but for the necessity of cigarettes. So rather than a full shouting matcht, the pair of them hurled vile comments at one another, assured that the last comment would be sufficient to quell the other. But this was not to be and foolishly whilst the two women were on the terrace exchanging sharp comments Terry decided it was just perfect timing to move in on Christian. This was also not logically the best thing but Terry being Terry and a vast amount of alcohol having been consumed rather rapidly this avenue now loomed up in front of him and his conceit was that Christian had waited for him all his life. Be it true or not, Christian's sexuality was what one could describe as cloudy, especially in front of his employer and all the staff, not to mention a very aggressive Kylie, who had just returned from the terrace to find Terry in her seat with an arm around Christian's shoulder and to Kylie's annoyance Christian did not seem that concerned. That set off the alarm bells in her system.

'Get your hands off,' she cried, unfortunately very loudly. It may have been the result of her sharp discussion with Estelle but it was clear and determined. Terry should have backed down and left with a joke. Goodness knows, it would have been easier, but he didn't. He saw Kylie as a social light-weight and in his mind he saw Christian as his for the evening. He also made an error, as Estelle had the same aim in view for the evening. She had received the highest bonus this year for lifting a branch up from the lowest to second from the top in earnings - even if she had to put up with Terry going on about it that it was his marketing with the 'possum' in the sales window that did it for her. So the night was explosive.

'Find another seat for that fat arse of yours,' was the start and the slap Kylie delivered was hard and sharp. To her utter surprise, as Terry rose from his chair he repeated the exercise on her. The shrill shriek was heard by all. It was here that Maggie took over and majestically strode across the room.

'Go out onto the terrace. Drink, smoke or kill yourselves but not in here.' She emphasised, 'Not in here – do you hear me?' No one spoke a word and the seating was re-adjusted without too much trouble as Maggie returned to sit beside Catherine, saying, 'Don't worry – same old Christmas drama,' and laughed. But underneath it all even Maggie saw a very tricky situation developing before the evening was to finish and she knew before a few more bottles were consumed that Estelle was going to be the most uncharitable person in the world, due to Rodney Taylor's new companion. She was absolutely right. Estelle had seen from where she sat that Christian had had no problems with a man's hand on his shoulder and especially with Terry's precious banter and so she decided to check out the rest of the atmosphere of the evening. As she had been given the highest bonus, she was floating high and so, moving amongst the tables, she found herself face to face with Rodney.

'Well,' she said, sarcastically, 'how are you coping at Head office?'

'Very well,' he replied with a secure smile.

'How nice, that we have managed to pick up something from an old filing system!'

Rodney's new companion did not find this comment either flattering or necessary as she knew quite well that the two of them had been lovers at some stage.

'How well you dress for a woman with such over-sized hips,' smiled the younger blonde girl by the name of Joan. 'You were so clever to dress in stretch black jersey this evening, but don't worry, Estelle, we all know the Titanic sank years ago.'

Estelle was furious and if Joan thought that her glib line about Estelle's broad hips was funny she was most alarmed at the electric reply. 'Oh, Joan dear –'

Rodney sank. He knew when Estelle was going to be difficult and this evening he was absolutely correct.

'Dear,' Estelle repeated, in the most patronising manner, 'at forty something, don't you think you should be looking at your make-up?

'I happen to be thirty four,' snapped Joan, somewhat foolishly falling straight into Estelle's trap.

'Oh, Rodney, can you believe it?' Estelle exclaimed in a very dramatic way. 'She must have made a mistake. Thirty four! I would have said closer to fifty, but as I said, Joan dear, a good make-up lesson and not too much of that ghastly foundation colour. You really do look like something out of an Egyptian tomb. Rodney, would you come with me. We must have a word with Catherine. Sorry, Joan, just us. It's business, public relations, as I'm sure you know. I'm sure that in the future O'Brien and Company will give bonuses for mice in the records section. Come along, Rodney.'

To say Joan was anything but pleased was an understatement. She had known Estelle at Head Office and disliked her. Now she was more than happy to make a public declaration of extreme hate and to her horror and annoyance Rodney dutifully went with Estelle to offer Catherine and all at the head table their best wishes for a happy Christmas.

So although both Terry and Estelle had made their social moves public, the best or as one sees it, the worst was to come. Whether this had a great deal to do with a determination to achieve or win, or whether it was due to a vast consumption of alcohol is unsure but if one puts the two possibilities together anything is possible.

Christian had had a lot to drink and when watching from one side Terry saw him slump into the men's toilets he was on his feet in an instant.

He moved across the room casually, without raising an eyebrow, but the moment he arrived at his destination he recognised his prey. Both had had a lot to drink and that generally heightened Terry's libido. Even if for a moment Christian said no it was not repeated a second time and both men realised that their explicit sexual act had been something neither had disliked at all.

'You go back first,' smiled Terry. 'We don't want Godzilla getting upset, do we? By the way, here.' And he handed Christian his telephone number ever so smoothly printed onto a pale blue calling card and smilled. 'Call me. Or I will call Godzilla to find out where you are.'

Christian just smiled back. 'Don't worry. You call me when you are free,' and left Terry feeling that staff parties were not so unbearable after all. When eventually he did return to his table he noted, after another drunk and another sarcastic comment, there was no George. For the moment he was confused, but the satisfaction of gaining exactly the prize he had wanted for a long time meant the empty seat beside him was nothing at all.

The large space emptied out between courses; the smokers were alive and living and it was at one of these breaks that a little drama all of its own was enacted outside.

'Really,' said Estelle in an extremely hearty manner, as both women had moved to the large terrace system overlooking the river to take another drag. 'The necklace you are wearing is just so unsmart.' This had been a gift from Christian and it was a long length of the most perfect white porcelain beads that stretched down almost to her waist, and had originally been the property of his favourite aunt. So the gift from Christian to Kylie was something very special and she was very aware of it.

'My dear,' exclaimed Estelle, drawing on her cigarette, 'I don't know why you wear these awful white poppet beads. They make your teeth look even more crooked and more yellow.'

That was it! Kylie threw down her cigarette and as, with her usual air of superiority, Estelle moved to the railing of the terrace, totally sure that she had destroyed Kylie with a few choice words, she was totally unprepared for the consequence. It took all of five or six seconds for Kylie, in a state of fury, to move across to Estelle and bend down. Before Estelle had a moment to adjust her position, with all her strength Kylie grasped her ankles and thrust upward. As a result of this, an exceptionally large splash was heard, followed by an equally dynamic use of expletives to describe Kyle. The noise on the terrace obviously brought most of the festive group out to see the damage. The laughter was infectious and a very bedraggled Estelle was hoisted out of the river and over the balcony railing.

'Thank goodness Christmas comes but once a year,' laughed Maggie. Estelle, absolutely saturated with water, dripped herself into the ladies' toilet to dry off. Terry, laughing hysterically, managed to get her a garbage bag in black plastic in which to deposit her wet clothes and to offer her, on behalf of the management of the establishment, a partial chef's outfit. Estelle took on quite a look as Terry said to her, 'Darling, relax. Now you are in uniform, just open another bottle.'

'You be careful,' was her sharp riposte. After all this, Maggie declared later the rest of the evening was tame.

It was next morning that Terry awoke with a slight hangover. He noted George was not there and it wasn't until late afternoon and feeling a little better that he realised that all of George's belongings were gone. He then worked out that as he had left the Christmas party early he must have gone back to the apartment and taken all his things but why, he mused? He consoled himself that this was all for the good as it left him with the apartment to himself to share with Chrsitian. Sometime later the word got about that not only had George disappeared from the social scene but also the entire contents of Jenny Walls's security safe had gone as well.

* * * * *

Catherine was so relieved to see the trees surrounding Donegal as they drove in from the road and genuinely gave a sigh of relief. The last fortnight in Melbourne had been hectic and she was looking forward to a quiet restful two or three weeks if she could manage it.

'What do you mean, the hotel caught fire?' she asked, as Gerald poured drinks.

'Yes, an electrical fault, so we all have five or six days off and on full pay.' He laughed happily. There are carpenters, plasterers, electricians, the whole dining room complex in chaos. So what are we all doing for Christmas?' He looked at the group having drinks around the pool at Donegal.

'What if we have lunch here and dinner at Bona Vista? What do you think?' asked James.

'It think that's a great idea,' Gerald replied. 'Why not?'

'Well. That's settled,' Catherine said with a smile and at the sound of a car they all turned to see Faith and Keven arrive and once again the Christmas party antics were repeated with everyone in hysterics at the thought of a sodden Estelle being dragged out of the river.

The boys all left and went to see the new garden set-up at Bona Vista that Sammy had produced, while Catherine and Faith moved indoors and with a drink in hand began to recap on the extremely eventful year that was almost complete.

'I don't suppose it's the thing to say,' said Faith, 'but I don't miss Terry at all. In fact my life is now, without the drama between him and Richard, completely calm. I don't know why I didn't do it years ago. So much has happened this year. I have got rid of a husband and son and oddly found another son. It's just perfect.'

Catherine just looked at her. 'Yes, it has been an eventful year, with Demit passing on and now Mark and James filling in the void I thought would always be there. It's now almost invisible.'

'I think we have both been very fortunate, especially you, Catherine.'

'Yes,' she answered, 'I am very aware of my good fortune with the boys.'

'Catherine!' came a cry and James entered. 'Gerald and Martin have invited us all to dinner this evening. I suppose Sammy will pop up somewhere.' He laughed at the thought. 'He always does!' As predicted, he did, organising everything whether they wanted it or not. The evening passed with the usual hilarity, with Sammy telling one funny story after another.

The next two days before Christmas Eve were seen to be rather busy, with supplies being brought in to tide them all over the Christmas period. It was in this period that everything and everyone seemed to fit comfortably together. James had never been happier. His and Jean O'Brien's dream had become a reality and everything that went with this fantasy fitted neatly together, especially Mark. He and James were inseparable, each supporting the other. Catherine had seen this relationship develop and was very proud to be part of it.

'Come on, Mark, I will race you to the end and back,' called James, and they plunged into the pool each determined to win, but they had in fact won, and won well, in one another. They had found the one thing that they both lacked, love, and the security of this showed visibly in both of them.

* * * * *

'Hurry up. We shall be late,' James shouted. 'I can see Gerald's headlights at the gateway.'

A quick scramble and a dash to the cars and everyone followed Gerald's car in the lead to midnight Mass.

'What are you carrying?' Catherine asked, as she noticed James with something in his hand.

'Oh, it's Miss O'Brien's missal. When you told me I could take what I wanted from the house in Lakes Entrance I took this. She always had it with her.'

The conversation moved on to lunch and what was now becoming a very large group for dinner and the evening. Catherine had been very strict. Her table for lunch was not to be extended beyond what she considered her close circle and that meant seven people only.

The cars parked, they made their way into the church, which was packed, and as they were seven people they had to divide to find a seat. Windy had seen them come in and smiled at Gerald and her cousin Martin as she sat beside her elderly parents. Gerald scanned the church and noticed Colleen and nodded and then, without knowing why, grasped Martin's hand without looking at him.

The Mass began and the usual carols were sung but it was a very observant Catherine, who had a clear view of Martin, and remembered so clearly someone who wasn't with her now.

James realised that the missal he held in his hands was a Latin one and as Mass this evening was not in Latin he casually flicked over the pages, filled with tiny cards of saints Jean O'Brien had placed in between the pages, obviously marking out special prayers or certain saints days. It was then, as he turned another paper-thin page that a newspaper cutting fell to the floor. He bent over and picked it up, feeling a little embarrassed at having dropped it and when he placed it back in its original place he noted that the first words in the missal were 'Holy Saint Michael, trusting in thy intercession' and then he looked again at the newspaper clipping. The heading read 'Local Lakes Entrance resident wins 750,000 dollars in the lottery. The resident has remained anonymous'. He raised his head suddenly as if he had received an electric shock. Catherine was most surprised and turned to look at him. He turned and looked forward as the Mass went on and a wide smile formed across his face. So this is how the dream of two completely opposite people came to happen and then he looked at the top of the page where the news clipping had been kept in safety for years. 'Holy Saint Michael, trusting in thy intercession.' James kept Jean O'Brien's secret, just that.

Windy came up and wished everyone a happy Christmas and unexpectedly invited them all back to her home for smoked salmon and champagne, so it was a very tired group that returned to Donegal and Bona Vista prepared to make Christmas Day for everyone a very special day.

And a special day it was. Catherine had insisted that just she, Mark and James, Gerald and Martin, Faith and Keven were to gather for lunch with no others and that was how it happened. She reflected that it had been a year of great change but decided not to dwell on it. The future lay ahead. When all were seated, she stood and glanced at them all. There was dead silence.

'You will always be welcome at my table, be it at Christmas or at any other time of the year,' she said, and quietly sat down. It was James who began the spontaneous clapping and this was the sound to which Christmas lunch at Donegal resounded. After years of being abandoned, Donegal was once again a family home, celebrating Christmas though the term 'family' was a much broader term than is usually used.

Needless to say, the evening at Bona Vista was much noisier and the laughter spilt out into the garden as the party began, with the addition of Windy and Marcos, and Sammy with the effervescent Phyllis. It began slowly, with Martin and Gerald organizing the kitchen. The moment Windy arrived with Mario she took over Martin's role and he automatically became the barman. It was a very elated Gerald, when all were assembled, and before Sammy and Phyllis arrived, who related the most hysterically funny story that had everybody laughing. Sammy had called Gerald to say that he, Phyllis and Niel would be at Bona Vista about 8.30 and went on to relate the most hysterical hijinks she had got up to earlier in the day. Phyllis had woken up on Christmas morning, for some reason out of sorts and found the false Christmas behaviour of Marion and her husband to be quite unnecessary. She dressed for a Christmas Day service at the Anglican church. Why she dressed completely in black, with a large picture hat, is unclear but among the people she knew this should have been seen as a warning sign. She found the happy Christmas greetings to be decidedly grating as they were constantly repeated. As the three of the moved down the aisle she was confronted by a matron who thought, unwisely, to direct Phyllis to a particular pew.

'I will sit where I want, thank you,' she stated in a sharp voice.

To say the woman directing things was surprised was an understatement. Phyllis remembered seeing Niel, the young man who worked in the supermarket deck out and had been a guest at her most memorable party, so she decided she would sit next to him. Seating was tight in the pew, so she loudly said to an overweight matron, 'Haul your haunches in, dearie, and perhaps another three or four of us can have a seat.' Niel smiled broadly and she separated herself from Marion and husband and oddly felt quite pleased about the seating arrangements. But directly in front of her sat Ashcroft with wife and Sophie.

'It's not all real,' said Phyllis loudly to Niel. 'She stuffs a wigglet or two up the middle.' Niel began to giggle very quietly and winked at Phyllis. If she needed any more encouragement that was it.

The service began and the first hymn was sung. Phyllis leaned forward and jabbed Graham in the back with her hymn book. He spun around and to his horror saw Phyllis glaring at him. She said, unfortunately quite loudly, 'Oh, be quiet. You have a voice like a rusty gate.' If Graham Ashcroft disliked Phyllis before, especially the comment about the dimensions of his penis, his dislike now moved a step beyond, to despising her.

The vicar on this occasion was in fine form. Usually the church was almost empty. As Phyllis said later, it had everything to do with a dreary sermon that never ended and this was to be the case on this very warm Christmas day, a captive audience. Off the vicar went, but he was not unaware of the third front pew being at this moment inhabited by a woman he general believed to be the most ghastly person in the world. Like Graham Ashcroft, he was still hearing smart little comments repeated at his expense from Phyllis's party. On he droned. Phyllis took it for a while and then became bored. She started a conversation with Niel, asking him how was the piano player in bed. This had the effect of very broad smiles or the constant sound of 'Sh, sh!' Phyllis was oblivious to it all. She was bored and a dull luncheon to follow did nothing to make her think her Christmas day lunch was going to be much better than this service. She then asked Neil what he was doing for dinner that evening, again, unfortunately, quite loudly.

'Oh, you must come with Sammy and me to Bona Vista. It will be great fun.'

Graham Ashcroft spun around. 'Would you two shut up!' he demanded and turned back to face the vicar, who was quite aware of what was happening. Graham felt he had done his duty as a fine church attender.

The bang was loud and clear, and a confused Graham was now terrified to turn and look at Phyllis. But the top of his head was smarting from the excessive force Phyllis had put into slamming a hymn book down on the top of his head. Realising Phyllis was moving into top gear, the vicar for once cut the sermon short, rather than face a brawl in the third pew from the front.

It was the habit of the vicar to move to the front of the church and shake hands as everyone left. 'How nice of you to attend,' he said, sarcastically to Phyllis as she passed by him.

'Same dreary sermon. I might just see what's happening at St. Brendan's next year.'

Whatever he said under his breath was inaudible but it did not take, as Sammy said, much to imagine his sentiments. When clear of the vicar, Graham Ashcroft berated Phyllis on her unseemly conduct in church and a crowd of parishioners gathered to watch the fray. Graham made the error of assuming that because he was with the vicar and friends of his Phyllis would back off. This was a very foolish mistake and he should have remembered her performance at her daughter's party, not so long ago.

'What are you going on about, you worm?' she spat.

'I find your social behaviour appalling.'

'You're a fine one to talk!' retorted Phyllis in a louder than usual voice. 'I hear on the grapevine that your daughter is pregnant but hasn't lived with her husband for two years, though I find it odd that Sophie' and she spat the name out, 'as a prostitute didn't take precautions.' She turned to leave.

'You're such a bitch,' screamed a very nervous Sophie, who at this point hadn't quite worked out how Phyllis had found out she was pregnant.

'It takes one to know one. Oh, do have a happy Christmas!' Phyllis leered very superciliously at her, leaving Sophie to explain to her parents her condition and then wondering how to get out of telling them who the married man was who was the father.

This should have been enough for Phyllis, but strangely she felt much better now, so a family lunch looming ahead saw her in fine form, much to Mario's dismay. As Sammy was also invited to this luncheon, so he was able to give a blow by blow account of it later, between gales of laughter.

Phyllis, the moment she returned home and Marion began fussing about the meal as there were fifteen to sit down to it, instructed Sammy to open a bottle of champagne, so she was well-prepared for the relations and other guests. Marion had gone to some trouble preparing the dining room and an extension of an extra table had to be put in place to seat everyone. The large, white damask cloth covered it all, so it looked like one larger table but the small table was a trifle unstable and so, as the meal proceeded and the wine flowed, it became a problem. Some of these relatives Phyllis saw only once a year, something for which she was most grateful. She found the small talk boring and only addressed conversation to Sammy. A vague relative of Phyllis's, a certain Amy Thrushbottom, attempted to engage her in conversation about friends that they had in common who were now dead.

'If you don't shut up, Amy,' Phyllis snapped loudly, 'I'll buy you a coffin and nail you inside!'

This had the effect, Sammy said, of silencing the whole table. Phyllis was unfortunately seated at the end of the unstable extension. During the main course, with conversation stilted indeed and no one game to bring up a subject that might offend Phyllis's sensibilities, one of the men put a certain amount of pressure on the table and the other side rose about five centimetres. As quick as a flash, Phyllis said to the other man with the raised section in front of him that if he liked her that much why hadn't he said so. Sammy said the rest of the guests were horrified at her innuendo and the man immediately, from sheer embarrassment, applied an unnecessary force to level the table but it now lowered in front of him and everything slid forward into his lap. He let out a scream as the crockery and glasses, wine, the lot, according to Sammy, cascaded to the floor.

'I love an impetuous man,' smiled Phyllis, not altogether sincerely.

So by the time she arrived with Niel and Sammy, and having had a rest after the fatal lunch, she was ready to start again. But the Christmas evening was tame compared with her lunch. Gerald noticed Mario's arm around Windy's shoulder as they moved to the swimming pool where the table was laid out, and smiled. He turned to make a comment to Martin but he also had seen this gentle form of affection and moved to Gerald and kissed him. The laughter from the guests outside gave

Gerald the greatest satisfaction. Hand in hand with Martin, he went out to join them.

With funny story after funny story from Phyllis and Sammy the evening passed very pleasantly. At 12.30 Catherine said she was going to call it a night and so with Faith she headed back to Donegal. Half an hour later Mark and James, after saying their goodnights to all, also returned to Donegal, hearing in the background a very happy Phyllis, who cried out loudly, 'Happy Christmas and a great New Year to all!'

Printed in the United States
By Bookmasters